Pr

THE POSSIBILIT\

MW00810589

"This extraordinary book by world traveler Beth Harkins is a must-read for every woman seeking the courage to go further in her journey of exploring bigger possibilities than she can even imagine. By joining the book's heroine on her journey from Oklahoma City to Madrid to discovering the divine feminine in the power of Saint Teresa of Ávila, Sekhmet, Sophia, Kali and Isis, your own spark of greatness is sure to be reignited and amplified. I can't recommend this book highly enough!"
- Claire Zammit, Ph.D., Founder of FemininePower.com

"Wouldn't we all like to go on a journey that leads to the heart of possibility? Everywhere in this delightful novel from Beth Harkins, we encounter the rising divine feminine and discover that what it truly desires is that all women of the earth live free of self-doubt and discover their voice. Harkins takes us on a journey through the mysticism of St. Teresa de Ávila, the Hindu goddess of Kali, Karen Blixen and more as her precocious young heroine grows into a woman who finds the power of the sacred feminine is in where and how women gather, whether it's under a mango tree in Kenya or on the backroads of America. This novel soars!"
- Carolyn Dawn Flynn, author of *Searching for Persephone* and *Boundless*

"The book is incredible...so inspiring. The divine in me was stirred and there was a sense of homecoming, giving voice to a part of us that is universal, that is cosmic and sacred. And yet, seeing it grounded in what seemed your own life story made it that bit more real and poignant."
- Lizzie Foster, Wayfarer Yoga and Coach, Turks and Caicos Islands

"What a powerful storyteller! I am blown away by the texture and evocative tones of the writing. The detail is stunning. The writing style is rich and deep and colorful, but then somehow on top of that (as if it weren't already a beautiful bath for the senses!) Harkins layers in this exquisite and essential narrative of a young girl (and later of a woman's need) to understand her place in the world."
- Kirstin Laurette, Founder, Coach and Consultant of Women in Love and Leadership

THE

POSSIBILITY

OF

EVERYWHERE

Casablanca to Oklahoma City, Kathmandu to Timbuktu

Beth Harkins

atmosphere press

To Stanton
May your eyes remain open
to life-positive possibilities everywhere.

.

When you travel, a new silence goes with you,
and if you listen, you will hear what your heart would love to say.

The Benedictus: A Book of Blessings, John O'Donohue

Another world is not only possible, she is on the way. On a quiet day you can hear her breathing.

World Social Forum in Porto Alegre, Brazil,
January 27th, 2003, Arundhati Roy

CONTENTS

PART ONE

1
FROM BANANA TREES TO WINDY PLAINS

Casablanca, French Occupied Morocco, 1953

From a spot in the shade of the banana tree, I sat and watched Votna grip a silver sewing needle between her thumb and index finger. She bent her knees and lowered herself onto a cushion of bumble bee-yellow grass. From a tangled ball, she threaded a needle the way I'd watched Mother do before stitching a torn hem.

I sat up as straight as the bangs across my forehead. With my eyes closed, I waited for a miracle while inhaling the scent of bougainvillea on a trellis at the front of my family's white stucco house.

I remembered earlier in the day soaking up the sun as I ran in circles around the yard. Me, Cindy Hollingsworth, a six-year-old, green-eyed, freckled-faced, Scotch-Irish American girl with brown bangs and plenty of attitude. I joined Votna, a chocolate-eyed, tan-skinned, Moroccan Muslim with middle-parted-hair and lots of spunk. Age ten or so, Votna lived in a garage apartment with Hudah, our Moroccan housekeeper. Votna spoke Arabic. I spoke English. Together we spoke "girl talk." I adored my special friend with her earrings and the things she knew, even though she could not go to school like I did.

Votna followed me as I flapped my arms like a butterfly. Free today, I was not sitting on a hard wooden chair at Sunday School the way I did at the U.S. Air Force Base church. There I'd be told, "Thou Shalt Not" do this or that before I colored pictures of Moses holding the Ten Commandments.

"Votna, pretty please," I pleaded. "I want to be a queen today. You can choose who you want to be tomorrow."

Votna's dangling earrings bobbled up and down as if to say, "Okay." I pretended to be Queen Elizabeth of England on her coronation day. My middle name was Elizabeth—making it easy to imagine I was a queen making important decisions before dashing off to grand balls wearing a satin gown and earrings.

Later, I pretended to be powerful queen Cleopatra. And then the Egyptian Goddess Isis. I knew their stories because Mother had read them to me. Queens and goddesses wore earrings. That's why I needed them!

Mother insisted, "Wait 'til you're older. Your father does not want you wearing earrings at your age."

I needed earrings so that I would look beautiful and so everyone, including my father, would realize how wonderful and important I was. As Votna and I played, I pointed to her ears with beads hanging from them. Then I pointed to my ears. Soon she disappeared before returning with a sewing needle, brown thread and two tiny, sky-blue stone beads. With the magic objects spread on the ground, we sat huddled together looking at them, shaded by the banana tree.

Soon Votna leaned toward me as she squeezed my ear lobe between her fingers. I felt a sharp pain and wanted to yell "ouch" or "stop." Instead, I sat motionless. Votna then squeezed my other ear lobe as an even sharper pain pierced through me. Bees buzzing around the bougainvillea broke the silence I did not allow myself to break.

That's when I raised my hands to my ears. Moving my

fingers down the threads, I could feel one round bead dangling below each ear. "Thank you. Thank you," I said, standing up to grab Votna's hand as I pulled her toward the house.

Like ballerinas dancing to the *Sugar Plum Fairy*, Votna and I floated through the open front door, moving across the tile floor, down the hall and into my parents' bedroom. When we arrived at the tall mirror hanging above the dresser, I saw my earrings dangling.

Excited, I didn't notice Mother napping on the bed. Jarred awake by our disruption, she sat up, stretched, and turned toward the mirror. I heard a gasp before Mother's glare landed on me and then fell onto Votna.

"Votna, did you pierce Cindy's ears? Germs! Cindy's ears could get infected!"

Sensing Mother's distress, but not understanding her words, Votna stood in silence, her eyes looking down. With her lips quivering, she raced from the room. The response sent darts to my heart. Votna did nothing wrong. I wanted earrings and she gave them to me. I got Votna into trouble.

"Hold still!" Mother ordered.

I squirmed to get away as the hair on my arms and the back of my neck stood up straight. From deep in my throat came my favorite word—the one Mother told me was "an ugly word little girls must not say." I folded my arms, stomped my foot, and yelled, "damn, damn, damn." I had heard Daddy say that powerful word many times.

"Straighten up! Be sweet and nice! Your father will be home soon," Mother said.

I squirmed as my mother retrieved silver scissors from her sewing basket. With my jaw clenched, I felt the cold scissors graze past my cheek and up to the thread and the bead hanging from one earlobe. I heard scratching scissors open and close before a soft "ping" sounded. The first bead hit the tile floor, disappearing like lost treasure in the ocean. Another snip and the other bead suffered the same fate.

When Mother pulled the threads from my earlobes, I shouted, "My earrings! They made me special!"

Touching my face, Mother tried to calm me. "You're special just as you are," she said.

Her words brought no comfort. Mother left and returned with a small bottle from the medicine cabinet. I knew what was coming. She poured orange-brown liquid onto a cotton ball and rubbed it across my ear lobes. I felt a sting like a burn from popping grease.

"Ouch," I yelled, to get her attention.

"Iodine kills germs," Mother said with the cotton ball held between her fingers. "Soon you'll be fine."

"Nothing is fine," I wailed. "Everything is awful!"

At that moment, my three-year-old sister Sarah dashed into the scene of my disaster. She clutched her Betsy McCall doll and looked around.

Mother locked her eyes on me. "Why don't you and Sarah play with your dolls? Like you did on the ship."

I sulked and began to play a pretend version of the real voyage, a year earlier, when Mother, Sarah and I took a train from Oklahoma City to New York before boarding the *S.S. Constitution* for a cruise from New York to Gibraltar, Spain. From there, we had taken a smaller ship to Tangier before landing in Casablanca. During the long journey, I had practiced saying the names of these places where we stopped.

With commercial jet travel a rather new thing, the train and the ships provided the best options for uniting Mother, Sarah, and me with Air Force Lieutenant Colonel James (Jim) Archibald Hollingworth, Mother's much-missed husband, and our much-missed father, stationed at Nouasseur Air Force base outside Casablanca. Since there was no place for us to live on the base, it had taken Daddy a long time to find a home for us.

On this day in Casablanca, having agreed to play dolls with my sister, I assumed the must-please role that had become familiar to me. I wasn't too worried about pleasing my mother, but pleasing my father was as important as pleasing God Almighty. If I acted sweet and nice and played dolls with Sarah, Mother might not tell Daddy I had yelled a bad word. And he might not be mad at me.

Grabbing my Madame Alexander doll and dragging her by the hair down the hall, I wanted to scream. How did I end up without earrings and stuck playing with dolls?

Soon, I heard the door open, and footsteps sounded in the hall. I looked up and saw my father, dressed in his olive-green Air Force uniform. He stood tall, the brass buttons and bright medals gleamed on his jacket. I imagined Daddy bending down, scooping me into his arms and squeezing me tight. He had never done those things, but today he might pinch my cheeks and say in his deep voice, "You're my special little girl."

I guess Daddy had important things on his mind because he didn't say one word. His eyes went through me, as if I were cellophane covering the orange slices Mother kept for him in the refrigerator.

I followed Daddy into the living room where he dropped into his rocking chair, picked up his newspaper and disappeared behind it. The last ounce of my "Somebody Special" dreams disappeared like my father's face behind his newspaper. I became "Nobody Special," a girl as useless as the Tooth Fairy without money.

I chewed around my thumb nail. The raw skin bled. I wished the throbbing would cover something worse—the hidden pain a Band-Aid could not cover.

That evening, my father invited fellow officers to our house. I wished Daddy would let me sit beside him to hear the important things the men were discussing. Instead, I was forced to sit outside the door, hidden and invisible. I couldn't talk, only peek in silence through a crack in the door of a smoke-filled room. I strained to hear what was said about their work at Nouasseur Air Base. About bombers pointed at the Soviet Union.

Daddy poured whiskey for the officers, but he did not drink any. The whiskey smelled like hay stacked in a barn. Mother would not want the men to drop cigarette ashes or spill whiskey on her rug, but I knew she wouldn't say anything.

I heard the officers say some people in Morocco did not want girls in school. I could not imagine why anyone would think such a thing. Later, I heard the words riots, strikes, and massacres before one officer said, "French soldiers killed fifty Moroccans."

I was terrified. Would the French soldiers shoot Votna and Hudah? If not, would Votna get to go to school? I ran to the kitchen to ask Mother to explain. She looked at me, at Sarah, then down at the floor and said, "It means a hard life for Votna and Hudah."

I was worried and sad, but Mother told me, "Everything will be fine. Let's enjoy the mountains. The oceans. The desert..."

Weeks later, remembering Mother's words, I looked out the window of our family's car as we crossed desert lands. I watched two nomads covered in long white robes slap their camels' rumps to force them down the side of the road. Behind them, donkey-cart drivers used their sticks to force the poor creatures to clump along as we sped by. I could tell by the way the camels and donkeys lowered their heads that being forced to obey did not please them any more than it pleased me.

I asked, "When will we be there?" Before I got an answer, I saw the city of Marrakesh appear—a rose-colored desert oasis where the sun made snow-covered Atlas Mountains sparkle. The wonders amazed me, but my excitement was dulled by the fear of French shootings, anger that animals had to obey or get hurt, and disgust that Moroccan girls like Votna could not go to school.

After we checked into our hotel, my mind turned toward Jemaa el-Fnaa Square, a magical space. Swirling belly dancers made music with finger cymbals. Fire-eaters swallowed fire! A snake charmer coached a cobra to bite his tongue for some strange reason. An old fortune-teller with dancing monkeys told customers their futures.

I wanted to know my future, but Daddy said, without looking at me, "No one knows what the future will bring." Mother stood behind Daddy without adding her thoughts.

If only I could know the future, I could see my grown-up life. I had decided that no matter how hard I tried, a girl like me could never become a queen or a goddess. With the exciting, important roles saved for boys, the possibilities for my life seemed dull and boring.

Outside a blue tiled Muslim Mosque, robed men removed their backless, pointed-toed, leather slippers before entering carved wooden doors. No women went inside. The men had come to pray, called by wailing muezzins. I wondered why women weren't called to pray.

On a street corner, I smelled a skunk. Mother said it wasn't a skunk, it was hashish smoked by men squatting around water pipes called "hookahs." Why weren't women inhaling from the water pipes? Was it because they didn't want to smell like a skunk? Because their faces were covered with veils? Or because they carried babies and bundles?

When the end of a mesmerizing weekend in Marrakesh arrived, my earlier worries had slipped into the background. I rode along in comfortable silence while Daddy drove us back to Casablanca, until Sarah started bugging me something awful. "Let's play dolls," she begged.

"No dolls!" I told her. "I want to look out the window." Sarah kept pestering me. I reached over and pinched her arm with my fingernails. She screamed. Daddy jerked his neck around and yelled, "Stop it, Cindy!" It was strange to hear him say my name, and I did not like the tone in his voice.

I watched as my father jerked his head back toward the front windshield. In a minute, he held his hand around one side of his neck while he drove the car to the side of the road and stomped on the brake. "You drive," he told Mother as he got out of the car to move to the passenger side.

Sarah and I sat as silent as dead people while Mother started driving. I was afraid of upsetting Daddy. I should have known better than to pinch my sister. Now Daddy was so upset that his neck got stiff. He couldn't even drive the car. It was all my fault.

Soon the world I had known disappeared the way an Arab woman's face disappears behind a veil. The way my first earrings disappeared on the floor.

Daddy came home one day and told Mother, "Morocco's ready to explode. More bombings, shootings, and protests." He loosened his tie and added, "The base commander ordered us to leave for Oklahoma City as soon as possible."

Mother packed our bags. Daddy loaded the car. We rushed to leave for the airport. When Votna watched and drew a two-thumbed hand in the sand. I asked Mother about the hand. "It's a symbol for Fatima," she told me as she shoved a suitcase into the backseat.

"Who is Fatima?" I asked. "She's a goddess who guides people through difficulty," Mother explained.

I waved goodbye, wishing with all my might for Fatima's hand to guide us all. From some place inside me, I remembered my lost dream about becoming a goddess. It would have been wonderful to guide people through difficulty.

Our family left Casablanca huddled inside what Daddy said was a Douglas C-54 Skymaster four engine, non-pressurized, transport plane. My stomach lurched. This was my first airplane ride. It scared me to climb into the sky unsure what would happen next.

Sitting on a cold, metal bucket seat, faced away from the windows, I couldn't see the moon, the stars, or a last sight of Morocco. I wondered if I would ever see Votna again. Would she be safe in Morocco? Would she ever get to go to school? Would I ever wear earrings again? Would girls in Oklahoma City insist on playing with dolls instead of imagining themselves as queens or goddesses? And why had I never heard of a queen or a goddess who lived in Oklahoma? And what did Mother mean when she said I had sand in my shoes when I didn't see any? I was not very smart, or I would be able to figure out more things.

Oklahoma City, Oklahoma, 1953

On a dark and dreary Monday morning, Mother and I walked down Hamilton Drive, toward Mayfair Elementary School, on the next block. Wearing black and white saddle oxfords, a cotton plaid dress with a Peter Pan collar and a sash tied at the back, I blended in with the other middle-class baby boomer girls.

Stepping inside my new school, I felt dizzy looking at a corridor lined with glossy gray linoleum tiles covered with a million tiny dots. The place smelled like a baloney sandwich covered with chalk dust and trouble. A hall door opened. Mr. Baumgartner, the school principal with slicked down hair and a pointed nose, directed Mother and me to take seats inside his office.

Mother, with her North Carolina bred Southern grace and charm, soon announced, "Cindy is a mature and precocious child. I'm sure she's ready for second grade."

Mr. Baumgartner raised his chin, using it as a pointer to move Mother's attention towards me. As if sitting on a pin cushion with needles stabbing me, I put my thumb in my mouth to make everything better. That's when Mother turned her head and saw me sucking my thumb. She accepted Mr. Baumgartner's decision that it would be best for me to return to first grade.

At that moment, shame covered me. I vowed never to allow myself to look stupid again. I would get smart, or at least pretend to be smart.

My life unfolded in a city where the wind came sweeping down the plains. Where tornado alerts were certain to interrupt shows like *Father Knows Best, Ozzie and Harriet* and *I Love Lucy*. Where TVs were packed with black and white images of white families like ours. Where J.C. Penny and the Sears Catalog provided my clothes—except the ones Mother made for me. Where I spent Sunday mornings and Wednesday nights at the red-bricked, tall-steepled Central Presbyterian church. Where each Sunday I would sit on a church pew, holding my legs together like a proper little girl wearing a hat—a red felt one with ribbon around it in winter and a white straw one trimmed with flowers in spring.

Here I learned God was powerful, like my father. That Mary, gentle, meek, and mild, was Jesus's mother—a mother like mine. That Eve sinned and so had I, and that she got blamed for everything bad. The same way I got blamed.

Mine was a world where women baked cookies for events in the church parlor. Where men counted money from the Sunday offering. Where a quarter would buy a Coke from the machine in the church basement. Where, after church, Sunday dinners with roast beef, rice and gravy, green beans and strawberry Jell-O would fill our plates. Where Daddy blessed the food. Where Mother prepared the food and washed the dishes afterwards.

Each night when I went to bed, I would follow a ritual and repeat a prayer taught to me long ago: "Now I lay me down to sleep. I pray the Lord my soul to keep. If I should die before I wake, I pray the Lord my soul to take."

I wondered, where was my soul? And why would the Lord want to keep or to take my soul? Without a soul, I could never become important. My soul needed to stay with me.

In time, I stopped saying bedtime prayers. When I entered high school, I had forgotten my dream of becoming a goddess or a queen—not even a prom queen seemed an option for me. A popular girl would fill that role. However, I held hope that by learning to drive, getting a driver's license, and driving friends for hamburgers, I would feel special. As one of the oldest in my class, I could get my driver's license before most others.

One Saturday afternoon, my mother persuaded my father to let me drive through the neighborhood, my first time behind the wheel. With great trepidation, I stepped inside the driver's seat of my parent's vehicle—a white Chevy station wagon that seemed the length of a city block.

My hands shook as I started the car. I felt the movement as I steered the station wagon down the street. All was well until I came to the intersection and attempted to turn the corner. As I twisted the steering wheel without allowing it to straighten, I sent the vehicle over the curve and into a row of hedges that lined our neighbor's sidewalk. I heard the front end of the station wagon scrape against the curb as I somehow managed to lift my foot and stomp on the brake. The sound of air leaving the front passenger-side tire made me feel as if the last ounce of breath was leaving my body. I waited in silence, steering wheel in hand, nerves jangled, wondering about my father's reaction. Tears wanted to burst from my eyes, but I held them back.

Daddy did not scream. He did not berate me. Instead, in a flat voice he said, "Move over." Those were his only words. Two words that seared into my memory. I was mortified. I'd wrecked the car, yet my father said nothing. His silence filled me with shame, but since he had never physically or sexually abused me, I felt ashamed to blame him for my deep self-doubt or for a strong need to please male authority.

A good provider. A retired army office. A respected banker. A leader in his church. A man who served drinks to friends but never drank himself, Daddy appeared to have become everything my grandmother wished her alcoholic husband might have become.

My father's childhood, the war and cultural expectations must have blocked him from the ability to be emotionally available. It would have been helpful to talk about these things with Daddy, but I did not know how to approach such a conversation. I lacked the words, the voice, and the courage. But someday, maybe...

2
DUENDE

Spain and Oklahoma, 1967-1968

On a sun-drenched September morning, as soft breezes blew through my hair, I stood near an Arabic-style arch—one that turned back in on itself like a keyhole. The arch rose between massive stone walls surrounding Toledo, Spain. The city, a medieval marvel, about an hour north from Madrid, lured me to visit before my classes started at the University of Madrid. Pausing at the arch threshold, I remembered another Arabic arch, one leading into the magical Medina in Casablanca.

I suppose it was no coincidence that Toledo reminded me of Casablanca, since Moorish Muslims from North Africa laid out Toledo's alleyways. The Moors brought cultural, architectural, religious, and intellectual influences beginning in 711. By 1492—when Queen Isabella and King Ferdinand introduced Spain's heinous Inquisition—Muslims and Jews, living in peace for centuries, were forced to convert to Catholicism or be tortured, imprisoned, exiled, or killed. The facts I remembered from college world history. At the time, I longed to visit faraway places, not to be lectured about their histories. But today what I'd learned had context.

Sitting above Morocco, though separated from it by the Strait of Gibraltar, Spain would be my home for a year. I had settled into the center of Madrid, living in an apartment shared with a Spanish family. I found myself outside the U.S. for the first time since age six.

Rarely had I felt so excited. Never had I felt lonelier. Isolated from everyone and everything familiar—except the Arabic arch and Moroccan memories. I looked down at my yellow cotton A-line dress. Mother made it for my travel wardrobe. I watched my black patent leather Mary Jane pumps hit the cobblestone path. As I did so, a familiar voice popped into my head: "Are you trying to look like a sunflower? And why did you bring pumps for walking shoes? Such poor judgment! What makes you think you're ready to live on your own in Spain?"

I forced myself to lift my shoulders and move forward. As I did so, my mind flooded with self-judgment and reminders of what I had come here to forget.

The Friday called Bid Day arrived—the day when sorority bids were to be delivered. I had waited in my dorm room for the cherished bid to be slipped under my door. A quick look in the mirror confirmed my ratted and sprayed hair looked the way a sorority girl's hair should look. Dressed in a beige linen dress, my outfit met the rush code. Not too short, too long, too tight, or too loose. Perfect for the celebration soon to begin.

As girls' yelling echoed down the hall, my heart throbbed. I could almost taste the thrill tonight would bring.

But soon the noise stopped. When an envelope failed to appear under my door, a sensation as strong as an earthquake shook my world. No objects dropped off the shelves. What dropped was how I pictured myself. Not wanted. Not popular. Not worthy. I wished I could disappear.

Weeks later, a rush committee member approached me in the student union where I stood with sorority rejection emblazoned across my chest, like Hester Prynne's scarlet letter. Daring to violate a cardinal sorority secrecy rule, the girl revealed with a scowl that my blackballing happened because I acted "way too forward" around fraternity guys. I "advertised wanting to go all the way." Her scrunched nose pointed up as she turned and walked away.

Me, forward with guys? Go all the way? I just wanted a date despite my self-consciousness. Had joining my roommate at the guy's table in the student union caused my blackballing? I'd added an additional item to my failure list. Though growing up hearing I should "love one another," I had no desire to love girls who blackballed me. The girls I had tried to imitate until they showed me I had failed.

I ran to the library and dropped down into a chair behind a bookshelf where I thought no one would see me. After a while, when sick of slumping in the chair, I trudged to the exit. A brochure tacked to the bulletin board by the door called to me. Bold orange letters read: "Study Abroad in Madrid, Spain."

Abroad? Spain? Forget sororities. Forget being labeled "too forward."

Back at the dorm, I called Mother to say how much I wanted to apply to study in Spain. Her voice echoed over the phone. "A year in Spain! It would be good for you. I'll tell your father you're applying."

With Mother's encouragement, I completed the application and rushed to get my ears pierced for my grand adventure. Two weeks later, I received a letter from the program. My body shook when I read it.

Accepted! My junior year would be spent studying at the University of Madrid. I suddenly understood my determination to learn a foreign language. I would now reap the benefits of studying four years of Spanish in high school. Why I majored in Spanish in college, despite the fact my father questioned what I would do with that degree.

Along with my excitement, I realized the costs with airfare would be much more than my current college expenses. Finances could block my dream escape. Our family budget was tight. I could cash in my savings bonds, but that wouldn't help much.

I went home to see my parents. When they gathered in the living room, I showed them the acceptance letter with the costs totaled. Daddy's eyebrows pulled together. I waited for a reply. That's when I heard Mother say, "I have money tucked away from a small inheritance. It'll cover everything."

Surprised. Thrilled. Profoundly grateful and uncomfortable about Mother's sacrifice, I asked what she was giving up for me to study in Spain.

"Don't worry," she said. "Go find what you're searching for." With that, she changed the subject.

My father, as usual, did not say much. However, when my big departure arrived, he drove us to the airport. He and my mother waited for me to board the plane. I noted Daddy seemed more distant than usual, and I saw his hands shake. Maybe he was nervous. Or maybe he wished he were taking this trip. From a man whose emotions stay wrapped up tight, I had learned to operate as if I were a search light, hunting for clues as to what he thought and felt. I decided to believe my father, though nervous, was happy for me.

I realized I was smiling. My mind left Oklahoma City and returned to the present moment in Toledo. Holding a travel guide, I looked around to orient myself.

Within moments, a wavy-haired Spaniard caught my eye. His shoulder leaned against a stone building while he gripped a notebook and pen. When I approached, this good-looking guy turned towards me, arched his eyebrows and grinned. An irresistible urge to stare at him stuck me to the street.

As I sensed my boldness, I looked down and noticed the European shoes. Slate gray trousers. An open-collared blue shirt. Sleeves rolled to the elbows. I touched one of my gold hoop earrings, holding it like a magic talisman that had delivered this magic moment.

"*Hola*," the handsome figure said.

I turned my head in his direction.

"Are you an American?" he asked, in accented English.

"I guess Americans stand out like crying babies. *Soy de Oklahoma*," I added to let him know I spoke rather fluent Spanish.

"I've seen the movie *Oklahoma*. My name's Ángel. Actually, Ángel Torralba Ruíz."

"Mucho gusto, Me llamo Cindy, Hollingsworth."

As I spoke, I understood that peering into a stranger's eyes on a street in Spain and without hesitation offering my name seemed crazy and scary, like Holy Toledo. What was this girl thinking? However, something assured me I had encountered a guy with a loving mother who gave her son the name Ángel. With this name, how could he bring anything but joy? My gut told me this. The same gut that assured me I would become a college sorority pledge.

"I took a bus to visit Toledo. My classes at the University of Madrid start tomorrow," I said, not knowing what else to say.

"Good 'ole Universidad Plutense de Madrid," Ángel replied. "I'm a Spanish history major there. I've been in Toledo a few finishing my research paper. It's about Santa Teresa de Ávila."

I nodded.

"Writing a paper about a saint is required for history majors. An example of Catholic high-ups controlling the education system."

"I don't know anything about Saint Teresa," I admitted in a halting voice.

"She's a sixteenth century Spanish saint. I'm fascinated by her."

Pointing to a simple wooden sign mounted on the front wall of the stone edifice, Ángel translated the words, "Barefoot Carmelites. Fifth Foundation of Saint Teresa of Ávila, 1569."

One of many reformed Carmelite convents Saint Teresa founded. "Still active."

I wondered why Ángel was fascinated by a saint and her 400-year-old convents. Did Ángel believe women should live contained, cloistered lives?

As if reading my mind, he pushed a strand of wavy hair off his face and said, "Saint Teresa might be the most respected female saint and mystic in the world. I'd label her a medieval, mystical activist."

"Wow!"

Ángel smiled in a way that made his eyes light up. "I'm drawn to Teresa's story," he told me. "A Catholic nun who used her smarts, her charm and her grace to convince the hierarchy to agree to her reforms."

Ángel intrigued me with his intelligence. I clung to his every word.

"Teresa lived during the Inquisition. She could have been labeled a heretic and set on fire for her bold ideas." Ángel pointed out. "But she learned to speak to her superiors in ways they accepted. A bold woman. Ahead of her time."

Looking straight into my eyes, Ángel added, "A city in Costa Rica and one in Brazil bear her name—so does a specialty rum!"

"Incredible," I said, imagining what it would be like to be a brave, feminist mystic, though I had but a faint idea what the word mystic meant. "I'm not Catholic, Ángel. I come from a Protestant background. Convents, saints and mystics were not discussed in my church. Nor were feminists. I haven't been to Costa Rica or Brazil. And I'm not into specialty rums."

After my little speech, I heard two songbirds chirping from their perch on the convent roof. I imagined them serenading Ángel and me. I squeezed my hands together to brace for Ángel's reply, afraid he might imagine me uninteresting and uninformed.

"I walked away from the Catholic Church a while back. The Franco regime's control of the institution was more than I could take."

Turning his head in a way that made me wonder if he heard the songbirds, Ángel added, "I wanted a career in law to help change Spain's archaic legal system, but I knew there would be no opportunity for a guy like me. I wasn't born into an elitist, Franco supporting family."

I thought back to Casablanca. How I had decided the world's interesting work was reserved for men, leaving few opportunities for me. I empathized with Ángel. Despite male privilege, he was denied opportunities due to his social class and lack of support for Franco.

Putting his hands in his pockets, Ángel explained that with a Spanish history degree, he could work in the main industry—tourism. "But tourism won't stop my political protests."

"Is protesting safe?" I asked.

"Protesting is not a choice," Ángel said, his voice convincing. "But enough of that; let's go to the Cathedral. You will see Santa Teresa's original manuscripts. Most people miss them, but you'll appreciate her words."

"Sure," I said, wondering how Ángel concluded I would "appreciate" a saint's words.

A mimosa tree caught my eye. I paused to inhale the pink blossom fragrance. The softness helped me forget dictators and my controlling inner voice. When I raised my head, I saw the limestone Gothic Cathedral's tower pierce the sky and cast its shadow over the ground. Ángel explained the iconic tower stood in the place where an Arabic minaret once stood.

"A magical co-mingling existed before it turned tragic," Ángel said, touching Arabic tiles on a storefront. "Look at the architecture. Much of it Mudejar—created by the Moors while under Christian domination. European styles with Islamic elements."

"I like the lines and colors," I said, focusing my camera and knowing I was attracted to much more than Mudejar architecture.

With his hands dancing, Ángel told me, "Teresa connected with *duende*, energy that moves up the spine and makes a person seek freedom and dignity. It's hard to describe, but flamenco dancers, musicians, bullfighters, artists, poets like Federico García Lorca and mystics like Teresa seek it."

"Can anyone experience *duende?*" I asked.

"Yes, it's possible."

The words excited me. "My first day in Madrid," I said, "standing in Plaza Mayor and hearing the flamenco guitarist. His strumming. His deep singing. I think I felt *duende*. It made me sit up straight and lift my chin."

What I didn't say was how much I sensed the same *duende* moving up and down my spine when I stood next to Ángel and when he leaned into my body.

"Some know *duende* as an elf who comes and goes. You'll come to know the deeper meaning that comes up from within. It brings longing and love. What if we look for *duende* at a flamenco *tablao*?" Ángel asked as we walked close enough that I could feel his skin against mine. "How about next weekend in Madrid?"

"Terrific!" I said, stopping myself from jumping up and down.

"See the Cathedral?" Ángel asked.

"It's huge. Looks imposing," I said as we approached the

entrance.

Ángel continued talking about Saint Teresa as we entered. "She found *duende* through her intimate experiences with the Divine. Hers was an immanent spirituality—one found within herself."

I was drawn to the spiritual concepts Ángel mentioned, ones I had vague intuitive understandings about. But more to the point, I was drawn to everything about this guy.

"*Duende* and ecstasy inspired Teresa's writing and her life. I'll discuss these ideas in my research paper. I don't expect the professors will like them, but that's fine," Ángel said as his brow wrinkled.

"I admire how you are willing to accept that your professors probably won't like what you write," I said, wondering if someday I could overcome the need to please authority figures.

Further inside, I saw what seemed endless columns reaching high above. Flying buttresses supported a cavernous stone ceiling. The space made me feel small and insignificant. White marble walls and floor. Enormous paintings by world masters. Overwhelming sculptures. Opulent gold and jewel encrusted objects.

A multi-story chapel with an ornately carved altar rose behind a locked wrought-iron gate. The sight convinced me such sacred spaces were to be approached only by priests with keys. The musty smell of old stones and votive-candle smoke clogged my nostrils. I preferred Mother Nature's sanctuary, filled with trees and flowers, rivers, and ocean scents.

"Granted, this is the first European cathedral I've visited, but I don't feel close to anything sacred here," I said surprised by my openness.

"Follow me," Ángel said, directing me toward an inconspicuous space where Saint Teresa's portrait hung above a glass case. "Here's Teresa's handwritten manuscripts. Her words helped my family cope after my father's death a year ago."

"I'm so sorry for your loss." I could feel his tender grief.

A brown veil framed the saint's face, her eyes connected with mine in a comforting way. I imagined they did the same for a young man grieving his father's loss.

Peering into the case, I noted Teresa's inky scratches. After minutes of silent reading, I turned and said, "Teresa's handwriting looks messy, like mine."

Ángel laughed. I continued reading from her book, *The Interior Castle,* where Teresa described stages of her spiritual growth, comparing them to rooms in a castle. The Spanish words had a beautiful flow. Made me appreciate my years studying Spanish.

"I'm amazed," I said, "by the intimacy Teresa used to describe her relationship with God. For me, God is removed. A distant judge who makes me feel guilty."

"I understand," Ángel said as he rested his eyes on a stained-glass window. It depicted two soldiers in battle with a winged angel rising above a fallen body.

"For years, I blamed a cruel Father God," Ángel said, clenching his fists, "for letting my father suffer in prison after fighting the evils of fascism."

The intensity of his words made me wonder if Ángel lived with an anger-filled heart. No, that was not true, because I sensed his soft, yet wounded, heart.

"After my father's imprisonment, he suffered survivor's guilt. Millions died fighting. During the rest of his life, he was withdrawn, despising Franco's brutal dictatorship. My mom provided the nurture my sister and I needed."

"My father wasn't a prisoner," I said, "but he went to war twice. I don't know what he thinks about those experiences. Really, I know little about what he thinks about anything. I'd like to know more."

To change the subject, I whispered, "Saint Teresa intrigues

me." My words echoed across the space.

Ángel touched my arm to move me toward her portrait. "Imagine Teresa in her twenties. Beautiful. Smart. From a wealthy family. After her mother's death, she ran away and joined a convent, refusing forced marriage. Her first spiritual awakening happened about our age."

Looking at Teresa, I thought about an Oklahoma girl named Cindy, the part of me I left behind days earlier. How this Cindy had obsessed about her sorority blackballing. She never imagined attention from a sexy Spaniard, or connecting with writings from a medieval, mystic saint, or the words *duende* as a description for what she felt.

Ángel interrupted my thoughts. "Let's get some *marzipan*. It's made from almonds. We Spaniards love it."

"Sounds divine," I said, wishing to infer how divine this day had been.

We left Teresa and strolled from the Cathedral to Pastería Santo Tomé. Once inside the shop, Ángel pointed to a four-foot-tall marzipan cathedral. And to a counter filled with various shaped marzipan. After tasting a star-shaped almond paste morsel, I whispered, "I'm in love. With marzipan, I mean."

Under a moonlit sky, on Saturday night in Madrid, the promised date with Ángel began. He met me outside my apartment, as was the tradition in a culture that considered it not proper for a young woman's date to enter her residence. We wandered toward a *tapas* bar on *Calle Preciados*, translated in English as precious or treasured street. The name reflected how I felt about this night.

"I'd like to call you Alma," Ángel said, his shoulder touching mine. "It's a Spanish name, meaning soulful."

"Soulful, I like that, but I've never thought of myself that way."

Words from my childhood prayer came to mind, "I pray the lord my soul to keep..." The word "soul" I had not spoken for years. Whispering the name "Alma," I imagined myself as "soulful," connected to an invisible, almost forgotten, inner force. Whispering "Alma" and "Ángel" one after the other excited and calmed me, as if both emotions and both the soul force and the attraction force belonged together.

I watched young and old lovers meander near us. Locked arm-in-arm, Ángel and I entered the flamenco *tablao* and got comfortable at a corner table. The room was dark except for candlelight. A guitarist, a drummer and three male singers performed hauntingly beautiful, moving music. The sounds filled the room.

A Spanish beauty arrived on the stage. Dressed in a red satin dress with a red rose tucked behind her ear, her feet stomped to the guitar and drum rhythms. As she moved, the ruffle trimming her skirt hem brushed the floor. The music's intensity grew. We watched the woman's hips raise and lower before she wrapped her arms around her body in a sensuous movement.

When the guitar strumming and the singing grew louder, a tall dancer in dark pants and an unbuttoned black silk shirt emerged. His lightning-fast foot-stomping caused the audience to shout *olé* in a passionate frenzy. The couple turned and danced face to face.

"That's the sexiest dance I've ever seen," I announced.

"Por Arriba. Por Abajo," (over the top and up from below) Ángel said as he offered his Spanish toast with a wine glass in one hand and his other hand touching my thigh.

"Ole!" I repeated, wanting to run my fingers through Ángel's hair

We drank *chatas de vino*. Shared a Spanish potato tortilla. I wished the sorority girls could see me now. Yes, I wanted to "go all the way."

When Ángel turned toward me, we laid our eyes on each other. I wished we were in a private place. Where was the pill when I wanted it? I knew about birth control pills, but I wasn't taking them. I couldn't easily get a prescription at home without being married. Anyway, "nice girls" didn't need the pill. And in Spain contraception was both illegal and criminalized.

Ángel tapped the flamenco beats; his fingers touched mine. Why couldn't we be together—be together in the way we both wanted—enjoying the thrill rather than the fear of getting pregnant?

I remembered overhearing Mother tell a friend that she thought it unfortunate that our evolutionary journey had come this far without reproduction and sex becoming separate functions.

This Monday morning, I forgot, for a moment, about loving Ángel. The soulful, contemplative prayer practice Saint Teresa introduced me to also slipped from my mind. Instead, a school history test consumed my thoughts. Without a Santa Claus-style God to deliver an "A" on my test, I struggled to remember enough facts to make a good grade.

As I left my apartment for class, the textbook weight I carried matched the heavy clouds that bore down on me. With an aching back, I boarded the University-bound bus. Because there were no empty seats, I balanced myself with one arm anchored around the pole behind the driver's seat. My other arm clutched my belongings against my chest. As the bus maneuvered through traffic, I repeated dates that might appear on the test. 1939, the year the Spanish Civil War ended. The year when General Francisco Franco's fascist dictatorship took control of the country. While I repeated the date, grief pangs struck me. It was what Ángel must feel for his country.

When the bus parked by the University, I saw two Spanish army tanks advancing to block peaceful student demonstrators. I shook off my shock and fear, determined to arrive at class on time. When I stepped onto the pavement, a policeman on horseback with a baton in his hand shouted, "*Está cerrado.*"

Due to demonstrations, Franco had closed the University with no indication as to when it might reopen. I turned around with my stomach churning and waited at the bus stop, desperate to get back to my apartment. Startled and unnerved, I'd never imagined finding myself surrounded by tanks blocking a peaceful demonstration. I had come to Spain to escape being shut out, not to discover I could be shut out of my classes.

Later in the day, Ángel met me for a stroll through Retiro Park. Once home to royalty, today it stood as a fairy tale space for the public to enjoy. As we passed ivy and rose covered trellises, peaceful waterfalls, and bronze mermaids, I explained the horror I had witnessed outside the University.

Ángel listened. "Arrests are routine," he said, "and torture or execution by Franco's *Guardia Civil*. Any perceived threat to the regime will spark action. But protests grow."

On the placid park lake, we watched boats with their passengers rowing with abandon beside swans and ducks while political repression hovered everywhere. Ángel put his arm around me. I tried to feel safe.

As orange, pink, and purple sunset rays touched my skin, Ángel lowered his head.

"Yesterday," he said, "the *Guardia Civil* stopped both my sister and me."

I gasped, never imagining Ángel in a situation like what I'd witnessed.

"They seized our pamphlets that called for civil rights." Ángel cleared his throat. "We waited to be arrested. Instead, we were ordered to leave the campus immediately."

As Ángel spoke, both his voice and rigid jaw convinced me he would no longer tolerate the regime's abuses—no matter the consequences.

"I'm scared. For both you and your sister," I said, my pulse racing.

"I didn't mean to frighten you. But now you understand."

I felt Ángel's soothing presence. "I respect you for protesting," I told him, "but I don't want you to be arrested."

"It's appalling," he said, "a woman, if accused of having sex outside of marriage, can be arrested, while rape arrests for men are as unlikely as eliminating bullfighting. The double standard must no longer be tolerated. Women are entitled to roles beyond enforced, pious domesticity."

Frightened for Spanish women, I realized that not only could Ángel and his sister be arrested, but I could be harassed, too. Injustice for one is injustice for all.

Admiring the courage to resist injustice, I considered asking for pamphlets, but the thought of protesting petrified me.

Through underground information passed to Ángel, I learned about expanding worldwide protests of the American war in Vietnam. Spaniards protesting the war had some cover for their anti-fascist protests.

"I'm overwhelmed," I said. "Frightened to open myself to so many new concerns and realizations. Some wonderful, some terrifying. I hardly know who I am anymore."

"We're both on quests, Alma. We can't avoid or ignore them. I refuse to forget that Franco holds back Spain's progress. The regime tried to block not just our political freedom, but our spiritual freedom, too."

I heard these words with inklings of understanding as to the full power of a fascist regime. In order not to feel overwhelmed or scared, I turned my eyes to enjoy the tranquil lake, watching the boats. On one level, I knew at some point I would need to use my voice to speak up my beliefs. I could not forever turn my gaze toward a calm lake.

Ángel's next words took me by surprise. "Alma, I love your spirit. You're an adventurer. A seeker. You could be unstoppable. Being with you excites me, but..."

I braced myself, waiting to hear what was coming.

"I'm concerned," he said, taking my hand, "about your *inquietud*. It could block your path forward. I wish you could respect yourself. Stop doubting your strengths and worth. You have a voice. Use it! You don't have to protest, but why not start by standing up to your anxiety and self-doubt."

Ángel's words made me defensive as if I didn't have the courage to face anxiety and doubt. Did he want to drag me into his battle? Forcing me to stand up to Franco's power, even if it meant I could get arrested or sent home? Breathing and pausing, I became less defensive. Maybe I was being asked to value and appreciate myself.

Ángel continued, "I've noticed you refuse genuine compliments. You don't accept when I say you're intelligent and interesting with new awareness to share."

A kiss landed on my cheek. I sat in silence, unable or unwilling to respond. Everything seemed confusing, complicated. Who was I? What difference did it make that I could no longer remain oblivious to threats to freedom and self-expression? And what were the implications of my restlessness, the uneasiness and self-doubt so obvious Ángel found them hard to tolerate?

Where did I belong? I had not fit into the conforming, conventional world of the sorority that rejected me. I was not prepared to take up the role of a Franco protestor. Or a Vietnam War activist. And I could no longer live as an unaware, twenty-something female.

The dangers Ángel and his sister protested represented

challenges for the entire world. Authoritarian squelching of freedoms through iron-fisted rule was clear to me. The repression and silencing of women had become real despite the progress women had made. I also realized that both external as well as internal emotional and psychological barriers limit women's power and potential. It was time for me to take a hard look at myself as I also opened my eyes to the world around me.

I sat on my bed this morning reading *The Book of My Life,* Saint Teresa's spiritual autobiography. The sun drifted through the window, covering the pages with light. I imagined Teresa when she was about my age. Not yet recognized as a saint or a spiritual leader and reformer. Someone actively seeking her life's purpose while also seeking love.

I had no interest in becoming a saint, but loving myself and being loved would be grand. I went to bed pondering such thoughts, but woke up in the wee morning hours. I turned on the lamp by my bed and reached for Teresa's book and gazed at her portrait on the cover. I wished we could talk. And that's when I felt as if the wise saint were present. As if she were smiling and asking me to visit with her.

I felt emboldened and began to speak. "Reading your writing excites me."

I imagined Teresa's mouth turned up in a smile.

"You spoke your truth to powerful male figures in the Catholic church," I said. "I'm amazed. I want your boldness and confidence. You traveled in a covered wagon. I know it wasn't easy. And you wrote about your spiritual life. About mysticism."

"I once wrote that just being a woman was enough for my wings to fall off," I imagined Teresa saying.

"I'd be amused if it weren't for how much your words ring

true today, four hundred years later," I replied and then continued, "The spiritual may be where the answers lie, but I've had doubts. About God. About my worth and my place in the scheme of things. Fears about oppression and suppression of human rights."

I could not stop talking. I felt as if I were being heard. Teresa seemed in no rush, so I said, "You describe things new to me. Words I don't fully understand. Mysticism. Ecstasy. The immanence of the Divine. Since coming to Spain, I've experienced what I'd call mystic moments. And maybe ecstasy and *duende,* along with my anxieties. I get the feeling you believe boldness, spirituality, and sensuality are connected. Physical love, spiritual love and seeking to bring change as sacred, to be honored and respected."

"Trust your experiences," I imagined Teresa telling me. "Allow yourself to be opened to inner guidance, to inner knowing. To the Divine within."

Hearing Teresa ignited me. Hers were ideas I'd not heard in church. Something different from Father in the Sky religion, from dogma and commandments. I could sense and feel a loving, sacred presence with me. With eyes as strong, as feminine and as affirming as Saint Teresa's. I put down the book. The wise mystic's understandings comforted me as I fell asleep.

All too soon it happened. After ten incredible months in Spain, it would soon be time to return home. School finals challenged me. As did the packing and shipping of a trunk that weighed twice what it weighed when it first arrived. The dreaded goodbye challenged me the most.

What would my life be like at home? Martin Luther King's assassination a month earlier sent shock waves around the world. His death. The war. The riots. The unrest. No peaceful solutions to racism, sexism or war. It seemed my country was coming apart at the seams.

What next for Spain? What next at home? What next for me? I wanted a significant, purposeful life with love and affirmation. Ángel had awakened me to these, but...

Despite my turmoil, the departure day arrived. Ángel drove me to Barajas Airport for my last ride inside his gray Seat 600. I had learned *"say aaht"* was the pronunciation for Ángel's Spanish-made vehicle. It had carried us back and forth across Madrid while sheltering us for goodnight kisses. And we'd day-tripped back to Toledo, where it all began. Then off to Ávila, Saint Teresa's birthplace. I treasured many magical rides with a *duende*-filled driver at my side.

I watched Madrid's streets disappear under a thick veil of clouds. My body tightened. I could not force a smile.

Ángel rubbed his throat as if his words were trapped there. He aroused the truth that we both avoided speaking aloud.

Once inside the airport terminal, I watched Ángel's feet drag across the tile floor. If only dragging our feet could stop time, and what we both knew must happen.

When I handed my suitcases to the agent, I did so with a heart heavier than my bags. Holding my boarding pass, I moved with Ángel holding my hand. Soon the boarding call came. I took my place in line. With my overstuffed purse hanging over my shoulder and a carry bag at my side, Ángel came close. We kissed our last heart-wrenching kiss.

While holding me, Ángel lifted a folded note from his pants pocket. After he handed it to me, I turned to board the plane. I could not allow myself to look back.

When the plane lifted above the clouds, the sights and sounds of Spain disappeared. Strapped into my seat while engines roared, I summoned the courage to open Ángel's note.

"I am amazed how much can be accomplished on this path by being bold while striving for great things. Even if a soul is not quite strong enough yet, she can still lift off and take flight. She can soar to great heights. But like a fledgling bird, she may tire herself out and need to perch for a while."

Saint Teresa of Ávila, *The Book of My Life*

I folded the note and placed it in my backpack. I felt love and gratitude for my time with Ángel. For his introducing me to *duende*, for giving me the name Alma, for sharing the beauty and delights of Spain. I wished for a balm to heal the darkness Angel battled because of the dangers and threats around him. Such darkness had become difficult for me to endure. I had to seek light wherever I could find it.

I touched my earrings and glanced out the window at the starry night. Yes, I would perch for a while. Soon though, I hoped to be bold enough to believe it possible I was encoded with possibilities as bright as the stars, even if I could not yet name those possibilities.

3
WINGS TO FLY AWAY

Oklahoma, Florida and More, 1969-1971

Hugs and "How was it?" met me in Oklahoma City. Friends and family sounded excited to hear about my experiences. However, I soon learned a dozen photos and a couple of stories sufficed to summarize my life-changing year.

What next? Unable to face another year at the blackballing college despite the academic opportunities there, I enrolled for my senior year at the University of Oklahoma. As school began, my greatest pleasure came in receiving Ángel's letters—thin folded aerograms that arrived in my mailbox. I answered each letter, until, in time, my mind came to accept what my heart knew. Ángel was where he belonged, and I was still looking for where I belonged. It was time to open myself to the possibility of new love, even if I did not know how to do that yet.

One morning, I dragged myself down the dorm stairs before rushing to class. Pouring rain appeared through the windows. Without an umbrella, a raincoat, or a plan for after graduation, what was I to do? My female career options—teacher, secretary, or Playboy Bunny—held no more attraction than getting soaked in the rain. But then I heard a voice. "Pan American Airways is hiring stewardesses. They fly only international routes."

I turned toward a blond gal cuddled on a couch close to her boyfriend. "Interviews are at the Career Center. But you have to speak a foreign language to interview."

A foreign language. I spoke a foreign language—Ángel's language. If I were hired as a Pan Am stewardess, I would get paid to see the world. Someday, I might write the book of my adventures and discoveries, like Saint Teresa did.

Inside the University Career Counseling Center, my Pan Am interview was about to begin. I sat up straight while my nerves jumped around inside. A male Pan Am interviewer sat behind a desk dressed in a suit and tie with glasses clinging to the tip of his nose. I could feel his eyes crossing my body as he emphasized, "Competition is stiff. We'll select about 5,000 applicants from 50,000 received worldwide."

I listened before registering the inappropriate nature of the glances and the condescending way I was made to feel it unlikely I would be selected. Though horribly uncomfortable, my internalized need to please male authority caused me to sit with my legs crossed ready to respond to whatever was asked. When the interview concluded, I was told to watch for a letter within a few weeks.

A photographer entered the room as the interviewer left. A camera lens focused on my face. "Why don't you turn your head for a right-side photo," the photographer suggested. "With your head turned, the space between your front tooth and your eyetooth won't be as obvious. Anything that detracts from a perfect smile could keep you from getting hired."

I turned my head and smiled from the right side of my mouth as I pulled my lip down over the teeth on my left side. Though self-conscious about the tiny space between my teeth, I had never imagined it would be a factor in getting a job or that it would cause me to feel humiliated.

When the camera clicked, I wished for a rabbit's foot to rub for good luck. I wanted this job. It would be a step toward the big life of my dreams.

A few weeks after the interview, a letter with a Pan Am return address appeared in my mailbox. I grabbed the envelope and tore it open.

"Congratulations," the first sentence read. "You have been selected to report to Pan American Airways Stewardess Training School in Miami Springs, Florida on June 1st. The program lasts six-weeks. Upon successful completion, you will become a stewardess employed by the largest, most respected international airline in the world. We will assign you to a base in New York, Boston, Chicago, Washington D.C., San Francisco, or Miami."

I trembled with excitement. Thanks to a college degree, hips not too wide, weight not too high, Spanish fluency and good eyesight, I had made the Pan Am cut, despite the space between my teeth. After telling everyone I knew my astounding news, I worried about passing the training. And would the other stewardesses like me? And where would I be based if I passed the training?

Wearing white gloves. False eyelashes. Pantyhose. Tan leather heels. A sky-blue bolo hat. A matching blue-wool Evan Picone suit. With gold Pan Am wings pinned onto my jacket. Wearing tiny round gold Pan Am earrings, engraved with a globe. I stood ready to see the world as I posed for a photo alongside twenty other newly hired Pan Am stewardesses, each of us based in Miami.

I'd passed hair and make-up codes—imposed as beauty and grooming rules. And I had passed the emergency aircraft evacuation test, simulated at a motel swimming pool. The cocktail mixing test proved challenging, but the Spanish fluency test I found easy. I'd also mastered serving a standing rib roast and caviar from a cart in the aisle of a mock-up aircraft. Now I could enjoy layovers in Mexico City, Buenos Aires, Rio de Janeiro, Barbados, St. Thomas, St Croix and more. My pride was highlighted by meeting stewardesses from around the world.

I thought about Susan Sontag's quote, "I haven't been everywhere, but it's on my list."

I settled into a furnished apartment in the Coconut Grove area of Miami with Emily, a new friend from my Pan Am training class. This smart, independent brunette I liked a lot. She put off graduate school to see the world. Good decision, I thought. During time off between flights, we discussed our separate trips and got ready for the next one.

My new hometown remained a stranger. Her beaches seen only from airplanes. Her boutiques yet to explore. Yet, before the sun showed its face Friday morning, I planted myself inside a cab headed to the airport. I was bound for the so-called "Nassau Turn Arounds." Today would include three less-than-an-hour flights over the ocean to Nassau, Bahamas and back to Miami. Then another return to Nassau and back to Miami. At each stop, jetsetters were loaded onto the flight. The glamor of flying faded fast on such trips, but my schedule next week would include a trip with a four-day-lay-over in Buenos Aires.

During my Nassau stops, I'd seen nothing of Nassau—except the airport terminal where I bought a bottle of rum during a dash into the Duty-Free Shop. Back this evening, at the curb outside my apartment building, I exited the taxi, tired while clutching the rum bottle, my tote bag, my Pan Am bolo hat, jacket, and purse.

When I got to the apartment stairs, I inhaled the scent of night-blooming jasmine growing by the stairs. For a moment,

I forgot my long day and instead looked forward to days off. I opened the apartment door where Emily greeted me, wide-eyed.

"Hurricane Watch!" she announced. "What should we do?"

As I bit my lip and fidgeted with the button on my uniform blouse, the room turned dark.

"The power's out!" Emily announced.

"Do we have a flashlight?" I asked, clueless as to what else to do.

Harried minutes followed as we considered our game plan. Without a car, hurricane shutters, a transistor radio, a flashlight or even a candle, what were we to do? As a citizen of tornado country, I had entered hurricane country without a qualifying visa.

Before long, we heard a knock on the window. Emily peeked outside into the now dark walkway connecting the seven units on our floor.

"It's a neighbor guy. I met him at the pool."

Standing in the now open doorway, wearing bell-bottom jeans and a Coconut Gove T-shirt, the fellow announced, "Grab food from your fridge. Head down to the pool. A Hurricane Watch Party is happening!"

I looked at Emily who looked at me. "Sounds good," I said with more confidence than I felt. A tightness in my neck and a queasy feeling in my stomach forced some awareness as to how stirred up and uneasy I was. I feared a hurricane with flooding downpours and 75- to 100-mile-an-hour winds. Was it safe to go outside? Should we evacuate? But where to? The air turned damp and humid. Wind blew through the door as the neighbor guy left to knock on other doors. A peek outside convinced me conditions had worsened.

Not wanting to reveal my hurricane panic, I slipped off my Pan Am uniform, put-on polyester pants with a peasant top and a rain jacket. Emily raced to the kitchen and retrieved wine bought on a Lisbon trip. I added my bottle of rum and some bananas.

When Emily and I arrived at the pool, I watched twenty-somethings gather. They chatted while placing their potluck offerings on a patio table standing next to lounge chairs. Hamburger patties, chicken breasts, chips, avocados, and tomatoes filled the table.

A beaming sundress-clad, curly-haired blond, with more self-assurance than I could muster, swaggered near me. Behind her, palm branches bent over at crazy angles before bouncing back again.

I tried to ignore the wind as I stood on the tile by the pool. A grill stood in a corner near me. Of more interest than the grill was the guy who stood behind the sizzling grill. He raised his head as he flipped a burger patty into the air.

A cute guy who could cook! I felt certain he would not plop into a recliner expecting a woman to serve dinner on his TV tray.

I stepped up closer to catch a better look at the appealing grill-master. I realized he was the same person I'd seen from the window a few days ago. That day, he had stopped at his mailbox, dressed in a gray suit.

"How do you like your burgers?" the grill guy said.

At first, I thought he was talking to the sundress garbed blond. But he turned toward me. Caught off guard, I searched for a light-hearted retort.

"I like my burger not to walk off the plate."

"Okay, that works. I'm Charlie," he said with a confident grin that excited my exhausted energy.

"Hi, I'm Cindy. My roommate and I live in apartment L."

"Cool. I'm in 'D' in the other building," he said, waving his grill tongs as a burger patty sizzled.

"Do you like to cook?"

"Been cooking since I was a kid."

I saw the way he turned his eyes to the ground.

"Wow! I never cooked a meal growing up," I said.

No more explanation came from Charlie.

"Are you from Miami?" I asked.

"No, I moved here a year ago from Pittsburgh. After I landed a job with an engineering firm. Got tired of the ice and snow. They call me a snowbird."

"You're an engineer?" I asked. A professional job is a good thing, I thought. "I'm from Oklahoma City. I'm a Pan Am stewardess."

"Great," Charlie said, setting his burger flipper aside as he looked my way.

"I started with Pan Am a couple of months ago. I've been gone so much; I haven't figured out what's going on around here."

"Well, we gotta change that," Charlie said, handing me a plate with a burger.

A sharp wind gust almost took the paper plate and my burger with it.

"Have you ever been through a hurricane?"

"No, but don't worry. We'll be fine," Charlie said, laughing. "My best friend lives a few blocks from here. His place has hurricane shutters. And food, water, and wine. We can head over there if this thing gets bad."

As more apartment dwellers stepped up to the grill, their banter kept me from talking with Charlie. As the party continued, I stuck close to the grill, or better said, I stuck close to Charlie. I spoke a word here and there, but mostly hung onto Charlie's calm confidence.

After a few minutes, Charlie took my bananas and the rum from the food table. He sliced the bananas, dropped them onto a skillet he doused with rum. Flames soared.

"Bananas flambé!" Charlie exclaimed as he scooped a huge

serving into a bowl. When he handed the luscious dessert to me, I almost spilled it, distracted by the energy I felt between us. Above our heads, rain clouds burst as though they couldn't contain themselves any longer. Emily rushed toward me with fright etched across her face. I watched Charlie shuffle through 8-track tapes stacked on the food table. Soon I heard Spanky and Our Gang lyrics blast through the wind-stirred rain. "I'd like to get to know you, know you. Yes, I'd like to get to know you if I could." Did Charlie mean that song for me?

Emily pulled me toward the stairs. I didn't want to leave, but she kept tugging.

"Let's get out of here," Emily said. "These people are crazy."

"Not all of them," I said as we ran up the stairs. Over my shoulder I said, "Nice to meet you, Charlie."

Inside the apartment, we wondered what to do. In a minute, we heard a knock on the door. It was Charlie.

"Call if you need anything," he said, handing me both a flashlight and his business card with a phone number.

Using the flashlight, I read the name Charlie Novokowsky. What a hard name to remember. What a hard guy to forget, I thought.

Charlie asked for my phone number. I hurried to give it to him. A few more words were exchanged before he left for his place.

Soon, the power came back on. We'd escaped a hurricane. Instead, a hurricane of stirring emotion had come my way.

"Hey! I like that outfit," Charlie said a couple days later when I opened the door and motioned him inside. Picking up my purse, I talked mindlessly and nervously as we left for our first date. When Charlie had called to ask me out, I fretted about what to wear. My Oklahoma clothes lacked a Miami flair, so I took a cab to Miracle Mile, a great shopping area. I bought wide-legged palazzo pants with a green and pink floral pattern. I paired the pants with a matching midriff-revealing crop top that also showed some shoulder. Other than wearing a bikini, I'd never gone out with my belly showing and rarely with shoulders showing. Anyway, Charlie said he liked my outfit, but what I really cared about was whether Charlie liked me. I felt sure he did.

I wondered if Charlie fretted about what to wear. I doubted it. He wore jeans and a white polo shirt. The kind with the cool little alligator logo. I liked his woodsy scented cologne.

"I'm like a tourist in Miami," I told Charlie to make conversation as I pulled on the hem of my crop top. I suddenly felt like a camera with an overexposure problem.

As we walked, Charlie hummed.

"You're fun, Charlie," I said, noting my sunglasses fogging in the humidity. "I've never had sunglasses fog over like this. That's not fun."

"You'll get used to it," Charlie said, slipping his fingers into mine as he took my hand. His firm palm and his strong fingers touching mine made me forget everything else.

Was it possible I was being drawn into a new romance as easily as my hands were drawn into this man's hands? Charlie was different from anyone I'd ever known. And I was more than a little intrigued by the difference. I didn't have to define what was different. No need to analyze it or scrutinize it, but simply to enjoy it.

A few steps later, Charlie stopped beside a red Mustang convertible. I squealed, "Is this your car? I love convertibles."

"This little buggy serves me well. A darn good moving van," Charlie said, motioning me inside the open door. "I hauled all my essentials from Pittsburgh. My blender. Turntable. Vinyls and a few clothes."

"Ha! Well, it helped that you rented a furnished place. Do

you have the same crazy floral sofa that came with our pad?"

Charlie chuckled as he got inside, adjusting the radio and the air-conditioner at the same time. "Same sofa," he said.

As Charlie drove along past tropical palm trees, he tapped the steering wheel to the Bee Gees' lyrics, "It's okay, it's all right." Charlie seemed to prefer silence to empty conversation. I absorbed his vibe without filling space with chatter.

In a bit, Charlie leaned back in his bucket seat. With a moist breeze blowing, he raised one arm above the open convertible top as if to touch the fluffy clouds. Meanwhile, purple jacaranda, red-orange frangipani, and olive tanned Charlie delighted me. Self-confident! Good looking! A bit older than me. A great cook! An engineer with a red Mustang convertible! What could be finer?

"Today," he said, "I'm taking you to Biscayne Bay, with a stop at Bayfront Park. Later, we'll eat Cuban food at my favorite Cuban restaurant." Turning the corner, Charlie waved at a bicycler.

"I've flown over Biscayne Bay, but never walked by it," I said. "By the way, do you know that fellow on the bike?"

"I don't know most people I wave to," Charlie said. "I wave anyway. It makes them wonder if they know me." He paused. "Ya know," Charlie added, "flying over Biscayne Bay and knowing the Bay is as different as having a dream and living one."

"You're right," I told him, stretching my arm outside the convertible to touch the balmy breeze. "I love the bay. It's so clear."

"As clear as a gin and tonic," Charlie said as he parked the car.

I liked his humor. Charlie seemed able to live without complicating life. In the face of a hurricane warning, he made burgers and bananas flambé. On a first date, he looked relaxed.

"The hippies at Bay Front Park! Lotta hair! Not a lotta clothes," Charlie added. "Smoking grass. It's a waste of time and money."

"I'll take your word for it. I haven't even smoked a cigarette."

"I prefer getting high on life," Charlie announced.

Sparks of intense attraction lit a fire in me. Yet, my burning desire to see the world, to be independent and to express myself in some important way tamed my fire until I looked at Charlie again. Another spark ignited. This one bigger than the last.

A cultural revolution in full display filled the park. Love and peace signs, guitar playing, singing and protestors shouting, "Make love not war." Another sign read, "Women want equality."

I sighed. "I'm remembering more than a year ago. At the University of Madrid. One morning as I arrived for class, protestors were demonstrating."

I tried to steady my thoughts. "Police and army tanks confronted the protesters. So frightening! The next day, Franco closed the University."

Walking toward the park, I felt the same anxiety of that day in Spain. I wondered how Charlie would respond to what I was about to blurt out. "I woke up in Spain realizing change must and is happening. I support it. Do you?"

Charlie turned his head toward me. He seemed to absorb my intensity without interrupting or appearing dismayed.

"I'm opposed to the war in Vietnam," he told me. "Thank God I have a high draft number. And I'm all for women's rights."

He pointed and nodded at a hippie waving a sign that read, "Men of quality are not threatened by women for equality."

"I'm glad we share the same values," I said, feeling as though my heart might burst with joy—right through my crop top.

"How about some lunch?" Charlie asked. "At my favorite Cuban place."

"I'm for that," I said.

Once settled inside, Charlie announced, "I'm in the mood for *picadillo*. It's made with black beans, rice, meat, raisins and spices. You're gonna love it."

"Raisins?" I said. "That's different. Okay, I'm in."

When our order arrived, I dipped my fork into the *picadillo*. The flavors combined in a sensory delight. I asked the waiter the spice I was tasting.

"Cumin, Señorita, mucho cumin. Es un aphrodisiáco."

I smiled and edged closer to Charlie. We glided into talk that covered our mutual liking of the Beatles and the Bee Gees, along with Charlie's interest in sports cars. When I asked about his family, he dropped his head,

"I was seven. I came home from school and saw my mother on the kitchen floor, not breathing. A heart condition, the doctor said. Life got tough. Just my dad, my brother and me. More vino please," Charlie asked the waiter.

A pang of anguish made it difficult to reply. With inadequate words I said, "Now I know why you started cooking so young. How hard to grow up without your mother!"

"Isn't the *picadillo* great?" Charlie said, changing the conversation.

"It's delicious!" I replied, taking another bite.

Charlie asked about my mother. Uncertain how to reply to someone who lost his so young, I said, "I have a wonderful mother. But I don't want her life. Raising kids. Doing the dishes. The laundry. Taking care of my father's every whim. No time for herself."

My words forced me to realize how much I valued holding onto my independent, adventurous spirit. And how priceless

Mother's love and support had been throughout my life. And how happy I felt with Charlie. And how sad to grow up without his mother.

For the next two years, my work took me on Pan Am jets across Central and South America, and the Caribbean. Layovers in Buenos Aires, Rio de Janeiro, to islands like Barbados, Jamaica, and Trinidad. The thrill of coming home to be with Charlie made life grand. I adored this sweet man. He said he loved me. We moved in together. Emily found a new roommate. She seemed happy, but she wanted a boyfriend.

I loved being with Charlie. Loads of girls in Miami he could have dated. How did I get so lucky? He was funny and fun, and I told him how lucky he was to be with me. I felt proud to have enough confidence to say those words, even if in jest. Charlie's manner made it easy to laugh with him. Easy to be myself, even as I was still figuring out who I really was.

On a day off, while Charlie was at work, I walked outside and sat under a sprawling banyan tree growing on the apartment property. I needed space to contemplate my excitement, my restlessness, and my *"inquietude."* I wanted time to explore the maturing love growing between Charlie and me. It was marvelous and frightening.

The sun's rays highlighted the banyan tree's aerial roots. It was odd how the roots attached to the branches before they cascaded to the ground like wooden stalactites. I had never seen a banyan tree before moving to Florida.

I wondered why I resisted any notion of putting down roots in Florida with Charlie. I looked up under the branches. Wind rushed through the leaves. I watched how the branches stay strong, undergirded by the aerial roots. Were the banyan tree branches trying to tell me something?

Later the same day, I heard that Pam Am's San Francisco's

base was open for stewardess transfers. Emily and I talked about how exciting it would be to transfer there. Without another thought, we both mailed our applications. We could share an apartment again. When not in the city, we would fly to Hawaii, Hong Kong, Bangkok, Tahiti, Australia and more. The allure of Asia, the Pacific and other exotic cities tugged at me. I could not allow my wings to stay attached like banyan tree branches. I wanted the freedom to see more of the wide world. Didn't Mother say I had sand in my shoes?

In less than a week after requesting transfers, Emily and I had ours. We'd committed to moving. Charlie had no idea. It all happened so fast. How could I tell him? I wanted to be with him, but the new travel... Was I selfish or smart to take advantage of what might be a once-in-a life-time opportunity?

That evening at Charlie's place, we sat on his couch. Charlie's arm cuddled across my shoulders. I fidgeted. My eyes turned to focus on framed photos of us arranged on the bookcases across the room. The wonderful memories I savored, reliving them in my mind.

The moment I would allow myself to reveal my decision to transfer, I feared shaking-up the beautiful, intimate relationship Charlie and I had developed. My decision would shock him. Could I bear to hurt Charlie? And I absolutely did not want to lose him from my life. I loved this man, but the world was calling me.

Charlie seemed certain and comfortable about our relationship. I, on the other hand, had to confront my wanderlust and my seeking for a grand purpose out there somewhere. It wasn't another man I wanted; it was something else.

"Whenever I travel to a new place, I sense I'm meant to be there." I could hear the sound of my voice ripple across the room as I spoke. "I sense I'm supposed to experience something important, to learn something new. It's hard to explain, but in each place I travel, I feel something rising."

"Do you mean the temperature?" Charlie quipped.

"No. It's something else," I said, as frustration made me tense.

"You think differently than I do," Charlie replied, pulling me closer. "MASH is about to start. Let's watch and not worry about other stuff right now."

I pretended to watch but heard not a word. My mind rehearsed breaking my news. Maybe Charlie sensed something he was not ready to hear. I decided tomorrow would be a better time. I needed to sleep on how to share what had to be told.

We found a corner table at a small Miami club where brass horns and cylinder drums created Cuban rumba and conga beats. Charlie loved this trendy, yet intimate club where young Cuban immigrants were introducing a hot new sound to Miami. He'd come here once before with some friends, while I was on a trip.

"You've got to hear this," Charlie said, tapping his foot. I realized how much he wanted me to experience what he had found. It was a bit like my finding *duende* in Spain.

On a warm, humid Florida night, I wore the same wide-leg pants and bare midriff top I had worn on our first date two years ago. The outfit brought back the thrill of that date. Seated at a table, with sangria in hand, Charlie wrapped one arm around me. I looked at his face and saw his foot tapping in beat to the music. He was one happy guy.

I felt the dark, painful side of *duende*. I thought about Teresa of Ávila. Since her Beloved was God, she didn't have to leave him when she traveled to create reformed convents. God could accompany her. Unfair comparison? Not to me, it wasn't.

When Charlie motioned for me to join a conga line, I joined

him. The dance floor filled with lovers, their bodies moving, swaying, and touching. I urged my body to move to the music until my mind took over and made dancing impossible. I had to speak up. I grabbed Charlie's hand and pulled him away from the dance floor. He threw me a frown.

"Don't you want to dance?"

I had to tell him. "I haven't wanted to upset you, but Emily and I are moving to San Francisco. We requested a transfer so we could fly to new places like Hong Kong, Australia, and Tahiti." The words flew from my mouth.

"We're supposed to move in two weeks," I said, spilling the news as fast as I could. "They didn't give us much time. I can't miss seeing what else is out there. You understand, don't you? We can still see each other. I'll fly back here. You can come see me..."

Charlie sat still for a minute. I watched his face tense. His demeanor changed. I had never seen Charlie look like this before.

"Sure, I get it," he said.

I wanted to hear Charlie say he understood. But when he spoke, I heard something different.

"For you, life's about putting pins on a map. For me, it's something more, much more."

Charlie's words triggered an awful, unplanned response from me. "Don't you understand the passion I have to discover more? Don't you want me to see the world? Don't you want me to find what's calling me?"

"What I want and what I know are two different things," Charlie announced. "Since I can't stop gravity, I can't stop you from moving."

He leaned back in his chair. I waited. Staccato words flowed. "You might as well know," Charlie told me while I saw pain written across his face, "I won't take the bridge if this thing between us doesn't work out. I want to be with you. I mean I want a life with you, but..."

The words were harsh, as was my applying for a transfer without telling Charlie sooner. I deserved every word he uttered, but hearing it hurt like I had never hurt before.

Charlie knew how to suppress his true feelings when he didn't want to feel them. He also knew how to get tough. I knew that. He wasn't going to tell me it was fine for me to leave. He was not about to agree to sit in Miami waiting for me to search the world for who knows what or for who knows how long.

I burst into tears. I wanted Charlie. I wanted the world. How could I have both?

"Cry all you want," the tough guy in Charlie said as he asked for the bill. "You've made up your mind. What's the use of crying? Let's go."

What had I done? My impulse to find something I yearned for, something to complement the love I felt for Charlie, was sending me to San Francisco. I might lose Charlie because of it. But Charlie knew me. I could no more stop myself than I could stop a river from flowing.

San Francisco, California, Luxor, Egypt, Istanbul, Turkey and more 1971-1972.

When Emily and I landed at the San Francisco Airport, we took a bus to the YWCA. Emily's thriftiness led us there. We left our suitcases in our room and hopped on a trolley in search of an apartment. After many steps up and down the hills, we found a one-bedroom apartment in the Mission district and rented it on the spot.

That night back at the YWCA, despite the thrill of a fascinating city, I could not think about anything except Charlie. I wanted love in my life, his love, but I had this quest that pulled me forward. I hated how I had made Charlie feel. How he had reacted. No matter his words, I never doubted he loved me. Did we have a future? Would he find someone else while I gallivanted around the world? Was it possible to be loved and to have space to grow and time to see the world? Could I know intimacy and sensuality and also pursue passions on my own?

I hesitated to talk to Emily about Charlie. She seemed a tad jealous since her dating life had not worked out well. However, I also knew nothing would have stopped her from transferring.

In no time, Emily and I were off on our separate flights. Hawaii, Hong Kong, Tahiti, Sydney and Guam, with long layovers in each place. Getting to these places required exhausting flights on 747s filled with passengers. But at each arrival, something exciting awaited. It was an affirmation signaling I had made the right decision not to miss this opportunity.

Over the next months, Charlie and talked on the phone the days when I was in San Francisco. I flew to see him several times, taking advantage of the free cargo flights that allowed one Pan Am employee per flight to travel from San Francisco to Miami. Charlie came to see me, but he had to pay full fair. We lived in the moment and never discussed tomorrow, but it was odd. Questions about the future filled my mind, both when the two of us were together and when we were apart.

Soon the annual one-month vacation Pam Am offered came around. Emily and I were both assigned the month of May. We got the news in early April and began making plans to travel together. Despite our separate flight schedules, we arranged for a round-trip ticket to Rome on Al Italia using a reciprocal arrangement with Pan Am. The ticket, at a cost of $99, allowed us unlimited flights for a month to anywhere Al Italia flew.

I could barely breathe imagining a month of travel to new places. I told Charlie and my parents we would visit Italy, England, and Ireland. Charlie would have loved to come along, but the cost for him would have been prohibitive. Besides, he didn't have a month he could be away from work.

"How 'bout Egypt rather than England?" I said to Emily after we entered the Rome airport, where I saw Cairo listed as the next departing flight. The flight to London had been cancelled. Why not jump on the flight to Egypt?

My pulse raced. I heard the announcement, "Passengers traveling to Cairo kindly proceed to gate 52." We were traveling stand-by with no hotel reservations or set plans. We looked at each other. Emily agreed. "Egypt sounds good." We ran to catch the Cairo flight, one that, lucky for us, had two free seats.

The fact Egypt did not appear in my *Europe on $5 a Day* travel guide did not occur to me—nor did the fact that not one person we knew realized we were bound for Egypt. It turned out England and Ireland, as well as postcards to inform loved ones about our change in plans, would have to wait. Phone calls were too costly and difficult. And one other thing would have to wait: awareness that Egypt ranked as one of the most dangerous places in the world for women to visit at that time.

He said his name was Happiness. The bearded, dread-locked American who greeted us as he smoked pot on the porch of our Cairo youth hostel—one better labeled a flop-house. We had found the place posted at the Cairo airport.

After a deep inhale, Happiness shouted, "Hell no I won't go—to Vietnam that is—but how 'bout joining me on the train to Luxor tomorrow night? They say the temples and tombs there are, like, far out."

Maybe he would help keep us safe, I thought. We looked at each other and Emily said, "Sure! Why not?"

"We can catch the pyramids later," I added, looking toward Happiness.

Except for one hiccup, the plan went well. It turned out that by the next morning Happiness had disappeared, and we never saw him again. But undaunted, Emily and I caught a cab to the train station where a muezzin recited the last Islamic call to prayer of the day, from a mosque minaret microphone. The sounds hung in the air, reminding me of the same call to prayer I had heard five times daily in Casablanca. Two decades after leaving Morocco, I'd returned to an Arab nation again. My childhood dream of becoming a queen had not come true, but the sand in my shoes had brought me far.

I wondered if during my vacation I could leave behind self-doubt—not doubts about traveling, rather ones about what to do with my life.

"There's so much to see," I told Emily, shaking my head. "Where should we go first? And how will we know what we're seeing? I'm clueless about Egyptian ruins."

On this first morning in Luxor, over breakfast in a café near our hostel, my nervous anxiety caused me to pepper Emily with one question after the other.

"Relax!" Emily snapped. "We can't afford a guide."

We had little money, but I didn't want to be reminded. Bothered that we had no plan for the day, I bit the inside of my cheeks to keep from irritating Emily. I talked about the weather. She was more direct than I knew how to be, but I really liked traveling with her.

An Egyptian woman, perhaps in her forties, stood up from the table next to ours. She approached us as she tucked her long hair behind her ears.

"Hello! I'm Ameera. I overheard your conversation." I greeted her with a smile that seemed to invite her to continue talking. "I'm an Egyptologist from Luxor completing my PhD thesis about Egyptian Goddesses," she explained. "But today I have no plans. I'd enjoy spending the day with Americans. You're Americans, right?"

"I guess it's easy to tell," I said, delighted at the thought of having Ameera to guide us.

Emily chimed in, twitching in her chair as if ready to head for the ruins at that moment. "A free guide. Sounds great!"

Did Emily have to throw in the word "free"? It felt insulting.

Anyway, we were about to join the first Egyptologist I'd ever known, and a delightful one at that. I could relax; we had a plan and a guide. "A free guide."

With winds blowing across ruddy, barren desert sands, Emily, Ameera and I jumped into a traditional horse-drawn buggy called a *calesh*. Our driver veered toward the Karnak temple complex.

"Karnak is one of the oldest and largest religious sights in the world," Ameera explained as we bumped along.

A cacophony of clip-clop horse hoofs, *calesh* and car drivers yelling over screeching horns accompanied us. Somehow, amid the hubbub, we talked about how hard it is to be a woman in a man's world.

"The freedom and independence you enjoy as American women makes me envious," Ameera told us. "In my country, I'm sad to say, women still contend with arranged marriage, child brides, and a huge lack of opportunities. Educating women and granting equal rights—such things really steam men, many to the boiling point."

"Speaking of boiling point, how do the women not burn up under those long black robes and veils?" Emily asked, wiping sweat from her brow.

"Years of accommodation, I suppose," Ameera said as her raven-colored hair blew with the sultry wind. "Some women and most husbands have decided the *hijab* is a symbol of adherence to the Koran. As a progressive Muslim, I find wearing the *hijab* a misunderstanding of what Muhammad taught about the equality of women and men."

I was unsure how to respond. I already felt uncomfortable about Emily's question about Egyptian women. It might have been acceptable for Ameera to make such a comment, but it felt less so for a non-Muslim American.

"Actually, things in my country were different in the '50s," Ameera added as we approached Karnak. "When Nasser came to power, many Arabs joined him seeking Western-style modernity. You even saw some Arab women wearing bikinis."

I was unaware and surprised.

"Today, *hijabs* have replaced bikinis," Ameera added. "And the education of women has been replaced by encouraging women to have more babies. Trust me, as women rise, male reaction will rise. I fear harsh consequences."

I looked at Emily, reading the same concern on her face that I had. Were we safe in Egypt? Was Ameera safe? And yet I understood the tension the rise of women creates around the world as well as at home.

After browsing through the magnificent Karnak Hierapolis, a hall containing more than a hundred massive hieroglyphic-incised columns, Ameera directed us toward an area with a sign that read, "Sekhmet's Temple." Pausing, Ameera said, "I often visit this mysterious, secluded temple. Many tourists miss it. It's a shame. Sekhmet represents sacred feminine power."

I halted at the sound of three words I had never before heard linked together. Sacred. Feminine. Power. Was it even possible to link those three words? Well, yes, certainly. But my mind had never combined the words together, nor had I ever heard the words spoken together.

Emily suggested I enter first. I got the impression goddess temples were not on her must see list.

After a jolt of energy rushed through me while filled with

curiosity, I entered the one-room temple. At first, everything looked dark. As my eyes adjusted, a black, granite goddess statue with the head of a lioness and the body of a woman appeared. I faced the larger-than-life goddess who stood with her right foot stepping forward. It did seem odd to meet a goddess with the head of a lioness. Yet I could not deny the solid black granite goddess had powerful energy encircling her. I could feel it. An unexpected sensation. I decided I had been directed to an archetype of sacred feminine power.

An orb of light covered Sekhmet's lioness face. I hesitated to speak aloud. Instead, I took out my journal.

"Sekhmet," I wrote. "I knew nothing about you before today, but I've learned from Ameera about your influence in ancient Egypt. I can't even imagine a female goddess playing such an important role in my country, not even in our so-called modern world. Though we do have the Statue of Liberty, our Lady Liberty.

"You stand strong and bold like a lion, yet calm and ready for what lies ahead. I must admit, I'm frightened, not knowing if Egypt is safe for young women. And I have other doubts and fears too."

As I wrote to Sekhmet, as uncanny as it seemed, a subtle shift came over me. I put my journal in my backpack and posed with one foot in front of me while I lifted my head like a lioness rising. As I held the posture, inner confidence moved up from the soles of my feet through my belly, my heart and lungs, up to my raised head. The feeling was powerful. I wondered if it would last.

For our next stop, Ameera invited Emily and me to gather underneath the dappled shade of an old sycamore tree in the open Karnak Temple space. "This variety of tree has through-out history represented power and protection," Ameera told us.

I had to make a comment. What I felt was too strong to

keep to myself. "For me, the sycamore symbolizes the power and protection I sensed in Sekhmet's Temple. Something coming from inside me rather than from the outside."

"That's it," Ameera said. "You named it. It's an energy and a principle. All people have it, no matter our gender. But most of us do not know how to name it. And we forget to claim it."

Having my words affirmed by this bright, aware woman opened me up to accept I was on a path of awakening. Nothing new, but my awareness of what was happening was greater than ever before.

"Inside a temple that once stood on this very spot," Ameera added, "the Forty-Two Admonitions—moral and spiritual principles of Maat—were written in hieroglyphics on the now forgotten walls."

Emily bent to sit on one of several large stones strewn in the sand. Seated nearby on another stone, Ameera asked, "Did you know Maat was the goddess who represented the idea of creating balance from chaos?"

"Heaven knows we need her today," I commented, imagining a temple standing beside me with Maat's Admonitions covering the walls.

Indicating her agreement with a nod, Ameera explained that the ancient principles of Maat honored the Divine Feminine. Scholars believe Moses condensed the Ten Commandments from Maat's Admonitions, created 2,000 years before his time.

I asked, "How come I know about Moses and the Ten Commandments and nothing about Maat and her admonitions?"

Ameera gazed around the ruins before she reminded us how feminine principles, myths, and wisdom have been disregarded, forgotten or attributed to males and masculine gods in countries around the world.

I felt my interest growing. Ameera shook sand from her shoes and described how, unlike the Ten Commandments,

Maat's Admonitions located personal power and responsibility with an indwelling divinity inside human beings. A change occurred when Maat's principles became those of a distant power over life that came from above.

"I call what happened a take-down of Maat," Ameera told us.

Emily and I looked at each other. What I was hearing inspired me to think of the immanent Divine presence that Saint Teresa wrote about. Maybe that was linked to what I felt near Sekhmet and beside the sycamore tree. Maybe I felt the same near the banyan tree in Coconut Grove and also inside of me.

Ameera sensed my interest. "The Divine Feminine is on the rise, but not everyone sees what is happening. Yet many of us feel Her presence. We're in the throes. And those of us with this awareness recognize each other."

I leaned forward, delighted to be with someone who could articulate my awareness. Moving closer to the lone sycamore tree, I touched the peeling bark.

"I need to do what sycamores do. To let the old bark peel away. Let my socialized mind peel away. For a start, I'm no longer wearing a bra like women are supposed to," I said with a laugh.

"Emily, what do you think?" Ameera asked, also laughing.

Emily shuffled around the scattered stone. "To be honest," she said, "I see ancient, tumbledown ruins. It's interesting, but not what I'd call divine."

I straightened my back to brace the next words. Rubbing her jeans, Emily continued, "I'm an academic, but also the kind of gal who feels divine in denim and while eating chocolate."

I got tickled and giggled.

But Emily was not done. "Don't get me wrong. I'm for female empowerment, but I got burned-out on religion long ago. I've struggled to find a spiritual path and gave up. But I am interested in the history of Maat."

Ameera nodded in Emily's direction. "I like denim, chocolate and female empowerment too. And I left behind patriarchal religious rituals and beliefs years ago. That's why I decided to learn all I could about ancient Egyptian goddesses and their wisdom. For me, the Egyptian goddess pantheon represents archetypes of a lost treasure more valuable than the jewels found in King Tutankhamen's tomb. I've discovered it inside many religious traditions, but often buried in dogma."

Ameera had Emily's full attention as she said, "Life in ancient Egypt did not create women's equality or freedom from oppression, but what I call the archetypal feminine was revered in myth and story. This feminine was strong and active as well as loving and receptive. Anyway, I'm hungry. Let's go eat. I know of a place where they have divine chocolate."

With that, we rushed past the tumbledown stones to find our *calesh*.

As we rode along, Ameera mentioned that Florence Nightingale had visited Karnak back in 1850.

"In her diary," Ameera noted, "Florence wrote that, 'you feel like spirits revisiting your former world, strange and fallen to ruins.'"

"So, Emily," Ameera added, "you aren't the only one who experienced Karnak as strange and fallen to ruins."

Emily looked at Ameera without response, as if waiting to hear more.

"You can read Florence Nightingale's diary, *Letters from Egypt*. She was about your age when she came here. Florence's mystical and spiritual motivations unlocked and ignited her calling."

"Ameera," I commented while bouncing inside the *calesh,* "it's interesting that you know so much about Florence

Nightingale."

"Right!" Emily said.

"After I found Florence's writing, I was amazed at how she managed to escape her conventional British life and the pressure to marry. How ancient Egyptian religion piqued her curiosity and led to her mystical insights."

As our buggy came to a stop by a charming restaurant, Ameera motioned for us to climb out. Standing on the street, we settled with our driver and watched him lead his horse and buggy down the road.

"Now, let's enjoy lunch with chocolate for dessert," Ameera said.

As we waited for our food, Ameera repeated quotes from Florence's writing, "For what is mysticism? Is it not to draw near to God, ('or the Goddess,' Ameera added), and not by rites or ceremonies, but by inward disposition?"

But soon it wasn't mysticism—but our love lives, or our lack of—that dominated the conversation. And I suppose it was not an unusual segue from mysticism, with its longing for love and union, to the love longings of three women.

"I thought I'd found the perfect guy," Emily announced, "until I realized he wasn't emotionally available. But he sure was sexually available. To any female who looked his way."

The waiter arrived to distract Emily with hot *falafel*, a deep-fried chickpea treat Ameera ordered for us to try.

Ameera took a bite then put down her fork. "Try finding a lover in Egypt!" she said. "I mean one who wants a free and independent woman. Finding such a man is rarer than two American girls heading to Rome and ending up in Cairo. And besides," Ameera admitted, lowering her head, "to find love, we must love ourselves. I'm working on that. Some men know how to love both themselves and a woman. At least that's what I've been told. But it might be a rumor."

I laughed. But as I did so, I understood this was nothing to laugh about.

"We want freedom and love. Finding the right relationship could require help from all the goddesses," I said, though it was not lost on me that I'd experienced a love neither Ameera nor Emily had known. Yet, I had left that love in Florida as I sought to seek something more.

Later, after much conversation, I was struck when Emily insisted she pay for dinner. Emily knew how to watch pennies. And how to spend them to show appreciation. Ameera had made an impact on my travel companion and dear friend.

On our way to the hotel, I realized it was hard to say goodbye. Ameera walked with us inside the lobby. She took our addresses and promised to keep in touch.

"Next time you come, you must visit the Temple of Isis at Philae. It's one of our most precious treasures, though it had to be dismantled to save it from flooding while the Aswan Dam is being built. It will be rebuilt on higher ground. When you return one day, you will see it."

"I'll be back," I said. "Someday I'll float the Nile and visit the Temple of Isis."

Istanbul, Turkey, 1972

"My shoulder hurts from carrying my backpack," Emily said with a grimace. "Do you think this place is worth the wait? What about the covered bazaar shops?"

"Istanbul's Hagia Sophia, one of the wonders of the world...," I said, my back turned to avoid Emily's face. I opened my guidebook and read aloud, "Built as a Byzantine Orthodox Christian Church in 532 CE, the basilica became a Muslim Mosque. Today the Hagia Sophia, with minarets piercing the sky, serves as a secular museum, though many believe it continues to encapsulate Sophia's sacred wisdom."

A female traveler about our age turned from ahead of us in line. "Hi, I'm Monique. From Paris. I came to the Hagia Sophia after a split with my fiancé," she said, straightening her sunglasses. "Sophia's wisdom and mystical presence..."

Intrigued, I introduced myself and said, "I never imagined being here. We jumped on an unplanned flight to Istanbul at the Cairo airport, and here we are. I must confess I've not heard about Sophia."

"You must know the Female Divine. The feminine counterpart of God. I need to meet Her to heal my broken heart."

Emily's eyes opened wide. She moved toward the entrance.

A female expression of God. Why had I never imagined such? I felt a reinvention, or at least a huge expansion of my concept of the Divine. And was it even possible I left Egypt and arrived in Istanbul to hear these comments?

Once inside, we lost Monique in the crowd, or she slipped away to be alone. A need to connect with Her stirred in me. As I looked around, I had the sense my body was absorbing more than my mind could comprehend.

Byzantine tile mosaics. Many with feminine faces. Bronze oil lamp chandeliers producing shadows of light around darkened spaces. The womb-like rounded basilica guarded me from the invisibility I'd felt inside most churches and cathedrals.

Emily and I lingered inside for a long while. In the silence, I imagined Sophia's wisdom encircling me. I sensed Sophia could understand my struggle to know if Charlie and I had a future. The answer to that question felt like the most important question in my life at the moment. I wanted to ask if I was ready to give back the love Charlie offered me.

When we left the basilica, no flash of light from inside the Hagia Sophia had appeared to answer my question, but I trusted an answer would make itself known. For now, I could stop worrying.

Our vacation odyssey would soon come to an end, but it felt more like a beginning. I pictured my six-year-old self with sand in her shoes and my twenty-something self now traveling the world, not yet understanding my life's purpose, not yet knowing if a life with Charlie was an option, but I could take in the wonders around me, knowing the Divine with a face like mine might understand my quest.

Interrupting my deep, calming thoughts, two Turkish men appeared, hissing and curling their fingers like claws. Without hesitating, I took off running. Emily sprinted down the street beside me. It was painful as well as frightening to consider that because we walked unveiled in jeans, we had become the target of the men's rage. I was reminded of Ameera's concerns about the rise of women. As I glanced behind me, I could see the men decided not to follow us.

"Thank you, Sophia," I said, rushing inside a coffee shop. There was more for us to see in Istanbul, but all I wanted to do at the moment was to picture Charlie. So far away. I wanted him close. The pull to transfer to San Francisco suddenly felt like a push to have time with him. What was he doing today? Why were international phone calls so complicated and expensive?

In two nights, after more time in Istanbul, Emily and I would leave for San Francisco. Once inside my apartment, no matter the time, I'd call Charlie. I had no idea what I'd say.

San Francisco, 1972

As much as I loved the excitement of visiting new places and having new realizations, it felt good to be back home. I called

Charlie as soon as I walked into the apartment.

I held the phone, wishing I were holding him instead. "I love you. I missed you. I have so much to tell you."

"I love you too. More than you know," I heard Charlie say. His harsh words and tone of voice from when I announced my move a year ago were gone.

"A few days to catch up," I said. "Then I have a flight to Tahiti."

"Why don't you come relax with me for a few days?" Charlie said. He knew I'd say I didn't have time. I said nothing. Charlie soon ended the call. I felt his disappointment as I put down the phone receiver, but I did need time to wash my clothes and to relax away from airports. But had I made the right decision?

During a year getting to know San Francisco, between flights to see the world, I had flown many times to be with Charlie, and he had flown to San Francisco to be with me. Each time together was better than the time before, though the goodbyes were painful.

While unpacking, I kept thinking about Charlie. That's when Emily's comments before my last trip rang in my ears. I didn't like what she had said or how she said it, but her words stuck with me.

"You run a big risk leaving Charlie alone in Miami," she told me. "Single guys like him don't stay on the market for long."

I could not bear the idea of Charlie as just a guy "on the market." But maybe Emily had a point. Had he been looking around to see who else might be available? My heart and my mind did flips. Why had I been so naïve and so sure that Charlie would never leave me? That night I lay awake picturing what life could be like with the man I loved beside me.

"You did what?" I said the next morning on the phone with Charlie.

"I broke my leg."

"Yeah, right," I said. "But are you hurt?"

"Damn sure I'm hurt."

Charlie wanted me to come to Miami. He felt hurt, if not really hurt.

"Let me check tonight's cargo flight. If the jump seat is free; I'll be on the flight."

Charlie stayed quiet before he put down the phone. About the broken leg... I wondered if there was a different translation for that story. What about, "I love you. I want you with me. But don't expect me to beg."

I pictured this great guy with his eyes falling over me in a way any girl would love. Everything inside me said I wanted to feel those eyes soon.

With the jump seat confirmed for the midnight flight to Miami, I requested an emergency cancellation of my upcoming Tahiti flight. I'd never canceled a flight, but I needed to get to Miami. I wasn't sure exactly the reason, but it felt important. I knew Charlie well enough to know he was not good at manipulation, but he was good at getting both my attention and my heart.

The thrill of Tahiti with a four-day layover at the Moorea Club Med had once seemed like a dream come true. However, despite the turquoise ocean and my own thatched roof bungalow, I'd felt terribly lonely on my previous trips there. It was awful not to have Charlie sharing the time with me.

4

SURPRISE AND POSSIBILITIES

Miami, Florida to Oklahoma City, 1972 to 1995

Stepping off the plane in the early morning light, I walked across an almost empty cargo area at the Miami Airport. My eyes landed on Charlie's round, tan face and sparkling eyes. When he crossed the tarmac about six feet from me, I heard these words: "Will you marry me?"

No broken leg. Nothing visibly hurt. No props. No pretense. Straight forward in a way that would not travel well across telephone lines, I heard Charlie's proposal. I knew I wanted to travel my life with him. I'd relished the experiences of the past year. However, I was ready to bid farewell to the long fights. "Nassau Turn Arounds" and being at home at night with Charlie sounded wonderfully exciting and simply satisfying. Charlie and I would create a world of adventure together.

"Yes!" I said, dropping my bag. "I'll marry you, but first fix me bananas flambé for breakfast."

The next day I asked Charlie what he would most like to change about me if he could do so. "Just don't wear that blue eye shadow," he said without a pause and with a grin.

Was that the only thing he wanted to change about me? A powerful affirmation of what I already knew about Charlie. I no longer needed to follow the Revlon blue eyeshadow fad, and loving Charlie was for me much more than a passing fad. This man accepted me. He loved me and I loved him. Charlie would with ease allow space for me to become who I came into the world to be. San Francisco was not the only gateway for my discovery of that woman.

A year later we got married! We bought a house in Whispering Pines Estates in Miami. Pine trees filled the neighborhood. Our mortgage payments paid not for an estate, but for a home sweet home where I had the tile floors covered with avocado shag carpet. Charlie cooked in a kitchen with gold appliances. Married life was good. A few heated arguments, about I can't remember what, turned into greater acceptance of each other's foibles. Charlie continued his engineering work, and I continued my Pan Am flights. With spouses allowed free airline passes, Charlie and I traveled to Madrid, Jamaica, Mexico City, and Buenos Aires. To Denmark, Norway and Switzerland.

In time, we were ready to start a family. I wondered how I'd manage being a wife, mother and a seeker too. Three years later—a positive pregnancy test! The thrill of a new direction in life brought Charlie and me even closer together. Since Pan Am continued to ban stewardesses with baby bumps—as if we carried contagious tumors—a forced furlough unfurled. The next month, the firm Charlie worked for folded.

Touching my belly and the new nursery dresser before dropping into the rocking chair, I cried, worried about our future. Like Mary and Joseph, we needed a stable for our baby with a stable income to pay our mortgage.

A sudden relocation to Oklahoma City provided Charlie with an engineering position, and we secured a place to welcome Abby, our precious pride and joy. With olive skin like

Charlie's, our daughter would not have my freckles. Now we had roots and we would raise our daughter to have wings to fly away when needed, and to put down roots when the time was right for her. I dismissed those who called my home state "fly over country," and accepted I could not easily commute to Miami to continue my Pan Am job, so I might not "fly over" the state for a while. But I could not leave Abby to pursue my former life.

I never imagined I'd move back to Oklahoma, but it was grand to have grandparents close by. I trusted my ability to parent would do less damage than that done when I first drove a car. Actually, what helped me most as I moved into parenthood was discovering that mothering myself was as essential as mothering our daughter. Through the process, I discovered the option to call on the Great Mother for wisdom and guidance, finding the Female Divine easier to connect with than Our Father in Heaven—remembered as someone to please and appease.

Twenty years flew by. How did it happen? Abby's birthday parties, Santa Claus moments, teaching her to ride a bike, to play tennis and to handle upsets. All too soon, she was ready to leave for college. We trusted she was ready for life on her own as well.

Many friends were made among parents while raising her. Many dinner parties we hosted. I set the table. Charlie fixed the food. At times we fussed, but because of Abby we never thought of not working out our issues. Instead, we would kiss. Makeup. Start over. Big love and laughter held our family together.

As a mother, a wife and working woman with a new career, I struggled to play my roles to perfection, ever pushing to do and be more. I moved my thoughts, shifting my mindset from the "never enough" attitude—away from not enough money or time or confidence. I trusted Charlie and I had given enough of ourselves to help prepare Abby for a fast-changing, confusing world. And to assure the gaps we missed passing to our daughter were filled, I asked the Great Mother to connect Abby to her inner wisdom and intuition, the truest guidance possible.

When the day came to take Abby and her gear to the university dorm, I watched as she arranged her new bedding and other stuff inside the small space she shared with her roommate. I looked at the confident tilt of our daughter's head, at her beautiful face and young female body. Abby was about to belong to a much bigger sphere of life.

In a way, I was ready to do the same. I searched for a name for my feelings while Charlie searched for a screwdriver to tighten the pulls on Abby's dresser. As I stood pondering this strange unknown, I saw my husband wipe a tear from his cheek, acting as if it were a bead of sweat. I felt his emotion and found words to name what I felt. Pregnant Empty Nester, that's what I would call myself. I was ready to give birth and to mother something new, but as yet unnamed. This while staying close to our daughter and her new path.

Oklahoma City, 1995

On Monday morning, arriving at my school office, I hurried to settle at my desk to review the latest addition of my *Possibilities Newsletter*. I'd left it spread across the center of my desk, not proofed yet.

I'd created the monthly newsletter as encouragement for parents. The focus was guiding children to become life-ready emotionally and socially, as well as academically. As I wrote this issue, I'd reflected about Abby and her life-readiness I felt certain she would carry as she started college.

Before rereading the newsletter, I paused for a moment to consider the past eleven years working as the school's curriculum coordinator and parent educator. Many challenges and many rewards had come my way through relationships with both students and their parents.

Traveling to see more of the world's wonders had taken a backseat during these years of parenting and working. I knew there were parts of me waiting to be claimed, more to my life purpose than I had fulfilled. As compensation, I had delighted in seeing Abby thrive through her high school years. I also celebrated my accomplishments at my workplace. I'd seen the benefits of a supportive, encouraging, and diverse school culture. The same culture we had endeavored to provide for Abby.

While I reminisced, I struggled to make sense of previously unimaginable events. First a school counselor told me Dr. Douglas, our headmaster, had complained about our school growing "soft and feminized." We heard that Dr. Douglas wanted to "beef up and clean up" the curriculum. That same day, a memo went out to the staff stating the student reading lists were to come "under review," without naming who would review the lists or for what reason.

Then came the eyebrow raising male speaker Dr. Douglas brought in, unannounced, to speak at a parent event. The hour-long presentation closed with a reference to an "important book" for parents and teachers that proclaimed the merits of corporal punishment and authoritarian parenting with fathers as the "dominant authority" and unquestioned "head of household."

Remembering how I'd shuddered during the presentation, I asked myself why we would change the parenting program offered at our school, a course based on a book by an esteemed Nobel Prize-winning author. Receptive parents and teachers were shown skills other than extreme control or excessive permissiveness to equip children to make responsible decisions and to feel good about themselves.

During a staff meeting the day after the parent presentation, I mustered the courage to question why no time had been allocated for questions following the speaker's appearance. Why no explanation had been offered about our school's reading list review.

Dr. Douglas did not reply to my questions. Instead, I heard him say, "I need to read your newsletter as soon as possible."

At that point, he ended the meeting. Both Dr. Douglas's behavior and his request dumbfounded me. Never had he asked to read my newsletter before it went out. And never had I imagined Dr. Douglas inviting such a shocking speaker to address our parents. My agitation at seeing a never-imagined side of Dr. Douglas made it hard to breathe.

My jolting concerns grew more unbearable after delivering the newsletter to Dr. Douglas's office. Soon I heard footsteps outside my office. When I turned my head, I saw Dr. Donald Douglas enter the room. Dressed in his usual navy suit, red tie and black shoes, his expanded chest and raised chin made him appear even more threatening than when he spoke at the staff meeting. I squirmed in my chair and watched his figure approach within inches of my desk. Not knowing how to react, I stood up and stepped backwards until my back touched the wall.

"Hello," Dr. Douglas said as the furrows between his eyebrows deepened. "How's everything?" Without allowing a moment for a reply, he continued, "I've decided we have a problem in our school and in the culture. Men have ceded too much power to women."

What? Adrenaline rushed through my veins.

Dr. Douglas straightened his six-foot-plus frame and stretched his neck. Within a millisecond, a wave of heat moved through my body.

"I'm recommending changes to the curriculum with a

focus on traditional subjects and American values. I'm suggesting a new book for the parenting classes," he added with his hands clenched at his side.

Sweat poured into my armpits. Words to respond stuck in my throat.

"Our students," Dr. Douglas added, "will be better served if we encourage women to maintain their roles at home and if fathers are encouraged to assume their proper role as the head of household."

Waves of uncontrollable emotion flooded me. I was drowning. I could not move or speak.

Dr. Douglas turned to leave the room. But first, he paused, looking back over his shoulder. "And come on Cindy, you had a typo in the first sentence of the newsletter. So unprofessional. I didn't even finish reading it. I don't want that newsletter mailed."

With that, he left.

I got dizzy as I tried to stand. My office turned fuzzy. I thought I would faint, but I forced myself to breathe deeply. Finally, my body began to cool, my heart rate slowed, and I was able to lumber out of my office. Somehow, I drove home.

In the safety and comfort of my bed, I fell asleep. When I woke up, a barrage of intrusive thoughts overwhelmed me. It was as if I were listening to a closed loop of Dr. Douglas's comments. Interspersed were my unshared concerns, including the belief that "power with" rather than "power over" stood as a core value in our school.

The title "headmaster" and the speaker invited to the parent gathering were clues I had not fully grasped. Had I unconsciously tried to please this man, overlooking his true nature? Or had he changed?

I picked up a pen to write a resignation letter but was blocked as I saw a little girl's face struggling to get her daddy's attention. Shut out, she felt helpless. I felt her suffer with shame when her father got a crick in his neck and she thought it was her fault. I saw her suck her thumb in silence as her elementary principal glared at her, saying she needed to return to first grade. I saw this child become a teenager, eager to please her father, as she sat mortified after driving his car into a neighbor's hedge. I watched a college girl striving to conform to the expected sorority rush code. I felt the failures at each stage of this girl's life rather than the accomplishments and growth I had accumulated.

Blinking my eyes, I saw the reflection in my dresser mirror of an adult woman. Bright, hard-working, a professional school curriculum coordinator. She too had failed, and the failure included not having found a way to declare that healthy masculinity is beautiful and essential but toxic masculinity must change, or not only our boys and girls but everyone will continue to suffer.

Or why could I not forget what had happened and simply move on? What had happened to the part of me who once felt as powerful as a queen or a goddess? The little girl who yelled "damn, damn, damn" and stomped her feet when wanting to be heard. Where were the wise muses like Sekhmet or Isis or the fierce determination and inner faith of Saint Teresa of Ávila, or the Divine Feminine wisdom of Sophia? Unable to conjure their strength and guidance, I fell into utter despair.

I worried about our school's future. About the world's future. I worried that without two incomes it would be hard to help Abby pay for college. I worried about finding another career. I worried about a dark cloud of hyper-masculine energy emerging to suppress authentic feminine energy. How to bring balance and healing for us all?

I slumped down, took a book off my shelf and flipped the pages to these words: "She doesn't make speeches anymore. She has become speechless. She stays in her home, but it doesn't seem to agree with her. How furious she must be...."

Serena Joy's thoughts from *The Handmaid's Tale* seeped into my reality as I imagined standing with her in history's long line of subjugated women.

Part of me, not the devastated, strangled victim part, but the hidden unstoppable heroine inside me, imagined seizing the courage to speak with confidence. Because like Serena Joy and like strong women around the world through the ages, becoming speechless did not agree with us.

Charlie came home from work. I told my story. His impulse to fix things welled up in him at the dinner table. "I'm calling Dr. Douglas," he said, dropping his fist on the table, "to tell him what I think. He can't talk to you the way he did."

"No way," I shouted. "Don't you dare speak for me!"

Not to be deterred, Charlie followed me into the living room. "I'm going to tell that sorry son-of-a bitch he's wrong about everything. Look at Abby. She's off at college, happy, confident. Day care and your working didn't ruin her."

"You're not telling that guy anything," I yelled. "Besides, he won't listen."

Later, when I calmed down a bit, I wondered why I had gone off on Charlie. Why had I not spoken directly to Dr. Douglas when he silenced me, but instead hammered Charlie, who loved and encouraged me? My sharp words probably hit Charlie the way Dr. Douglas' words hit me. But I didn't have the energy to apologize. I went to the kitchen, grabbed doughnuts and stuffed my mouth before plopping onto the living room couch, waiting for a comfort food high.

Time passed. My job search and the doughnut ritual continued. With each donut I swallowed, Dr. Douglas' voice would echo through my body. He became an intruder occupying a room in my mind. Not knowing how to cope, I went to the bathroom to soak in a bubble bath. As the water rose around me, I considered holding my head under the bubbles to end my pain and confusion. But no, how could I consider such a plan with so much love in my life? What was the matter with me?

I slipped down into the water, letting the warmth and bubbles soothe me. As I lay there, I began to breathe deeply for the first time since the deplorable incidents began. As I did so, an inexplicable realization came over me. My overactive mind began to slow down and get still. I lifted my head and leaned it against the tub to enjoy new aliveness flowing over me. My obsessive thoughts began to disappear like bubbles bursting in the air.

With my eyes closed, one blessed moment of peace, ease and lightness came to me. In my bubble bath, I seized the power to believe in myself, if only for a while. I felt the same inner power and strength I'd tried to share with Abby and with the students in our school. Could I hold on to what I felt?

Soon I heard the door open. Charlie appeared. "The phone is for you," he said, handing me both the phone and a towel. Surprised and wondering who was calling, I took the phone while in the tub covered with bubbles. "Hello," I said.

"Hi, Cindy. It's Stephen Edwards from Change of Possibility." Before replying, I remembered weeks ago I saw that Change of Possibility had an opening. I knew about the organization because my father sent them checks. It supported grassroot, community development programs in rural villages of Asia, Africa, and Latin America. Fantasizing about working for such an organization to expand their reach to women, I mailed my application, not expecting to hear back.

I sat in the bathtub with the phone in my hand, listening as Stephen said, "How about interviewing for our Travel with a Purpose Coordinator position?"

What? Was this a prank call?

Stephen explained he had read my resume and wanted me to interview for a position leading supporters and potential supporters on trips to visit Change of Possibility programs. "If selected for the position and if you accept our offer," Stephen said, "you would lead a group to Nepal with trips to other program areas to follow."

Would I accept the position if it were offered? Did Elvis move his pelvis? Did Cinderella want the fella? I thought these thoughts and rushed to say, "Yes, yes, I would absolutely accept."

"Well, I like your enthusiasm!" Stephen replied with a laugh. "Meet me at our office for an interview. How about tomorrow at nine o'clock?"

"Sounds perfect," I said, not believing my ears. After thanking Stephen, I jumped out of the tub, wrapped a towel around me, and ran to hug my husband.

"They liked me. They want me. I got the job," I told Charlie when I flew into the house after the interview. I watched his face light up as bright as mine.

I told how Stephen had offered me the job, saying, "I have no doubt you will catalyze others to support Change of Possibility." He went on to say, "Be sure your passport is up to date. Get trekking boots and malaria pills. Take typhoid, tetanus, diphtheria and hepatitis shots. And don't forget polio and cholera shots. And remember you'll be trekking in Nepal through rough conditions. Your first trip leaves in a month."

"No problem!" I had exclaimed as I reminded myself to pack my earrings.

With my future up for grabs, without concern for typhoid, TB, polio, or anything except the chance to travel and to pursue important work, I decided I had fallen into my next act the way Alice fell into a rabbit hole. Or maybe I had proven myself bright and capable enough to pursue meaningful, important work in the world.

Charlie cheered me on by fixing bananas flambé once

again. I could see he was glad my pity parties and slide into depression had halted. I called Abby at school and heard her say, "Mom, that's great! Rock on. I'm proud and happy for you."

The next evening, standing in the kitchen, I enjoyed the comforting aroma of basil in Charlie's slow-cooked tomato sauce. I felt no need for a doughnut. Instead, it occurred to me, I hadn't run away from the school. I had broken away from a man with a fragile ego who set off my intimidation. Parents and staff at the school with stronger voices than mine would deal with what I had abandoned.

I thought about Abby. She would speak up to male domination when encountered. We had instilled more assertiveness in her than I had mustered for myself.

I headed into the kitchen where Charlie was stirring the spaghetti. I lifted his hand and squeezed it. "I'm sorry for the things I said. My misplaced anger spilled out. I love you. And thanks for loving me."

Something had to change. I could not treat Charlie or myself the way I had been treating both of us.

5

ON TOP OF THE WORLD

Nepal, 1995

At the break of day, as a crisp breeze brushed my skin, I sat on an ancient stone bench beside a garden pond. I was outside an iconic hotel in Kathmandu, Nepal. Enthralled by pink and purple lotus blossoms opening above stems as tall and straight as a yoga mountain pose, it amazed me how the petals had pushed through the pond's mud and muck to reveal their exquisite color. My fascination seemed to reflect my rising above the mud and muck Dr. Douglas and his ilk represented to me.

Charlie and Abby and the love we shared grounded me. I would miss my family during this journey, but coming to Nepal seemed important, really important. At the same time, my stomach knotted as I felt the ongoing tension between being a good mother, a good wife, a good employee and a seeker of a larger life purpose. I sensed supporting the voice and value of women and the feminine was at the core of my calling.

Lifting my gaze above the pond, I watched light in shades matching the lotus blossom colors illuminate a world wonder—Sagarmatha, meaning Goddess of the Sky, the Sanskrit name for Mount Everest. Her mighty presence compelled me to ask her a direct question.

"Sagarmatha, why do you suppose British men, like Sir Edmond Hillary, took it upon themselves to change your name to Mount Everest? Today, most of the world has no idea of your sacred name."

From the strong, silent majesty of Sagarmatha's face, I received a response to my query. I understood that for Sagarmatha, having her identity replaced with a male British mountain surveyor's name was but one shocking incident in her long life. Eons and eons ago, continental plates collided, thrusting Sagarmatha and her sister peaks to rise above Kathmandu. I realized rising above shocking situations was not unfamiliar to Sagarmatha.

With my eyes on the sacred mother mountain, I dug deep for confidence to trust myself as a catalytic leader of the five Americans soon arriving for a two-week Change of Possibility Travel with a Purpose.

The closer it came to the time for our group meetup, the more my garden enchantment shifted to questions that made my nerves jitter. Though excited to meet the group, was I prepared to be their leader? Would they like me? Would the group leave motivated to support Change of Possibility programs?

Each group member had provided me with a photo, their age, health, and a short bio. I'd discovered each was bright and accomplished. I longed to appear the same to them.

The first to arrive at the designated garden spot was a tall, slender American fellow with comb-over hair, a V-neck sweater, and khaki pants.

"You're Dale!" I said, rushing to meet him. "How was your trip? Did you sleep well last night?"

"Hello," Dale said in a soft monotone voice as he gripped

his water bottle. "All is well."

A three-word response. I remembered Dale's sparse bio: Sustainable Agriculture Professor U.C. Davis. That was it. Though Dale might be an introverted academic of few words, I sensed he could be guided to open-up to the group during our time together. No need to push him.

Margaret, a strawberry-blond photographer and grandmother from Richmond, Virginia, arrived next. Wearing a vest covered with pockets to store her film and her camera lenses, her preparedness reminded me of my desire to be prepared both internally and externally.

Bridgette, a vibrant red head, was Margaret's friend. Like Margaret, Bridgette's bio expressed her love of nature. Margaret photographed nature and Bridgette sketched it. I hoped the trip would show both women ways Change of Possibility programs helped protect Mother Nature while also improving the lives of those relying on Mother Nature.

"Hi, I'm Genie. Quite a trip to get here!" the forty-something, blond corporate consultant from New York announced. She greeted me with an embrace so intense I almost lost my footing. Her energized spirit made me certain she would be a great addition to our group.

"You've got to be Jack," I said moments later when another member arrived. Jack shook my hand as he cordially greeted me and the others.

Jack, a surgeon from Seattle and an Ernest Hemingway look-alike with a short, white beard, had listed his interests as quantum physics and neuroscience. His interests concerned me, since I knew almost nothing about either subject.

Gopal, the Change of Possibility country director, entered the garden last. His head was topped by a geometric patterned *dhaka topi* — a traditional hat shaped like a rectangular tissue box squeezed into points at both ends. Gopal held degrees in international development and agronomy. He greeted us by placing his palms together with fingertips pointed to the sky. As he bowed his head, salt and pepper hair protruded from under his *topi*. "*Namaste,*" he said.

The Sanskrit greeting Gopal translated to mean, "I honor the divinity in you that also dwells in me and throughout the universe."

In response, I resisted my usual, "Hi, how are ya?" Instead, I lowered my head, placed my palms together and repeated, "*Namaste.*" With one word, I acknowledged our shared divinity, something I wished to recognize in myself and in all humanity.

After a high-energy exchange of group chatter, I knew what I wanted to do.

"As we begin our time together," I told the group, "I invite you to join me in a short focusing meditation. It will guide us to leave our ordinary world and concerns behind and to enter the extraordinary world of new people and new discoveries."

As I spoke the words of the mediation, a surge of energy coursed down from the top of my head, through my hips, to the tips of my toes and out to connect with each of my companions.

Moments later, Margaret told me, "Your meditation. A perfect way to begin." Others agreed or did not complain. I had confirmation that following my intuition was the way to move forward, come what may.

Later in the afternoon, in the ancient city of Bhaktapur, eight miles outside Kathmandu, sixty-five-degree Fahrenheit weather welcomed us. The temperature represented a rare recognizable feature. Pigeons, the other recognizable feature, clapped their wings as if applauding us on our arrival to an otherworldly place.

In front of us lay Pashupatinath, a medieval five-level, pagoda-shaped tantric temple with tarnished-gold roofing that thrust above throngs of reverent worshippers. Considered one of the most important holy sites for Hindu devotees, we watched as they circled while other locals continued their daily lives, accustomed to the sight and apparently unaffected by it.

Sunlight shafts struggled through dust and pollution to illuminate the exotic and erotic Pasupatinath Temple. The same light fell over dreadlocked, ash-covered, skeletal-bodied Sadhu holy men. They sat on the temple steps dressed in loincloths and nothing else. While gazing at the Sadhus, Jack, with his ever-engaging smile, pushed his wire-rim sunglasses up to the top of his nose and said, "I'm not much different from these fellows."

As I imagined Jack in a loincloth, I felt my face turn bright red.

Moving closer toward the Sadhus, Jack added, "I don't have dreadlocks or wear a loincloth, but like the Sadhus I seek enlightenment, even if I'm unsure what enlightenment is."

I looked at the others to catch their responses.

Jack continued, "I came to Nepal because I needed to get away from how I was living life."

Without offering more detail, Jack nailed something that resonated with me.

Pushing her dark-brown hair out of her face, Genie said, "I'm a bit like the Sadhus, myself. I follow a life of spiritual discipline and yoga. But I don't push away the world like an ascetic Sadhu. I pursue both worldly and spiritual pleasures."

"Sound good to me," Jack said, his eyes wide open.

"I like tantric yoga," Genie added. "It teaches me that if I want to change the world and the things that happen to me here, I've gotta change thoughts within me. That's a big job."

Dipping my head in agreement, I said, "From now on I'm calling you two 'Swami Jack and Genie Yogini.'"

"That works," the two agreed as laughs echoed around the group.

I liked the way our group had begun to bond. I even saw Dale grin as he listened.

Gopal pointed to the copulating couples carved into Pashupatinath's roof struts. "The carvings symbolize the sacred union of Shiva and Shakti, the divine masculine with the sacred feminine energies."

Waving his arms to point out various carvings, including the copulating couples, Gopal continued, "Many Westerners associate tantra with wild, unbridled sex, yes? But tantra, as Yogini Genie knows, is a spiritual practice that recognizes the feminine aspect of Divinity." Pausing to look around the space, Gopal added, "Tantra teaches harmony of mind, body, and spirit while acknowledging everyone and everything as connected."

The words Shakti, Shiva, and tantra were new to my vocabulary. But I admitted the fact only to myself. Everything and everyone connected. That was a concept I'd tried to impart to the students at school. I had no idea the relation to tantra. How far away I was from my school experience, and yet still connected. The sacred masculine and sacred feminine flowing together and uniting. I contemplated that beautiful notion.

While examining the carvings, Gopal motioned us closer. Nepalese women draped in colorful saris, Nepalese men, some in jeans and T-shirts and others in traditional white pants and tunics, passed by. "Whether Hindu, Buddhist, Christian, Jew or of no faith," Gopal announced, "anyone can use tantric mantras, meditations and rituals to aid in finding a path toward balance and wholeness."

With closed eyes, Gopal offered a chant to Shiva, the masculine divine, transcendent force in Hinduism. "On namah shivaya," he prayed and then offered the Adi Shakti chant to what he described as the immanent, sacred feminine, creative force.

After offering the mantras, I caught Gopal's gaze and bobbed my head to acknowledge I'd heard his words. I felt a deep inner intimate connection to the sacred, one like Saint Teresa of Ávila first awakened in me in Spain.

As we sauntered around Pashupatinath, I heard various languages and observed diverse people. I was inside a multi-language, multi-religion, multi-caste nation. One wedged between China and India with the Himalayas at the northern border. Closed to the outside world until about 1960, Nepal was now gripped by forces for reform colliding with a 2,000-year-old feudal, authoritarian, corrupt and oppressive monarchy. Remembering this information I'd placed in our group's orientation packet, today I felt gripped by my awakened contradictory and curious feelings about what I saw and heard.

"King Birendra," Gopal said as we guided us through the crowds, "among the richest kings on earth, rules one of the poorest, most oppressed countries on earth." Lowering his head Gopal told us he loved his country with his heart and soul, but deplored the grinding poverty endured by the masses, the rigid though illegal caste system, gender inequality, a lack of rural sanitation systems, running water, and health systems made worse by the intolerable environmental degradation.

I felt Gopal's pain about the conditions we were about to discover, beginning with Kathmandu's polluted air, worse than any I'd ever experienced.

"I've read," Genie said with her brows wrinkled, "how Maoist insurgents fighting against the government wave guns at trekkers before they rob them."

Margaret and Bridgette's faces froze.

Gopal straightened his *topi.*

"Yes, my country is on the brink of political revolution. Violence in our peaceful kingdom grows daily as needed change struggles to be birthed."

Without stopping for Genie to speak, Gopal continued, "The marginalized, especially women, want the monarchy gone. Toppling King Birendra is essential. He's ruled for twenty-four years."

After clearing his throat, Gopal added, "I'm not a Maoist, but our corrupt king, in power for such a long time, must go. We must add civil rights to our constitution. Yet women who join with the Maoists must not become pawns as they fight for what is right. They must know Maoists have no interest in improving women's lives."

With my mind as heavy as the fodder wood strapped on the back of the stooped Nepalese woman crossing in front of us, I absorbed the context into which my dream job would unfold. A thought struck me: I was not a bold trekker here to conquer a mountain or prepared to face robbery at gunpoint. I had arrived as a seeker posing as a prepared travel leader. After showcasing Change of Possibility-supported agriculture, preventive health, and micro-credit programs in impoverished villages, I needed the group to write checks to support the work. Could I assure that would happen? And could I also satisfy my search for a significant life? A full, risky agenda stood before me. Was I up for the task? And wasn't it rather late to ask the question?

We rode in motor-powered rickshaws along an alley lined with shopkeepers in open-front stalls, as bicycle bells mixed with car horns, motor scooter vrooms, monkey chatters and mooing holy cows. We were headed to another temple while breathing the heaviest pollution I'd ever encountered.

"It fascinates me," Jack said, "how the ancient tantric

concept of the connection of all things fits with twentieth century quantum physics theory. The idea that everything is a part of everything else."

We plodded through a jammed street, but I craved hearing every word about tantra and quantum physics and what to expect next in Nepal. The rickshaw stopped in front of a red brick structure framed by gold and turquoise pillars. Two large open eyes painted black decorated the white stucco entrance.

"Here you see Guhyeshwari Temple," Gopal told us as our group gathered again. "The powerful tantric site, sacred to both Hindus and Buddhists, symbolizes Shakti as the counterpart of Shiva symbolized at Pashupatinath. We would have visited the Shakti temple first," Gopal added with a self-conscious chuckle, "but I made an exception due to logistics. Another example of modern concerns creeping into my life."

In a hushed voice as we scurried forward, Gopal said, "It's nothing new to pass over the power of the creative feminine and defer to the masculine. Right?"

Genie, Margaret, and I applauded in absolute agreement, while I appreciated Gopal's need to keep us on schedule.

"See the eyes painted beside the pillars? They symbolize the third eye."

I sensed by the way the group listened, that each felt drawn to and comfortable with Gopal as our guide. So was I.

"For most beings, the third eye sleeps," Gopal said, placing his index finger at the spot on the center of his forehead just above his eyebrows. "Such beings remain blind unless one day the third eye opens. That opening we call awakening."

Genie stepped forward and said in a matter-of-fact tone, "Yogis understand that higher consciousness emerges through the third eye. Both feminine and masculine energies merge there."

Hearing this, Bridgette rubbed the spot on her forehead. I

decided to do the same. While wondering if my third eye would ever open, I watched Margaret snap photos before rubbing her third eye.

"At Guhyeshwari we honor the female creative space," Gopal told us with a grin. "You call it a vagina, yes?"

Hearing vagina, Bridgette lost no time in announcing, "Yes, a vagina or a womb. In my hometown we could use sacred womb temples to honor the feminine creative force."

I wanted to second the idea for my hometown, but I kept my thoughts to myself. I did know that Hindu temples existed throughout the U.S. and perhaps in Oklahoma City, though I had not visited one.

Gopal glanced at each of us. " 'Where the feminine is respected, gods reside,' our Hindu teachings say, 'and the heavens open for angels to sing paeans of praise.' In Shakti's presence, it is possible to release worry, fears and doubt."

The heavenly thought recalled our upcoming trek and my occasional fear of not being capable enough or smart enough to handle the physical or mental responsibilities of my dream job. As I turned toward the temple, an unusual thing happened. The harsh, haranguing, critical voice that traveled in my head became as still as the stones beneath my feet, replaced by a surprising confidence. Perhaps my Shakti energy had given me a much-needed relaxation response.

When it was time to say goodbye to Guhyeshwari Temple, I walked alongside Genie as we stepped toward a souvenir stall. Numerous brass sculptures stood in neat rows. I was drawn to a six-inch tall goddess figure whose dangling earrings drew me to her. The shopkeeper lifted the statue and presented her to me. "Lakshmi, goddess of good fortune and abundance. Good for your journey," he said, a wide smile covering his face.

To create an abundance of funding for Change of Possibility programs, I needed good fortune. So, I touched the

Lakshmi statue without holding her. A surprising sense of some big connection to a larger field of power came to me. My amazement must have been obvious, because Genie looked at me and smiled in a knowing way. "Lakshmi is an aspect of Shakti. Of the Divine Feminine," she said, glancing at the statue in the shopkeeper's hand.

I felt curious, but I said nothing.

"For me," Yogini Genie added, "Lakshmi represents the energy that awakens spiritually informed living and that brings both inner peace and outer prosperity."

"The sounds great," I replied. "No wonder she needs four arms."

I wondered if both inner peace and outer prosperity could be gifts from a goddess. Many ideas introduced this day were new to me, but they resonated with what I was feeling.

I sought a deeply spiritually informed life of peace and prosperity. At this stage, my life was in transition from an old career to a new one, from young age to mid-life, from mothering to launching my daughter on her way, from living in my head to trusting my body, soul and spirit. I decided to leave the brass statue in the stall, but I trusted that Lakshmi's powers could guide my way.

The next morning as the sun shone across freshly harvested rice paddies, our group lined up for our first day of trekking. With walking sticks, trekking boots and back packs, we crossed beneath mountain peaks, walking by dry, golden-brown rice paddies. Stepping onto the mud-packed dikes around the paddies, we used our sticks to balance. It seemed much different from how I imagined the start of a Himalayan trek.

A couple feet tall and several feet wide, the patty dikes used as walking paths served during the growing season to retain water for rice seedlings. I tried to keep my feet from slipping off the dikes. Women nearby, graceful in their long flowing red saris, stacked their cut rice stalks into golden piles.

"These women," Gopal told us as he proceeded, "risked everything as they dared to experiment using less water to grow their rice."

What was I hearing? Women risking everything...

I listened as Gopal explained a process of spacing rice seedling in rows, planting fewer seedlings and allowing the seedlings to grow with less water. More production resulted, and with less labor and drudgery.

"SRI stands for a system of rice intensification!" Dale interjected, his normally silent voice ignited. "It sounds counterintuitive, but by using less water and fewer seedlings, it's possible to produce more rice. I've seen the study results!" He paused as if his excitement exhausted his breath. "That's why I'm here," he added, "to see proof of increased yields."

Gopal looked pleased and filled in more information. We heard how this season's ample rice yield would provide food for families with some left to sell. And without the women needing to plant bent in ankle-deep, muddy, disease-borne water.

I looked at the women as they worked. I felt the intensity of their risk taking, pleased to hear two men celebrating it.

"And if the harvest had failed," Dale added, "the women and their families could have starved. Talk about courage! Talk about trust."

After Dale spoke, an old message came over me. I could feel my deep need not to appear uninformed, dumb or inadequate. A voice inside tried to convince me I had no business leading this group. How had I not known about SRI before we came here? And why had I missed understanding Dale's interest? Rushing to get shots and boots. Trying to get my body ready to trek, I had missed understanding ways that Change of Possibility was empowering women rice farmers.

I watched one of the older Nepalese women tilt her head

toward me. Her eyes gave me the impression she understood how I felt. Maybe it is how she felt trying a new rice planting system, one different from what had been followed for centuries. I decided this brave woman was encouraging me to stop thinking I needed to know all the answers. When I smiled, I hoped she knew how much I wanted to acknowledge her. I felt she understood.

That's when I decided to trust my leadership skills on my first Change of Possibility Journey in a way similar to how the women rice growers had trusted their SRI trial.

I approached Dale to let him know I appreciated his enthusiasm for the women's SRI trial. He seemed anxious to make certain I understood that the women I saw represented 500 million rice cultivators worldwide. Together they provide the most labor-intensive work on earth. Work needed to feed the population. "SRI could lighten the burden they bear and help the health of the planet by not adding chemicals to the soil."

"Those believing women are the weaker sex should meet rice cultivators," Bridgette said, as she extended arms toward the women.

"I will never eat rice without remembering them," I said. As I watched the women work together, I thought about the power of women connecting. I'd never struggled to grow rice, but I understood grit. I used it when I accepted my new job and when I agreed to bring the group to Nepal.

After time to explore the area, the Sherpas who would accompany us throughout the trip prepared *Bhat Dahl*, a Nepalese vegetarian staple of rice and lentils. It was good to relax and visit about our day.

As the sun slipped behind the mountains and made way for the moon, Gopal focused his gaze on us. He proposed a mantra to honor Lakshmi's powerful energy. He called her the goddess who holds feminine power and energy. She releases her gifts for beings of all genders, when they are ready to receive what she brings. "The process is as certain as when a split uranium atom releases its energy," he said.

I pictured the brass Lakshmi statue from the shop with her earrings dangling. I closed my eyes and sank into Gopal's mantra.

That night, before I crawled inside my round-top tent the Sherpas provided, I looked at our row of tents. They reminded me of lost spaceships settled onto a harvested rice field. Though not lost, we were in a strange new place. What was the deep "why" for each of us coming to Nepal?

One thing seemed clear to me. I was here not only to secure financial support for Change of Possibility programs, but to gather stories to show the changes women are bringing.

The next morning, Sherpas prepared hot tea and toast over an open fire surrounded by morning mist. After breakfast, Genie stood and announced, "Most Americans suffer from shallow breathing. For us to trek up these mountains we must breathe deeply and relax our bodies. Now, let's practice some yoga nidra practices."

With that, Genie began to demonstrate deep belly breathing followed by alternate nostril breathing.

I was being introduced to many new things and decided not to feel dumb for not knowing such practices. Instead, I would stay curious to learn more.

Genie explained, "Yoga nidra is the name for alternate nostril breathing. It relaxes, calms and guides us on our journey to consciousness."

More relaxed and prepared to climb as well as to become more conscious, I heard Bridgette announce, "I thought we were going to Bandar. Is Consciousness nearby?"

This gal had a sense of humor. I heard laughter rising in the air, as I picked up my trekking pole. That's when I realized our group was decked out in fancy, waterproof leather boots.

Rather, five in our group were decked out in such boots; mine happened to be non-waterproof from a discount store. Would my feet get wet on my journey to Bandar and to consciousness?

When I noticed the Sherpas wore sandals, I felt grateful for my boots and most grateful the Sherpas would carry our heavy gear. My Stairmaster workouts at home had not prepared me to manage the weight.

Before arrival in Nepal, I had never carried a backpack or climbed anything higher than a kitchen stool. I was accustomed to breathing at an elevation of 1,200 feet above sea level. Soon I'd be trekking at 9,000 feet, and ultimately our trek would take us to the height of a 72-story building.

As we trekked, I felt the steep rise up the mountain. I struggled to place one foot in front of the other onto the rocky, narrow path. By the second hour, exhaustion set in.

At a curve in the trail after a couple hours of upward trek, I suggested it might be time for our first Himalayan potty-break. For the women, this involved the dreaded squat. I crept behind the biggest rock I saw where I squatted before lowering my pants. That's when it dawned on me that Margaret, a Southern lady from Virginia, had gotten it right when she dressed in a long denim skirt below her vest.

Back on the trail, I watched a petite sari-draped woman climb the path above us. Across her back, supported by a strap across her forehead, she carried a brass water jug. It must have weighed forty or fifty pounds, perhaps twice the weight of Margaret's camera gear.

Nepalese women walk miles, once or twice each day, to riverbeds or wells, where they fill jugs with water vital for cooking and drinking. Water for both family and livestock. Once filled, jugs must be hauled back to their villages.

Other women passed, loaded with fodder bundles on their backs. They resembled walking trees. Women's work included gathering fodder for outdoor fire cooking and for feeding livestock.

I could not imagine what it must be like to face such ordeals day in and day out. Did they dream of different futures?

Margaret stopped, raised her camera and with a slow, lilting drawl said, "I've long dreamed of photographing the Himalayas."

As I heard these words, my heart sank. Was Margaret capturing nothing more than mountains? After shooting more mountain views, Margaret turned her lens to focus on the woman with her fodder load.

"Now I know. It's the work of women I'm here to capture," Margaret said from behind her lens.

Margaret offered a smile as she motioned to the woman with her camera. The woman never stopped walking, though her nod indicated no objection to a photograph. I sensed her trust that Margaret would capture dignity amidst the toil of a woman's workday.

"You're not only a photographer," I told her, "but you're a sensitive one. I like how you requested permission before capturing her on film. I hope you'll share your photographs with Change of Possibility."

"Absolutely, I'll share them. I want the world to see the women's work."

I realized how much was stirring in me. The oppression of women, the effect it had on me. Hearing the impact on Margaret made it more real.

A couple more hours of uphill trekking passed before thatch-roofed, stone structures finally appeared on the horizon. The buildings defied gravity in the way they clung with determination to the mountainside. At last, we had arrived in Bandar, our destination for the night. Because my calves were about to go on strike, I could not have been more pleased by our arrival. Dale, with his shoulders sagging and his back bent, arrived with laughter that we shared. Thank goodness for a good-natured group.

Surrounded by green and gold terraced fields with snow-capped peaks and billowing clouds covering the sky, the village of Bandar resembled a *National Geographic* spread. However, the town lacked a phone, a motorized vehicle, or a paved road. Should we have an emergency, it would be almost impossible to get help. So far, we'd avoided Maoist insurgents, but what about the weather? Why was the sky getting grayer by the minute? It was not supposed to rain.

"Subha prabhat," Gopal announced his good morning in Hindi as he tapped on the guesthouse door after our night's sleep. The group had slept on cots inside a large room above Bandar's health clinic. Breakfast on the adjoining covered balcony was about to begin as rain, unleashed by a full-blown monsoon, pounded the tin roof.

Margaret held her teacup with both hands as she struggled to keep it from blowing away. "Our trip was planned for November because it's the dry season, right?"

A deep wrinkle grew across Gopal's brow. Unease etched into his face and into mine, too. "Our trek must be delayed," he told us. "Unseasonable rains have caused floods, and mud-slides."

"Oh, my!" Bridgette declared with a braver demeanor than I could muster.

"Don't worry, we'll wait it out," Gopal said as he poured us more tea. "Meanwhile, we'll visit the health clinic down-stairs. The only one for miles. Thanks to Change of Possibility, a trained nurse works there. You must meet her."

How could I not worry? I felt responsible for the entire group. Without trekking to the villages, how would we be impacted by the power of Change of Possibility projects? What if we had to stay here for days or for a week? Trying to dismiss my concerns, I remembered a Change of Possibility article I read about a Bandar nurse. How she worked with women's groups. A wild commotion outside the clinic interrupted my thoughts. A familiar voice in my head wanted to wedge a way into my day. "It's just like you to speed read and miss important points."

In my defense, I reminded myself I had a mere three weeks to prepare for coming here. Yet, my "not good enough" button had been pushed. It was still easy for me to touch that button. Hearing commotion outside the clinic interrupted my self-beratement.

"Hurry! Come with me!" Gopal said as together we rushed down the stairs.

I saw a Nepalese girl, maybe eleven or twelve, draped in a rain-soaked sari. A funnel-shaped straw basket the size of her trembling body was strapped from her forehead over her back. When she turned, her tear-stained, mud-soaked face and her haunted eyes met mine. As I trembled, concerned as to what we were about to witness, the young girl proceeded with great care to place the basket on the ground. As she unwrapped the cloth covering, a blood-soaked woman appeared coiled inside.

Gopal lifted the bloody fabric wrapped around the woman's head. A deep gash in her skull gushed blood.

"Saraswati, come quickly!" he called through the clinic door.

Would the woman die? In a moment, Saraswati emerged from behind the clinic door. She wore a red and gold sari and gold earrings with a red *bindi* painted between her eyebrows.

When she saw the woman, she motioned to Gopal. Together they lifted this distressed soul from the basket and placed her on a straw mattress inside the clinic's one patient room.

I noticed a brass water jug against the wall and said a

prayer of thanks for the women who fetch and boil water each day. Because of them, a supply of safe, clean water stood ready for the woman to drink and for cleaning her wound.

Our group waited outside the room. I watched Jack hesitate, wondering if he would intervene. Saraswati examined the woman using lantern light and said to Gopal, "Her scalp is torn. But the skull is not fractured."

Jack nodded without intervening. His manner assured me he trusted Saraswati's assessment. With sterile gauze, she applied gentle pressure to control the bleeding.

Another figure appeared at the clinic door. She wore hoops in her ears and nose. Multi-colored bird feathers sprouted from a white band wrapped around her head. She entered, raising a leather bag in one hand, and waved a long-handled, two-sided drum with the other.

Gopal walked close, and the two spoke before he told us, "Our respected local shaman heard about the injury and rushed to assist Saraswati. One healer brings western academic learning and the other Eastern inner knowing."

Our group stood and looked at each other. I remained quiet, astonished to see a shaman.

Saraswati motioned for the shaman to join her. As she approached the patient's bed, brass bells that hung from her neck rang softly. She tapped her drum as if to echo heartbeats, and blew long, steady breaths over the patient's feet. I sensed the fear and distress hanging in the air.

Opening her leather bag, the shaman removed a copper cup and a copper stir stick. After filling the cup with water from the jug, she stirred it.

"Energized liquid," Gopal whispered as the shaman rubbed the water across the patient's forehead. I heard deep breaths. I watched the woman turn her head in our direction and open her eyes. A slight upward movement at the corners of her lips formed a smile. The shaman held the woman's hand, gazing into her eyes before turning toward Saraswati.

I watched as Saraswati examined the wound again before applying an antibiotic cream—something rarely available in most rural clinics. She then covered the wound with clean bandages. The woman's face glowed with grateful relief.

With appreciation and respect for what I'd observed, I smiled. "From the beginning of time, women have been healers," I said to whomever might be listening.

The young girl who had carried the patient edged closer to the bed. Her shoulders dropped as if releasing both physical and emotional weight. With one hand she pushed her thick hair off her brow as she glanced into the wounded woman's face.

In a shy, halting voice, a less panicked young girl announced, as Saraswati translated, "I'm Urmila. This is my mother. We were walking home after gathering wood. Mother slipped on a slope."

Urmila told how the slope was covered with slick mud from the rain. How she watched her mother plummet to the bottom of the mountain, where she hit her head against a stone before Urmila rushed down the slope and found her mother lying on her back. Blood gushing from her head. When her mother's eyes closed, Urmila feared she would die.

I felt her urge to cry as she spoke about how she had covered her mother's head with a cloth unwrapped from her own sari. Despite fright, Urmila vowed to save her mother's life. She emptied the basket and placed her mother's wounded body inside. Lifted the basket with her mother inside before placing the basket over her back and configuring the leather strap around her forehead. The weight of her mother balanced inside.

It was hard for me to imagine what Urmila had endured.

"I started walking," Urmila said. "Only because of my mother's cries did I know she was still alive. The whole time,

I prayed someone might be here to help us.

My mind reeled. This young girl had carried her mother up the same steep paths I struggled to climb without a load on my back. I turned my attention within and closed my eyes at the image of a terrified, isolated, barely conscious mother entrusting her life to her daughter.

In a gentle, direct voice, Saraswati said to Urmila, "You made a good choice coming here."

"Saraswati shares the name of the Hindu goddess of healing and knowledge," Gopal said. "She comes to us like a river flowing to wash away our fears and replace them with comfort and healing. Today, nurse Saraswati manifests the Goddess Saraswati's qualities. Together with the shaman, they treat inner as well as outer obstacles to healing."

Nurse Saraswati repeated a soothing mantra. I was coming to understand how she treated patients combining Western medical practices with time-honored sacred knowledge of life practices known as ayurvedic science. I caught sight of Urmila's shoulders dropping and her face relaxing. It appeared her trauma as well as her mother's had been eased by the mantra.

With Urmila's mother resting, Saraswati stepped outside the patient's room. I complemented her on her composure and confidence. She looked me in the eye and said, "I was nineteen when I first arrived here. I feared failing as a nurse in a rural village. Despite a good education, self-doubt consumed me."

I was amazed to hear the words "self-doubt" coming from such an impressive nurse, but I related. It was good not to feel alone with my doubts.

"My father disapproved of my leaving Kathmandu," Saraswati added. "With modern Western medical training, I was expected to find a high-paying job at the city hospital. My father insisted that ignorant, low-caste hill people would never accept me. He called working in a village clinic a waste of my education. But I was determined."

As someone who had sought male approval my entire life, Saraswati's determination inspired me. While born in a country and culture on the surface far different from mine, Saraswati and I shared similar feelings and desires. I also wanted to heal wounds. Not physical wounds as much as emotional, psychological, and spiritual wounds in myself as well as other women. Those, like a little girl's childhood wound no bandage could cover. Or at least that was the old story I had told myself. Maybe a new version was possible.

Saraswati paused and told me, "At first no one visited the clinic, and I began to question my decision. People believed an unmarried urban woman had no place in their village. I worried if a patient died, I would be blamed. After several years, I have gained the people's trust. We proceed forward together."

I got near enough to touch Saraswati's arm, in a way that would not interrupt her. I simply had to show an indication of my respect for her perseverance.

Gopal spoke up after standing nearby, listening. He seemed anxious for us to know that Change of Possibility funds had made it possible for Saraswati to train, hire, and equip female birth attendants. The clinic now provided preventive health and first-aid workers for twenty local rural communities.

"Astounding," I said as others in the group echoed me.

"Low caste women and girls, like those in this area, face lack of education, health care, clean water and adequate nutrition," Saraswati said as she examined a woman who arrived with a swollen eye and a black-and-blue face. "Women have few rights," she told us. "They can't own land. They see little recourse from wife beatings or from having acid thrown in their faces for supposed offenses. Women can be murdered if a man wants out of his marriage. Or because a man seeks revenge when a family doesn't pay the demanded dowry."

I cringed, absorbing the terror women must feel with little recourse.

"As you walk the paths," Saraswati continued, "you will see sheds called 'chhaupadi.' Women must live in such sheds when menstruating because they are considered unclean. Pregnant women often deliver children alone in the sheds, remaining for days, facing the possible death of their newborns, or facing their own death."

I looked away, avoiding the faces of our group, not wanting to see their reactions while trying to cope with my own. The cruelty inflicted on women and girls sickened me. How could a woman's life-giving blood serve as a reason for isolation? Females need time alone, but not forced isolation. The thought of such blatant control of women's lives and bodies made my body contract.

Saraswati leaned toward me as if she sensed my anger and rage. She described how she organizes women into small groups where they share their problems and seek solutions. She told how the literacy training, income-generating projects, and the savings and loan programs combine to improve women's economic situation as well as their self-confidence.

Yes, women's circles, women's groups! Women connecting, changing, rising. That's the hope I held as I heard clapping.

"The women are bright and eager to learn," Saraswati said as she glanced into the women's faces gathered near us. Moving to yet another patient, she added, "As women gain a voice and respect in their villages, real change can happen."

"Voice and respect," the words resonated in my body like temple bells.

I asked myself, "What if after rescuing her mother from the fall, Urmila would return home to face a *chhaupadi* shed each month? Or someday to deliver a baby alone inside a shed?"

With those thoughts, my mind shifted to myself. It felt both selfish, under the circumstances, and important. A clear sense that I was seeing a wider vision for myself and my life came to me. When and how that would crystalize, whether it would happen on this trip or later, I could not say. Wonderful new work had landed me in Nepal. I had agreed to guide my group on this journey in hopes of encouraging them to fund Change of Possibility programs. At the same time, I felt my purpose was about much more than that one goal. Holding the tension between the crisis of the moment, the need to generate funds, and my desire to have clarity about my purpose was a big task. And to be successful with my effort, I had to cultivate more self-confidence. I tried to convince myself I would not return to the dismal dismay and overwhelm that crippled me after allowing Dr. Douglas to silence and overwhelm me. After those thoughts, I pictured Urmila. After her display of courage, she likely would face a *chhaupadi* shed of limited possibilities. The world needed to change, and I wanted to step up as a changemaker.

The next morning, I awoke thinking about Urmila's mother. When I hurried down to the clinic, what should I see but a smiling mother standing with a bandage on her head. She was hugging Saraswati as bright-eyed Urmila lifted her empty basket onto her back. Mother and daughter would walk home side by side. With great relief, I joined the joyful community sendoff.

"The rain is almost gone. It's trekking time again!" Gopal announced after the women departed. He handed each of us plastic ponchos to protect us from raindrops. I had no idea where he came up with the plastic. We started climbing. The villagers hiking above and below us wore interlaced bamboo strips to cover their heads—the most ingenious umbrellas I'd ever seen.

How ridiculous our group must have appeared to the graceful local people we passed! Covered in plastic rain protection, wearing heavy walking boots and with water bottles strapped around our thick middles. They climbed a brisk pace, barefoot and surefooted, carrying enormous loads on their slender backs. All of this, protected only by bamboo and leaves. I had much to learn about resilience and re-sourcefulness.

After several hours of trekking, my feet began to drag. Bridgette looked ready to keel over. Halting in her tracks, she raised her head and announced, "Stick me with a fork; I'm done."

With that, she plopped down on a nearby rock. After sipping her water, she took out her red lipstick from her fanny pack.

A minute later, three Nepalese women passed Bridgette as she applied her beet red lipstick. The women glared.

"In my country only prostitutes wear red lipstick," Gopal said.

Bridgette recoiled like a snake poked with a lightning rod. She jumped up and wiped off her lipstick with the back of her hand. She hustled up the path. At first our group burst out laughing, but laughter shifted to shock when Gopal explained how more than six thousand young Nepalese girls per year were sold as sex slaves. Fathers would sell daughters to sex traffickers, who would cart the young girls to brothels in India. Other girls would be recruited, believing they were destined for a life of glamor in Bombay. Girls as young as ten or twelve would suffer until they died unless they acquired HIV, in which case they would be sent home to die.

Like Bridgette, I recoiled. I'd been poked into awareness of the unimaginable torment inflicted on unsuspecting young girls. What could be done to protect them?

Some forty sari draped women sat circled on grass mats covering a sunlit patio outside the village's health clinic. Our group had trekked to this village for the purpose of meeting those gathered. The women, Saraswati had explained, were Dalits—the caste at the bottom of the social hierarchy. Many arrived from a distance anxious to gather for their monthly group facilitated by Saraswati.

Due to circumstances of birth and occupation, the women bore the label of a Dalit, which indicated their "untouchable" status. Though laws officially prohibited the caste designation, the Dalit stigma continued to frame the women's lives, forcing them to endure the triple discrimination of caste, gender, and crippling poverty. Despite their dire circumstances, on this day the women chanted, clapped, and laughed. Many while nursing babies and some while keeping an eye on older children playing close by.

Once a month, the women would leave their harsh lives to connect with other Dalit women from villages in the area. While gathered, the women deposited small sums into their savings accounts or made payments on their low-interest, micro-credit loans. To ensure the success of their program, the women studied numeracy and participated in literacy classes. No longer would they be cheated in the marketplace.

Dalit women traditionally married within their caste, usually before age seventeen, some as young as nine. Few family-planning options other than self-induced abortions had been available. Through Change of Possibility programs, the women now had access to safe family planning options as well as reproductive health education and well-child programs.

The women learned the dangers of sex trafficking and sexually transmitted disease. Because Nepal faced among the highest birthrates in the world and among the highest infant mortality rates, such programs proved lifesaving, especially for high-risk Dalit women.

As I watched the women, I saw respect for Saraswati through admiring glances and warm handshakes.

When the women's chanting ended, I watched one woman lift her chin before she spoke. "My name is Sushila." With a rail-thin frame, wrapped in a turquoise sari, Sushila drew her spine tall. "I must feed eight children," she added. Though her eyes were smiling, they seemed to harbor memories she would prefer to forget.

"My husband," Sushila said, lowering her voice, "abandoned us a while back."

Sushila feared she and her children would not survive. The magnitude of women's burdens settled in me while I held hope for positive change through Change of Possibility initiatives.

When Sushila heard about a savings and loan group for Dalits, she knew she wanted to join. At her first meeting, Sushila heard how members could contribute a tiny sum to the group account and could also qualify to receive a loan to buy and breed a piglet. (Gopal earlier had told our group that some Hindus and most all Dalits eat pork).

Sushila said it seemed "a miracle" when she received a loan. Soon after purchasing and breeding her piglet, Sushila had offspring to sell. With her profit, Sushila bought food and was able to make a payment on her loan.

"My life was getting brighter," she said. "I no longer felt unworthy or feared my family or I would starve."

When she finished speaking, Sushila placed her hands on her thighs. She closed her eyes and the other women followed suit. They began a stirring chant, a reminder of the women's chant I'd heard in the rice fields.

When the chanting stopped, the sounds echoed inside me.

Margaret walked toward Sushila to shake her hand before she continued around the circle. The others in our group followed her lead. The process moved me. Historically Dalits had been forbidden to touch those outside their caste.

When my turn to walk the circle came, I longed to have Abby and Charlie with me to share the experience. Moments later came the time to leave.

When Gopal led our trek to the next destination, I trekked uplifted by the spirit of the Dalit women.

Inside a tiny, stone teahouse on a mountainside not far from where we left the women's group, a corner fireplace warmed us. Our group huddled on mats while the owner served tea with yak butter.

"The traditional tea will fortify you for your trekking," the animated woman told us as Gopal translated. As we sipped tea, I pictured the Dalit women's group.

Gopal fumbled with his words before saying, "There is more to Sushila's story." Lowering his voice, he continued. "One night a man from her village pushed his way into her small shack. It was the shack shared with her children and her piglets. Immediately the man grabbed the animal, stabbing and killing it with his knife."

A memory seized me. Perhaps it was not fair to compare an event I'd experienced with what Sushila had suffered, but as I thought about Dr. Douglas cornering me in my office with his announcements, I felt as if he had "killed my piglet." As if he had stolen both my income and my purpose. The thought connected me to Sushila's horror.

Gopal put down his cup. "You must know, Sushila persisted after her suffering. With her group's encouragement and support, she repaid her loan before securing a second piglet that she bred, selling the offspring. Her business grew, and because of the strength she demonstrated, Sushila's women's group selected her to receive training to become a preventive health worker."

Now Sushila had completed the health worker program and advised young women about prenatal care and preventive health. She speaks out about domestic violence. Because of the respect gained, people, both male and female, guard to assure no one harms her piglets or those of other women.

Gopal explained the Gayatri mantra, chronicled in the *Rig Vega* 2,500 to 3,500 years ago, was chanted by both women and men regardless of their station in life. Or it was until in the Middle Ages, when women, especially low caste women, were prohibited from chanting it. Men feared women would gain power from chanting.

"They told women the mantra would cause hair to grow on their faces," Gopal chuckled with obvious embarrassment, sharing such an absurdity.

"The truth is," Gopal said with his head tilted toward his heart, "the Gayatri mantra beseeches the Divine Mother Goddess to open minds, destroy ignorance and to bring possibilities to all."

"Lead us in chanting," Genie asked Gopal, her hands held in prayer.

As he chanted, heart opening vibrations spread without fear of hair growing on a woman's face. Without limitations placed by culturally instilled fears.

A glorious pink covered the sky as the sun prepared to leave for the day. Another arduous climb over rocky, ill-defined paths below Barunapadi awaited us.

Margaret and I, with arms over each other's shoulders, pushed up the ridge. Somehow, we were the first to reach the final and highest point of our trek. Exhausted, yet elated to glimpse the Buddhist village, we looked upward toward Sagarmatha to thank her for guarding our journey so far.

Standing next to Margaret, I appreciated her friendship.

She reminded me of my mother's Southern charm and warm heart. An ironic thought, as Margaret stood gripping her trekking stick while wearing her dusty boots. My mother had never owned either of these objects or had any reason to own them.

As we climbed, Margaret confirmed what I suspected. Like my mother, Margaret loved her husband, children, grand-children, her sterling silver, her hydrangeas, and Chippendale furniture. To the mix, Margaret added her love of photo-graphy, traveling and her life as a seeker. Her roles intrigued me. I wondered if my mother, who I believed was also a seeker, ever allowed herself to dream of traveling as we were doing.

After an arduous climb, dinner cooked and served by the Sherpas provided much needed time to relax. Under a canopy of stars and a crescent moon, I appreciated how the moon and the stars followed me wherever I roamed.

After a dhal and rice meal, a two-layer chocolate cake appeared with enough burning candles to turn on a smoke alarm. "Surprise!" Everyone, including the Sherpas, shouted, "Happy Forty-ninth!"

I was shocked that anyone knew about my birthday and surprised even more by the chocolate cake baked over an open fire. A birthday impossible to top. Near the top of the world, close to new friends, with a birthday cake to light up the night. The inner struggles strangling me before coming to Nepal lay as far away as the Milky Way.

While enjoying a Himalayan high, I felt humbled, realizing Sherpas hauled everything needed for our dinner, including the birthday cake, up the same treacherous paths I struggled to climb carrying only a fanny pack, a water bottle, and my determination. And I would not ever forget that a Sherpa woman about my age carried my gear on her back.

I wondered if this woman contemplated as I did what it

meant to be here now. I meant here in Nepal, and here on planet earth, and here inside our skin; she inside her olive skin and me inside my freckled skin. I also wondered if I could truly relate to the plight of rural women in Nepal. After all, I'd never hauled heavy loads on my back, been forced to work in a brothel, had to sleep in a *chaupadi* shed or to watch an income-generating piglet slaughtered. I should have begun a conversation, but the language and cultural barrier made my thoughts difficult to convey. The best I could do was to send smiles her way.

A few days later, with the trek behind us, our group rumbled in a rickety bus on a winding, rough road through a forest bordering the confluence of two streams. I assumed the drive would take us back to Kathmandu. Instead, we stopped in front of an isolated Hindu temple complex.

Crushing crowds, some carrying baskets of golden marigolds and red hibiscus lined up beside those carrying ducks, chickens, or goats. The women's saris matched the red canopy over the entrance.

"We're at Dakshinkali Temple, no?" Gopal suggested, addressing us from the bus. "We'll visit a revered temple dedicated to the Goddess Kali."

Surprised we had stopped some place not on our itinerary, I worried what kind of impression this strange, crowded complex would leave. Since today was our last full day in Nepal, I wanted the group to leave on an emotional high, ready to return home to write checks to support Change of Possibility programs. We'd seen temples. Another one seemed pointless. However, others seemed curious, so I followed along.

We began to climb endless stairs, smothered between Kali devotees. Men selling prayer beads, statues and marigold garlands worked their way into the crowd. Brass oil lamps alongside the steps burned to create a haze that blurred tantric symbols carved into stone walls.

After a half-hour, our group passed under the red canopy stretched over the entrance. I wished to appear reverent with my head bowed, but my shoulders and neck felt tense and the whole thing seemed bizarre and uncomfortable. Furthermore, I assumed the temple was reserved for Hindu worship

"Should non-Hindus enter?" I asked Gopal.

Gopal used his hands to motion us forward. "Here," he said, "people of all faiths or of no faith may pay respect to Ma Kali and ask for her blessing."

Before entering, we removed shoes and socks and stacked them at the entrance alongside shoes of every variety. With my bare feet touching the concrete floor, I peered through smoke encircling rows of burning candles. As I stumbled across the dimly illuminated temple, I smelled profuse incense. The crowd's push against my body made it hard to breathe. What was my group feeling? No one spoke. Was I prepared to open myself to this experience? My mind seemed to resist connecting to what was around me, but my body felt an odd desire to enter more deeply.

When I looked up at the Kali statue on her altar, I saw the face of an ancient goddess sticking her bright red tongue out at me. In one arm Kali brandished a mighty sword. Her other six snaking, muscular arms she raised high above her head in a warrior stance. Severed heads dangled from a belt around her waist. Skull earrings hung from gold chains pinned to her ears. In her presence all sounds disappeared. How odd! How bizarre! Why did Hindus worship this figure? I didn't even like pretending to find Kali inspiring. I didn't get it. Actually, I was completely turned off and ready to leave.

"We call her the Divine Mother of us all," Gopal whispered. "She holds *shakti* energy and power."

His words intrigued me while skepticism seized me. I

watched as Kali devotees gathered close to the altar, placing bowls of fruit, rice and marigold petals at the Goddess's feet before bowing before her.

My first encounter with a fierce, demon-destroying, compassionate, sacred feminine image left me without a full understanding of what I was experiencing. At the same time, I sensed something deep, powerful and essential had been ignited within me. Kali stood ready to battle the world's darkness, pain, and strife while sticking her tongue out and waving her sword at those who might resist her power. She personified the ability to destroy what must be destroyed inside and around us. I stood in awe of the transformational, feminine power she communicated. Yet another opportunity for me to connect to divine feminine power had presented itself.

In the silence, Kali's energy and her presence, along with Gopal's words, enveloped me. I felt armed like a female warrior ready to battle that which must be changed. I laughed, picturing myself wearing skull earrings to embody Kali's power.

I decided to offer Kali a prayer. "Allow me, Ma Kali to grow and become the person I am meant to be. A woman full of passion for a better world—one where women would be valued as strong and wise as well as loving, nurturing and compassionate. A world where I would not work endlessly to please others without pleasing myself first, where I would not doubt my talents and skills." I had come to Nepal without fear of traveling to a country I knew little about. The decision to accept a new job with the adventure of leading a trek in the Himalayas had seemed challenging, but not as difficult as speaking up to my former boss.

I continued my prayer-conversation with the benevolent goddess. "Until today I had never heard your name. But your presence makes me ready to battle the moments when I lack confidence. You demand sacrifice. For me, that means sacrificing or letting go of my hang-ups. My exaggerated need to please. My fierce self-judgment. I am gaining awareness that you represent the unleashing of all things taboo regarding the feminine.

"I must say, it never occurred to me to picture the Divine Feminine with your ferocity. I could picture Jesus as he overturned tables outside the temple in a demonstration of his righteous rage, but I knew of no stories showing Mary doing any such thing. What I had learned was that stomping my feet, yelling damn, or speaking my truth to patriarchal power was not acceptable or something possible for me."

I bowed toward Kali, then turned to follow our group back outside the temple. "Something that concerns me," I said as if I simply had to keep speaking to this goddess, "is the irony that the Divine Mother is greatly revered in Nepal, yet violence continues against women, almost unabated. And I find it pathetic that in a so-called developed nation like mine, violence against women continues."

Twenty-two kilometers from Dakshinkali, I browsed with my travel companions through *Abhaya* boutique, one of the best-known, most successful handicraft production companies in Nepal. *Abhaya* meant "lack of fear" in Sanskrit. The perfect name to fit the goal that the founder and executive director, Maya Sharma, imagined for her business. Here, female craft producers created the products sold. On a shelf of handicrafts, boiled felt purses caught my eye. One purse, chocolate brown with three pastel-colored felt flowers sewn to the top, seemed longing to go to the USA. Putting the purse strap over my shoulder, I chose to become the purse's adoptive parent.

I spied a jewelry case with silver and opal earrings also needing a home. I picked up the earrings and looked at a card attached. It read, "Earrings are more than adornment—they possess auspicious benefits. When a woman wears earrings, she honors the Divine in herself, the Divine in others and the Divine throughout the universe."

So that's it! Now I understood why I had adored earrings since my childhood, and why I would purchase the pair with the note attached.

I watched Genie drape a brightly colored Dhaka cloth scarf around her shoulders before placing three other gorgeous scarves in a stack to purchase.

Dale selected a Dhaka "topi" hat. When worn with his disco shirt, it made quite a statement, perhaps showing respect for Nepali culture combined with respect for disco culture too. Margaret chose a carved yak bone necklace. Bridgette, block print placemats and napkins, and Jack bought a lovely silver necklace. Who was it for? I wondered. Jack had never mentioned a woman in his life.

After shopping time, Gopal directed us to the product production area where sari-draped women gathered in groups seated on the floor. They chatted as they worked. Some knitted, others strung beads. Others stamped fabric using carved wooden blocks.

Seated beside wood and bamboo treadle looms, weavers wove intricate patterns into silk-like cotton called Dhaka cloth. Several women stitched together Dhaka "topi" hats like Dale's and other women stitched Dhaka scarves like the ones Genie loved so much.

One woman managed a machine where boiled felt sheets rolled off wooden rollers. The strips were made into purses like the one I would carry home.

Into this beehive of activity, a petite, sari-clad woman buzzed around. The woman was Maya, the heart and soul of *Abhaya*. Standing tall at less than five feet, for the next half-hour, Maya shared her story in English with a Nepali accent.

"One day I knew I wanted to establish an organization with stable incomes for unskilled craft producing women who raise children and manage farm tasks too. I offered flexible schedules and training and provided raw materials for producing traditional handicrafts."

To cover her expenses, Maya obtained a small grant from Change of Possibility. The funds enabled the enterprise to expand. Within four years, Maya, her board of directors and her staff had established a self-sustaining nonprofit entrepreneurial handicrafts venture. Starting with about thirty impoverished female producers, *Abhaya* now employed more than a thousand well-trained and well-compensated producers, including former sex trafficking victims.

Bridgette looked at me. I looked at her. We knew about Nepal's sex trafficking issues because of Gopal. And now we knew *Abaya* employed and aided once-trafficked girls and young women!

At that point, Maya paused and placed her palms together in a prayer pose. With her last three fingers interlaced, she pointed her index fingers upward. "With our hands shaped in a gesture, the Kali Mudra," Maya said, "we practice a ritual. During the workday, we take a deep breath. Then we repeat, 'I am strong! I am powerful. I can change what must be changed!' The ritual provides a calming, restorative and empowering practice."

Maya and the women producers needed strength to face many obstacles, including bureaucratic laws and corrupt officials who tried to block their work. We learned how the young women producers also had to protect themselves from police who had attempted to steal their wages when they left work.

As I shaped my fingers in the Kali mudra, I vowed to grow my sense of feminine authority to oppose the oppression of women. As these thoughts played in my mind, Genie turned to me and said, "I know how to help Maya market the young women's products at home. I'm familiar with international marketing."

I imagined what Maya and Genie could make happen and felt an adrenaline rush of excitement. I'd do my part by assuring both women connected. Such a partnership would give proof to the value in bringing women to visit the programs.

On the street corner outside *Abhaya*, we saw Nepalese women approaching. Several carried infants strapped to their backs. The women huddled together, chanting mantras while holding placards protesting the corrupt monarchy. I listened, soaking up the beauty, power, and energy the mantras produced while watching women raising their placards to protest the lack of children's immunizations—something the government has long promised, but never delivered. Despite the hard-won 1990 revolution introducing a constitutional monarchy, virtually no assistance or economic development has reached the poverty-stricken rural poor, and these mothers appeared determined to do something about that.

Moments after the women arrived, a dozen policemen, protected by both chest and head guards, surrounded the protestors with swinging batons. An enraged policeman struck one woman on her back. Stunned, we saw a second policeman strike a pregnant woman on the shoulder. A third woman received a blow across the back of her leg. Gopal's face tightened. He looked as though he would lunge at the police, but restrained himself to protect our group. "You could be killed if pulled into the fray," he shouted, "and the protesting women could be killed to show Americans the police are in control."

As the policemen's batons flew, other women received

blows. With no obvious recourse, the defenseless women dispersed. Gopal lowered his head and shoulders as if to hide his pain and helplessness. He explained how the women had walked hours from their mountain villages to protest local officials who dump medical supplies and immunizations into the river, rather than carry them up the mountain to the waiting villagers. Fury swirled inside me as I realized the reality of the corruption.

Jack turned to ask if I had any food in my fanny pack. Then he asked for my water bottle. I was shocked this man could think about food and water after what we'd seen. I handed Jack a package of crackers and my water bottle. He disappeared.

The police left. Not long afterward, I heard a chant rising in the air and noticed a woman around the corner lifting her placard and chanting as she had done earlier. This time she walked alone down the street. I imagined the woman was drawing strength from her companions who walked in opposite directions.

Gopal led us around the corner where I observed Jack handing water bottles and snacks to women still holding their placards. While I stood doing nothing, Jack had gathered water and food to share with the protestors. I sensed how his concern, without worries for danger to himself, impacted us all. The protestors bravely waved at Jack as they headed to their villages, safe from the police for now. Gopal assured us the women would be back another day.

"On behalf of each woman, I thank you," I told Jack as we paused at the site of the terrifying scene before the group continued toward our hotel. It would take time to absorb what we had witnessed. As dust from the street blew in our faces and mixed with the pungent smell of turmeric and cayenne used in street stall cooking, Jack fumbled with his fingers before announcing he had something to say.

"I've had my head in a book or in the clouds most of my life, but I left my heart behind somewhere. I've been absent without leave emotionally for a long time." He added, "Soon I'll be heading home to revive a long, almost-lost marriage." He paused, lowered his chin, and drew a deep breath. "My task will require tantric transformation of body, mind and spirit. The strength and trust of once-trafficked women and of protesting women. I'll need to heal old wounds. I hope it's not too late to ask my wife to accompany me."

Jack's voice trailed off in a lonely longing that reminded me even Swamis have issues. "If my wife were here, and I wish she were," Jack added, "she'd be advocating for the *Abhaya* producers. For the protestors and for the rise of women."

"I'm deeply touched," I told him, noting how filled with emotion I felt. "We each have wounds to heal. Women and men healing ourselves. What a world of difference that could make," I noted as I walked forward.

When we arrived at our hotel lobby, a young man dressed in a U.S. State Department uniform with a focused look on his face walked into the lobby. "Are you American citizens?" Without pausing for a reply, the official added, "Because of the tragedy, our Embassy must assure we've accounted for all Americans."

"What tragedy?" I asked.

"The avalanche," the official declared, "Forty-three trekkers died. Buried alive in their sleep. We're trying to locate survivors. Most people here have no idea about the tragedy. News from the mountain travels slowly."

My jaw dropped. My hands trembled. My knees shook. Forty-three people lost their lives, and we never knew anything happened. Snow fell above us while raindrops came to the lower areas where we trekked.

Racing with the others to the phones, frantic about our family's concerns, we discovered the phone lines were down, jammed after a barrage of calls.

The avalanche deaths rattled and sobered me. Human existence is fragile, and life can be over before we know it. The notion of my mortality made my desire to manifest my inner longings more urgent. I acknowledged how much our quests contain both what is promising and what is perilous. For those who lost their lives the perilous prevailed. I knew not why. May they rest in peace.

An image of the invisible equator came to mind. I saw it encircling the globe and encircling me to connect two halves of a whole—the authentic feminine and the authentic masculine, Shakti and Shiva, Yin and Yang.

A profound sense of absolute trust that my voice, value, impact and high purpose would emerge with the same certainty of aging, dying and death.

Oklahoma City, 1997

I searched the crowd outside the Oklahoma City airport customs area. In an instant, I spotted two shining brown eyes as appealing as when I first saw them twenty-seven years ago. Lugging my backpack, I rushed toward those eyes. As we hugged, I asked, "Were you worried about me?"

"Hell, yes, I was worried," Charlie answered. "I thought I might have to find another wife." With that, his eyes gleamed before he kissed me like in a soap opera scene.

I looked around to see who got to see our reunion before asking, "How's Abby?"

"Doing great. Had a big test today. We'll call her later," Charlie said as he rolled my bag toward the parking lot.

How would I explain what it was like on top of the world? I had a birthday there, returned with a new awareness of my mortality and of so much more. What would I do with what I had learned? How would it feel to see the world through a lens different from most of the people I knew? How would it be to inhabit a new stage of my life? One with a new career. Where parenting did not play the major role it once had.

On Monday morning, after a weekend cuddling, sleeping, and sharing stories with Charlie and sharing cherished time with Abby, I entered the Change of Possibility headquarters building. I imagined balloons and a welcome back poster. After all, here I was, not a boring middle-ager, but a wiser-wild ager with much to share.

Not seeing balloons, I wandered across the earth-toned, stained-concrete floors interspersed with green carpet patches. The architect suggested the floor coverings "added a world village feel to the space."

The office floor I saw needed a mop and a vacuum more than it added the "feel" of village pathways like in Nepal. But these facts did not diminish my euphoric mood as I approached Stephen's cubicle.

"Good morning. How's it going?" My words left my mouth with the exuberance I imagined Sir Edmond Hilary felt returning after his Himalayan quest.

"I'm good," Stephen responded in a monotone voice. Without looking up from his computer, I heard him mumble, "Glad you're back."

I noted this fellow didn't hold his breath in anticipation of my trip remarks, but I replied anyway, "Nepal was like a trip to the moon and back. Another world. You know what I'm talking about."

"Uh-uh," Stephen said without looking up. I got his message. I'd broken an unspoken cardinal rule of our workplace. Displaying emotion carried the same taboo as eating with your left hand carried in Nepal.

Go gather facts and figures for the Change of Possibility newsletter and bring back checks. That was my travel assignment. The fact that Nepal rocked my world did not matter. Nor did it matter that I intended to rock others' worlds with stories of what I had discovered.

After Stephen's lukewarm response, I left him alone to pound his computer keys. That's when Rick, our executive director, appeared. Did he intend to invite me for coffee to hear about my trip?

"Hello," Rick announced as if I were back from a lunch break, "I trust all went well. I'll need your budget figures Friday. Also, your trip report for the trustee mailing. Be sure to show indicators of progress in Nepal's programs," he added.

With that, Rick turned and sped across the stained concrete path back to his office. So much for a welcome back party. I was inside a culture of logical, linear rigidity and restraint. Despite accomplishments supporting grassroots development in marginalized communities, how could our office culture attract the needed funds and commitment to support the rise of the feminine? And how could this culture grasp the concept? With that thought, I wanted to finish my work and go home.

Once a month, on the third Thursday, for twenty-one years, I'd joined friends for an evening of Bunco. At a different member's home each month, the "bunco" game, played with nine dice and luck, allowed a dozen women to forget our responsibilities and worries for a while. We laughed and enjoyed connecting. We ate. We drank. We shared stories. We rolled dice while seated at one of three tables of four women. The object, besides enjoying ourselves, was to score points, taking turns to roll three dice in a series of six rounds. We'd yell, "bunco" if we rolled three-of-a-kind.

As the game proceeded, there was a time to rotate to other tables, according to the rules. This gave us time to visit with every woman in the group. By the end of the night, the member with the most "buncos" would get a prize, purchased by that month's hostess.

Glancing at my friends, I realized how important the group was to me. I felt close to these women, though my travel experiences made me feel somehow different.

I wondered when or if I'd hear someone ask, "How was your trip?" And would the question come before or after the same question was posed to Kay and Mary about their trip to New York? They shopped and watched *Hair Spray* on Broadway. A great trip I would have loved, but one unlike mine.

If asked a question about Nepal, I might be dipping chips into spinach dip. Would that be the time to tell how Nepalese women trekked hours each day over treacherous mountain paths to collect water? How they cooked over outside fires. Or would I tell how Nepalese women laughed when I explained that in my country women use a machine that lets us walk in place—a practice we call exercise.

Even if I fantasized about how fabulous it would be to introduce these friends to the importance of Sushila's savings and credit group, tonight would not serve as the forum. Besides, I was pulled between fitting in as one of the girls, versus standing out to share what I'd discovered. Another complicating factor—I was not perceived by these bunco buddies as an advocate for change. And being seen as a capable leader felt compromised when they had to help me search for my purse.

After a mere three weeks in Nepal, my perspective on the world had shifted. I saw everything through a different lens—

with or without glasses. I'd changed, though I lacked a warrior goddess tattoo or a protest placard to reflect the change. Under the surface of what my friends could see, I held an awareness unknown to me three weeks ago. How long would I silence what I knew to be true? I felt admired for being brave enough to trek in Nepal. While the boldness to speak my truth was what I needed.

I passed the dice to the friend on my right as my thoughts wandered again. Here I sat on a speed bump in the middle of my road of life. To keep my job, to travel, to learn and grow, to connect with and support women around the world, I had to recruit travelers to Change of Possibility trips.

Zero travel prospects appeared on the horizon. My plum job could be in jeopardy. Yet, hope was not lost. While Change of Possibility's mission might not appeal to everyone, if I found as few as six trip participants interested in a country where we had programs, I could lead them on a potentially life-changing experience that should lead to donations. In the meantime, I would indulge in a fun-filled evening with my girlfriends and with Mary's chocolate cream pie. Worries about trip participants I'd face tomorrow.

Near quitting time at work the next day, as I straightened papers on my cubicle desk, I felt like a dismal failure, a not unfamiliar feeling. I had still not recruited travelers to life transforming Change of Possibility travel. Suddenly, I heard my desk phone ring. I expected a telemarketer.

"Hello Sam, great to hear from you!"

Small talk ensued with Sam Edwards, a long time major financial donor to Change of Possibility. Everyone in the organization knew and respected Sam.

"I heard you have a new bride," I told him. "How wonderful!"

"I promised Ida Mae we'd honeymoon in Kenya before my upcoming 80th birthday," Sam chuckled. "And I have two friends about our age who want to join us."

I told myself I had two trip participants ready to travel! But 80-year-olds on their honeymoon traveling with friends the same age?

But wishful thinking allowed me to promise I'd be back in touch with trip details.

For the moment, thanks to Sam, I had four travelers and Sam's suggested dates. With two more travelers, I could lead a trip to Kenya. Change of Possibility had impressive programs there. I wanted to see them and to see Africa again forty-four years after my childhood experiences in Morocco and twenty-six years after my trip to Egypt.

For the next few weeks, I worked every lead I could imagine in an attempt to recruit two more travelers to Kenya. I enlisted help from the entire staff with no results. What was I to do? I put my head on the desk as the "I'm not enough" part of me took hold.

I sat with that victim in me until I sat up and told myself the Universe was on my side. I stayed curious about solutions as I worked on the trip itinerary. A few days later, I heard my phone rang at an unexpected moment. A thick Oklahoma twang soared over the line.

"Hey, Shelly Sanger here. My friend Patricia and I want to sign on for your trip to Kenya."

The Universe heard me! "Shelly, that's wonderful," I replied.

But who was this person? I asked how Shelly knew about our Kenya trip.

"I met one of your trustees at a party with some fellow lawyers. He told me you lead Kenyan adventures. I've always wanted to go to Kenya to see the wildlife. The dates fit, so I talked a friend of mine into coming along with me."

Logic required I suggest Shelly call a travel company about

one of their upscale African safari gigs. But I put logic aside for a moment.

Shelly added, "I know Change of Possibility takes people to visit African villages. We want to see native villages and their local color."

The demeaning terms "native villages" and "local color" used to describe encounters with those struggling to improve life in rural Kenya made me cringe—until my inner Sacred Feminine guidance made my body believe Shelly and Patricia could have their eyes opened in Kenya. The same way I had mine opened in Nepal.

Then the critic who lived in my mind spoke up, "These gals won't shift perspective. They'll infuriate Sam and ruin the trip."

With an impulse in my belly battling a haranguing voice in my head, I made an executive decision—though I was not an executive, only an entry-level employee desperate to keep her job. I asked for Shelly's credit card number to reserve two spots for the trip.

"Congratulations, Shelly," I announced. "You and Patricia are bound for two weeks in Kenya. I'll send a detailed itinerary and an information packet soon."

6

ON SAFARI

Nairobi, Kenya, 1998

"Nairobi must be Swahili for Shitty City," Shelly declared.

This I didn't need. Riding along with six Change of Possibility adventurers—who weren't that adventurous—and with Joshua, our Kenyan driver, we gyrated wildly through streets where skyscrapers loomed over minibusses called *matatus* packed with people, chicken, and goats. We'd seen women balancing straw baskets on their heads passed by chauffeur-driven Mercedes Benz carrying dark-suited businessmen. Trying to be a helpful tour guide, Joshua had pointed to an ocean of closet-sized, tin-roof shanties. "Kibera. Some say a million people live here," he said, locking his eyes straight ahead as if to avoid watching our reaction. Raw sewage flowed into ditches filled with plastic bags and other debris.

Responding to the scene, Shelly from Oklahoma failed to spare us her commentary. Subtlety was not her forte.

Ruth, a west Texas rancher's wife, turned up her nose at the smell. Her husband, John, two sheets to the wind after 20 hours and 18,000 miles of in-flight drinking, babbled a litany of complaints. Sam and Ida Mae, Texas oil barons, stared at the passing Kibera rubble in silence. Patricia, a banker from California, closed her eyes.

And so, we began our Kenyan safari—the Swahili word for a journey. Americans had arrived from a country believing itself exceptional, expecting sanitized, cleaned-up versions of real-life journeys. Though I knew Sam understood what we were seeing.

"I could be in big trouble with this group," I told myself. Seeking strength, I pulled from my tote bag Karen Blixen's *Out of Africa*. "The chief feature of the landscape," Blixen wrote, "and of your life in it, was the air... Up high in this air you breathed easily, drawing vital assurance and lightness of heart. In the highlands, you woke up in the morning and thought, here I am, where I ought to be." I felt a strong connection with Blixen's sense of adventure. As I thought of her, I decided to call her Tania, a name used by those close to her.

I pressed on through Tania's words, even as smoke from slum fires filled my lungs and the smell of sweat and foul water invaded my senses. I thought of the irony that the "farm" described in Tania's classic story remained now in a nearby high-dollar community named Karen, in her memory.

I wanted to believe, as Tania did when she arrived, "Here I was where I ought to be." As the leader of a Change of Possibility trip to Kenya, my job was to assure a memorable and impactful experience for everyone. If I failed to open eyes—and checkbooks—my dream job would be short-lived.

The Hotel Stanley showed no interest in cooperating with my need for a smooth group experience. Upon our arrival at this famed five-star hotel where celebrities like Ava Gardner, Clark Gable, Ernest Hemingway, and the Prince of Wales once stayed, we were greeted with scaffolding, wheelbarrows, broken rock, piles of dirt and construction. When Joshua stopped our vehicle, a dusty wooden sign appeared with barely visible letters spelling Hotel Stanley. Nearby, construction workers swung pickaxes.

A top-to-bottom remodel was underway. I led our exhausted group to check-in at a counter notable for its non-functioning computers and harried staff. Just when I thought I might scream, the manager handed me keys to our rooms on the fourth floor, then informed me the elevators were shut down during construction. Now I had to lead a weary, irritated bunch of jet-lagged travelers on a forced-march up four flights of stairs. I had no words.

Soon after we negotiated the nightmarish stairs, and I got settled in my room, before I could dial the front desk to ask about the fate of our bags, I heard a knock. Our luggage at last! But no, it was a hopping mad John, demanding I get his bags to his room and quick. It seemed obvious what I should do—cut my wrists. No, I should push my aching body back down the stairs in search of either our luggage or a seat at the bar.

Thirty minutes later. Bags were in our rooms, carried up the stairs by smiling porters.

"I considered heading 'Out of Africa' last night," I heard Shelly say as I arrived the next morning to join our group for breakfast. "But I'm no quitter. I've decided to stick it out."

John chuckled as the others joined in. Relieved, I took a seat.

Wariko Muthengi, the Change of Possibility program director for Kenya, joined us. I felt I already knew her, though we'd only communicated through email. Before I introduced our group to this bright, charismatic woman, I watched her thousand-watt smile greet us.

"Welcome a friend," I said, wrapping my arm around Wariko's waist. Turning my face to her, I added, "I'm excited about what we will learn from you."

As I spoke, I thought about the email I'd received from Charlie at home in Oklahoma. Reading between the lines, I sensed how much he was entrenched in his familiar way of life. That's when I worried that both he and Abby, the two people I loved most in the world, might not grasp the ways our Western lifestyles strangle us and strangle the Divine Feminine. Pushing men and women to assume distorted masculine ways in the workplace and even at home. Often making us depressed or sick, unable to imagine another future. By living life entrenched in Western society and its demands, despite its benefits, Charlie and Abby might not be open to what was opening in me. The thought terrified me.

"We're now leaving 'Nairobbery,'" Wariko announced as we embarked on the long drive to the Ukambani region. "Nairobi's crime is ignored or caused by corrupt police and despotic politics. Loans and aid to improve our economy benefit politicians, not the people. But you must know most Kenyans are honest and hardworking with burgeoning potential inside their hearts and minds."

"Why can't things change?" Shelly announced from the back seat.

"Perhaps your question is akin to asking why racial and gender discrimination and poverty don't disappear in your country," Wariko replied without a smile. "Here we contend with racial and gender discrimination. Population growth. Inadequate schools. Poorly functioning healthcare. HIV/AIDS. Severe job shortage. Plus, an aging president/dictator, who refuses even to fix our few paved roads. Instead, he and his cronies steal funds and squelch forces demanding democratic reforms. Moreover, we contend with massive World Bank debt."

I noticed Ruth buried in a book, *Under the Tuscan Sun*. A

book, not about the wilds of Africa or Africa's challenges, but about restoring a villa in Italy.

"We will travel close to the Kenya-Somali border," Wariko said as her eyes grew intense. "Be vigilant. Al-Shabaab terrorists target Westerners. They're dangerous fundamentalist jihadists. Should we be confronted, hand over whatever you have. Don't hesitate and risk death rather than submit your passport or sunglasses."

The skin between Shelly's eyes wrinkled. She straightened her back and said, "Oh, but I love my Armani sunglasses."

And then John leaned forward to proclaim, "Christ, Wariko, ya think we're fuckin' pansies? Sam and I fought in WWII. I fought kamikazes in the Battle of Okinawa, and Sam brought home a Purple Heart from his Pacific battles. We've seen it all."

When Sam nodded in agreement, John was off on a story about one dark night in a ditch holding a buddy as he died. "Nineteen he was. Gunshot to the head. And I can't count the numbers of starving children and devastated mothers I saw during the war. It's impossible to forget such things."

Sam braced against the seat. Looking at the strained faces of these two men, I was struck by the way men bear the world's pain and suffering. I thought about Charlie. How would he have reacted if he were here? Would he have his tough guy warrior armor on? Or would the cracks in the armor I'd seen lately have allowed him to show fear for himself, for me, or for all of us?

My awareness of dark forces rising had once again been ignited. How would I handle my growing awareness?

Haunted by drought, the Ukambani landscape lacked a single blade of grass. Into terrain as barren as photos of Mars appeared two women wrapped in African kangas balancing plastic jugs on their heads. One woman carried a baby strapped to her back. The woman beside her gripped bowls and scoops made from gourds while her toddler son walked beside her.

As we watched from the distance of our now parked van, the women stopped beside two truck-tire-sized holes filled with sewage-colored water. The younger woman placed her jug at her feet and bent to fill her gourd scoop. She lifted the liquid to her lips. Offered a few sips to her baby. Then filled the jug with more of the turbid water. The other woman did the same as her young son silently sat on the sand staring into the muddy water.

"They walk miles and miles to get here and the same distance back to their village," Wariko said. "Tomorrow morning, they will repeat the journey. Unless they or their children fall ill from waterborne disease. Which happens."

I would never forget the faces of the women or frail little boy. Backyard swimming pools, waterfalls, sprinkler systems keeping grass green, all the excess of the life I had left behind left me shaking my head. Where was justice and equity in this world? I did not have an answer, but I carried a visceral, painful reaction to the problem.

Back on the highway, intense silence filled the van. "In drought-stricken Africa, access to clean drinking water is one of our greatest challenges," Wariko said. "Water wells are needed, but they must be drilled and maintained. Limited government money is allocated. Change of Possibility and other nonprofit groups fund water well projects, but more are needed. We stopped for your eyes to be opened to reality."

"Good God," Shelly said.

What was good about God? My Source, the one that accompanied me as I carried these and other shocking images,

I had become disconnected from in my rush to get our trip together. Maybe I was in the midst of a spiritual drought, something that might not cost me my life, but could cost vitality, hope and alignment with my purpose and with a belief in the ultimate goodness of life, the goodness of the Divine.

Moving back into what was happening, I heard Wariko say, "As a young girl, I often walked twice a day to collect water from sites such as the one we just saw."

As we drove, Wariko shared her story. "I was the first girl born into a family of ten children," she said, passing bottles of clean water to each of us. "We were raised in a village much like the mud hut village homes of these women. When I turned six, I wanted more than anything to go to school, like my brothers."

"A dream of learning as big as the African sky propelled my hopes, but I heard it said again and again, 'Boys become warriors and girls become mothers.' No girl in my village had ever gone to school, so why would I imagine I could?"

I remembered how at age six, I started school in Casablanca while Votna, like the other girls in her village, could not.

Wariko pulled us into her words as she continued telling how her father, a laborer in Nairobi, understood her yearning for an education. "He decided I should go to school. At first, my mother objected, saying, 'A wild elephant or a lion could attack you or you could be raped along the way.'"

Wariko knew her mother's larger concern was that without her daughter's help, life for the family would be more challenging. But her mother did not argue with her father. Somehow, even with her husband away, Wariko's mother managed to pay for the books, fees, and uniforms—none of which were provided by the government. And Wariko became the first girl in her village to attend primary school, proudly walking across scrub brush four or five miles to school each day.

"When I finished sixth grade, I wanted to continue learning," Wariko told us. "Literacy would let me author my own story, one with more than poverty and the oppression of women as themes."

Because secondary school was too far away to walk, Wariko would need to live in a dormitory. Bedding would be needed—something not used at home where she slept on a straw mat. And more books and money for fees. The costs amounted to more than her family would see in an entire year. "I decided my school days had ended."

"For me, to go from sixth grade to junior high required simply that I get into my mother's car for a ride to a new school," I reminded myself.

Wariko explained that before the school term began, her mother decided Wariko must go and learn. So, she took her one bag of grain, what she had produced and stored, and she sold it at market. With money from the grain, Wariko was able to go to school.

Thanks to her mother's sacrifice, Wariko was not married off as happened to most girls her age. Instead, she finished secondary school and secured a scholarship to college in Paris. She even attended graduate school in London, though sadly her mother did not live to see her graduate. Now she focuses on both informal and formal education for rural women and girls. "It's the way I honor my mother's sacrifice," Wariko told us.

Hearty cheers for Wariko filled the van. I gladly joined in. Wariko offered high fives in reply. With my cheers for Wariko, I also cheered for her mother and for my mother, too.

For too long, I had associated power and strength with men. Craving what they had, I discounted my mother. Her feminine power and wisdom. Her support for me What a fool! Fooled as the world has been. My mother shared with me what

Wariko's mother shared with her—the chance to go and learn. Yet, I had not fully appreciated my mother and her wisdom and what she had contributed to my life. It was also time for me to claim the feminine within me. I'd felt it, longed to bring it forward, but I seemed to continue to rely on masculine push energy more than my creative, feminine energy.

"We're in a Dust Bowl," Patricia proclaimed, wiping red dust from her face with a handkerchief. Wariko informed the group that poor farming practices, deforestation and climate change had turned the soil to dust as water disappeared.

"Look," Shelly broke into Wariko's talk, "if you think you're shaking up privileged white Americans with all your talk about Kenya's problems, you won't be successful. We might be shocked, but we're tougher and more perceptive than you think."

Even from Shelly, this eruption was a surprise. I stepped in. "I see myself as an ally to Africa's women," I said. "Especially the marginalized. I'm here to have my eyes opened, though I'll see more than I can grasp—as may happen for all of us."

I turned to Wariko. "So, Wariko, you must decide if you view us as allies or accomplices. Representatives of a non-governmental development organization supported by private funds. White folks with savior syndrome. Imperialists. Or clueless tourists here for photos of villagers and African wildlife."

Emotion crackled like logs in a fireplace. Silence fell over the van. Taking a deep breath, Wariko lifted her head and threw her forehead back. "I stand for dignity and justice, for protecting land and resources. Democratic principles applied equally to all. It's my lifetime dream. All who share my dream I embrace."

Her voice dropped a notch. "Forgive me for unconscious distrust or bias. It's because of what I've seen and what I want to erase. It's patriarchal power that robs, whether it comes from British colonialism, Western governments, or multi-national corporations. From Moi our autocratic president. Or from unaware citizens of our shared Earth home."

With issues and emotions laid bare, we arrived at a guesthouse that seemed to resist the obvious need to collapse. Goats, chickens, and dozens of shaved-headed, barefoot African children approached, the young ones laughing with curiosity. They whispered "*wazungu*," their word for white people. The truth was, we looked more like red people with thick dust on our faces.

One by one, we passed under the shade of a sagging thorn tree while Akamba elders gathered around us. As greetings and handshakes continued, I turned to see a sour-faced John. "What do you mean asking Ruth and me to share a damn squat toilet with a cold bucket shower?"

While John's barking words rumbled through the air. I paused and looked at the ground, wondering how to respond to the pummeling of my sweaty, exhausted, anxious-to-please self. I wanted to fall into a hole to escape John's appalling behavior. I should have realized that the drive from Nairobi had taken a toll. I should have better prepared the group for where we would be staying, but I did not realize it would be such a modest place.

Shelly dropped her luggage and stretched to her near six-foot height. The feisty attorney in her became obvious. She towered over an agitated Texas rancher. Trying not to burst into laughter, Shelly said, "John, just ask them to change your room to the penthouse."

Quiet laughs allowed upset energy to flow. John got quiet and went inside. The others followed. Except before Shelly left, I stopped her.

"Thanks, Shelly." She laughed once more and said, "John just might come around like I did."

"Let's hope," I told her. "How 'bout coming with Wariko and me to meet Florence? She's a community trainer we did not expect. She's waited hours to see us."

"Well, I'm dead tired," Shelly said. "But, what the heck. I'm game."

I felt relieved. I wanted the others to sleep, but I needed some of us to meet Florence, and something told me Shelly should meet her.

Wariko and a slender woman wearing a sky-blue African kanga settled with Shelly and me on wicker chairs in a small room. Two objects caught my attention: the required photograph of President Daniel Moi hung on the wall, and a sole light bulb hung from the ceiling, flickering as if to announce electricity was not ever-present.

"My name is Florence, and I serve my people," the headscarf-wearing woman said, sitting tall and speaking formally. Casual greetings ensued before she began her story. "I work with six hundred members of nearby rural villages. Preventive health, agricultural training and gender relations courses are offered thanks to Change of Possibility support. Men and women are encouraged to join the training. The communities know and trust me. My work is difficult. Many footsteps, but the work is my life, especially now that my children are grown. For the first time in my life, I have dignity."

Shelly and I looked at each other. Despite a long day, I could tell we were both touched.

"I was widowed at forty-two," Florence told us. "I lost my husband to malaria, leaving me to raise six young children."

Wariko intervened to explain the custom that when a woman is widowed, she is forced to marry her husband's brother and grant him the land and home she had shared with her husband. For Florence, this could mean becoming one of her brother-in-law's wives.

"Yes," Florence interjected. "And to have sex to cleanse my husband's spirit. If I refused, I would have been beaten. Or killed."

We circled around Florence: Wariko, Shelly and me. It seemed we held our breath together.

"But I defied those rituals," Florence continued. "One night, I fled the village with my children. We came to Nairobi. I was determined to make my way. To get my children an education. Even though we had to live in Kibera's slums. Accepting life in one of Africa's worst slums was better than my fate with my brother-in-law and the laws of unweakened men."

Shelly shifted in her chair. The hard edges of her voice softened as she responded to Florence's defiance, "Florence. Where do you find your strength?"

Florence pointed to the moon in the dark sky and said, "She guides me. She's my strength even when I can't see her."

Shelly, her voice wobbling, said, "I'm a widow, too. My husband died in a plane crash when our daughter was a baby."

I was shaken. I had no idea Shelly was a widow who raised her daughter alone. Inside a transformative circle, we held the connection shared before turning our faces to the comforting face of the moon. Tomorrow Florence would need to leave for her work in a village a few hours from here.

As roosters crowed and goats bleated, women's singing echoed above all other sounds. Such was my Ukambani wake-up call. Despite stiffness from a night sleeping on a mattress the thickness of a cracker. Despite sleeping under mosquito netting with holes bigger than the buttons on my pajamas, I felt rested. After a bucket shower and a visit to the squat toilet, I dressed and headed to the modest kitchen for breakfast.

As I crossed the dirt patio, I saw Shelly seated at a table with her hands flying in animated conversation. I watched the others in our group listen. When I approached, Sam jumped up to grab a chair for me.

As soon as I sat down, Shelly announced: "Last night I heard something true and real. I got a whiff of one woman's strength, steadiness and resilience, and her life after loss." Moving forward in her chair as we waited to hear more, Shelly said, "Florence's story is like nothing I've ever heard."

I watched the faces and the way they put down their coffee cups, listening as Shelly repeated Florence's story in powerful, vivid detail. Shelly was quick to connect the place from which Florence rebuilt her life with the slum of Kibera we saw on our first day in Nairobi.

"The slum we passed going to The Stanley?" Patricia said.

"Yep, Kibera," Shelly said. "While living in a shack without running water, Florence and her children went to school during the day, then came home to make earrings and other jewelry from rolled scrap paper they gathered. On Saturdays and Sundays, they went to market or to the streets to sell their creations."

We nodded in admiration for Florence's perseverance. "When she completed her classes, and her children finished too, that's when Florence joined Change of Possibility," I said, picking up the narrative. "She's now a Change of Possibility paid community development worker in Ukambani. Her home. Where she'd lived among the Akambas most of her life."

Ruth, who rarely spoke, turned toward Shelly. "Widowed mothers from different worlds, under an African moon, find connection. It's the power of the feminine and of these trips."

When we arrived at the village, the "mamas" welcomed us. The exuberant, shell-rattling, kanga-draped Akamba dancers with their hair covered by white scarves tied low at the back of the neck, they shook and shimmied their bodies to the beat.

"Mama Wariko!" came the wild cries, using the title chosen for their revered, childless leader. As the music died down, Mama Wariko signaled it was time to tour the village. Our group trailed past a sea of smiling faces. This felt so different from the flashing TV screens back home where nonprofits sought money for poor people in Africa without awareness of their oppression, instead depicting them as pathetic objects needing charity, rather than agents for their own development. But that wasn't Change of Possibility. The contrast felt profound as we walked through her village, seeing it through Wariko's eyes. Earlier, she'd told us that such tear-jerk images of impoverished Africans could be labeled the "pornography of poverty."

Here, where two hundred Akamba people lived in mud huts with grass roofs, women coaxed millet, yams, and other produce from bone-dry soil, while caring for their children. Having finished their field work, some women sat weaving colorful sisal baskets to sell at market. Their daughters, wearing white blouses and blue skirts, scurried down the road, waving back to their mothers. "The girls are headed to school," Wariko announced as she patted one of them on the back. "The community organized to help build their building." We waved, too.

It felt good for me to wave at the young girls. An image of Votna in Casablanca came to me. I wondered if she ever had the chance to go to school. An image of waving to Abby the day she boarded a bus for first grade. Also waving the day she left for college.

Wariko led us to a circle of adults seated beneath a solitary baobab tree—a singular sight. It resembles an upside-down tree with gnarled and bare branches spreading like sprawling roots. An ancient baobab can be thousands of years old and stand ninety feet tall and about thirty feet in diameter. Though the baobab looks dead in winter, bare without leaves, in spring when it blooms it's covered with white flowers and a nourishing, tasty fruit. The leaves provide a treatment for malaria, and the trunk swells with springtime rainwater the villagers tap for drinking. They call it the sacred tree of life.

"For as long as anyone can remember, only men climbed baobabs," Wariko said, touching the leathery bark as fascinated villagers circled us. "The men would hang hollowed-log beehives in baobab branches. Later they harvested the honey they enjoyed or sold for a profit. Women were forbidden to do this because it was thought immodest for women to climb trees."

"Now that's a glass ceiling!" Shelly said.

The village's entrepreneurial women had set up white honeybee boxes around the baobab. "The women's box-produced honey sold for more than tree-harvested honey, bottled with bees in the honeycomb," Wariko said. "And, yes, women keep the profit from their box-produced honey. Most often they use the money to pay for their children's school expenses."

I remembered Sue Monk Kidd's *The Secret Life of Bees*, when the character August says, "Women make the best beekeepers 'cause they have a special ability built into them to love creatures that sting. It comes from years of loving children and husbands." I told Wariko this story.

While one of the women brought us samples of clear, golden honey, Wariko turned and translated August's words. The women clapped with uproarious laughter.

Wariko bent to lift a framed plaque from her bag and handed it to Sam, who was laughing with the women. Wariko pointed to the words of appreciation across the bottom, with signatures from the women beekeepers. "Because of support from people like you, the honey box project has become a reality reminding us of what men can do," she read. "Something that does not sting," she added.

Sam, a man of few words, held his shoulders back with a gleam in his eyes while Ida Mae reached for his hand.

"A honeymoon scene as sweet as honey," Patricia said, taking out her camera. Eighty-year-young Ida Mae, a West Texas woman with white hair and bright blue eyes, moved close to a gray-haired, dark-eyed Akamba woman and her granddaughter. Ida Mae smiled at them, pointing to the honey box. In that snapshot, I saw a world where grandmothers could forget, and where young girls would never know, that climbing trees or claiming profit had once been something only men could do.

John watched as women began removing the honey-laden frames from horizontal top-loading wooden bee boxes. "These gals know how to pull themselves up by their bootstraps," he announced. I looked down, noting the women's bare feet, and grinned at the irony.

Suddenly, the women beekeepers broke into song in their native Kikamba. A serenade for the bees in a gesture repeated each time they retrieved with gratitude the precious honey, always leaving some behind for the hives. The caring ways keep both bees and honey as plentiful as spring leaves on a baobab.

"What a great business—honey!" I imagined Charlie would say if he were here, meaning both honey and 'Honey,' the term of endearment he had used with me all these years. Oh, how I missed the sound of that man's voice. His touch. His presence. Reassurance that he was okay. Why I felt uneasy about him, I wasn't sure.

Wariko touched the ancient tree trunk and rubbed the bark. "Since baobabs lack growth rings," she said, "it's impossible to know their age. Wish that were true for us, but like the baobab, we have nothing visible to show what our experiences have given to us. We have but actions to reflect what we discover."

The next day brought us to a Teso village near the western border of Kenya, a hot, steamy morning on a plain surrounded by wheatgrass and brown millet stalks, parched banana trees and mud huts covered with grass roofs. It also brought an accident. Sam fell and hit his head, requiring stitches.

Wariko explained Sam could receive urgent care at the leprosy clinic. I gasped at the sound of the word "leprosy" and the fact I had to acknowledge the feared and forgotten disease must exist in this area. Sam and Ida Mae accepted the plan. Shelly took Ida Mae's hand, and they strolled with the others to meet our awaiting hosts. I hesitated to be certain they saw no need to return for something or other. I tried to trust that care such as Saraswati and the shaman gave Urmila's mother in the health clinic in Nepal would be given to Sam at the leprosy clinic for his less serious injury.

A few minutes later, I felt more comfortable to leave. I turned, surprised by a greeting from a woman standing among her tall corn stalks. I had paid no attention to her in the moments after Sam's fall. Her corn stood in lush, neatly lined-up rows. Brown, shriveled stalks withered in a nearby plot. The woman pointed to my camera. Not a good time for a photo shoot, I thought. I was anxious to meet our group at the women's gathering.

Pointing to a shovel lodged in the dirt, the woman again pointed to my camera. I relented and reached for my camera. A smile raised the high cheekbones of this farmer's svelte face. "*Jambo*," I said, repeating a Swahili greeting before I took the photo she might not ever see unless I had it printed and sent to Wariko to somehow deliver to this woman.

"*Biao bo apaaran*," she replied in Ateso. "Mary Marunga," she said.

I extended my hand and felt her calloused yet warm hand with the gentle, customary African handshake. I shared my name. Our powerful exchange of energy caught me off guard.

After I snapped a few photos, Mary's turned-down mouth signaled she was not ready for me to leave. Reaching down to the cracked dirt, she lifted a rope with knots tied every six inches. Holding it outstretched, she straightened with a satisfied smile. Strangely, a memory flashed in my mind. It was last spring when the begonias in my garden had bloomed so profusely that I'd insisted Charlie take a photo of me near my precious flowers. Mary must feel the pride I felt.

Tied around Mary's waist above a Western T-shirt was a bright orange cotton kanga, a pattern of white sunglasses printed across the bottom edge. I had to laugh. Kangas often display African designs or political sayings, but Western-style sunglasses printed on an edge of cloth worn by a struggling farm woman who may never own sunglasses struck me as ironic. Mary must possess a sense of humor.

When I arrived near a huge wild mango tree, the branches cast a deep shade over the women gathered beneath them. I was invited to take a seat on a wooden chair, where a white crocheted cover hung over the back. Two women poured tea, boiled over an outside fire. The gracious service in white plastic teacups made me feel welcome and comfortable, the way I would want the women to feel having tea if back home with my friends and me.

As we sipped our tea, Wariko said, "Considered sacred spaces where men claim their power, the limited shaded areas had long been off limits to women. Men told the women that poisonous snakes rested in the shade of trees—where men lounged, drinking beer and acting in charge. But things were changing in Teso village. The women had negotiated with the men for their time to sit and enjoy the shade. With snake sticks nearby, the women held no fear, only anticipation for what they would achieve as they joined to discuss community issues."

For these women, the snake represented a feminine symbol and reminder that just as snakes must shed their old skin, so must old stories be shed.

One by one the women of *Wasiwasi* Women's Group rose to speak. "Mercy Akoth, president, *Wasiwasi* Women's Group," the first woman proudly announced. Wariko translated, "*Wasiwasi* means sweat. It forms on our brows when we labor in our fields, labor delivering and caring for children."

We clapped and smiled, supporting proud Mercy and the *Wasiwasi* Women's Group. One by one the women rose to announce their name, each with the dignity of an ancient African queen.

It came time for the last woman to be heard. Drawing a slow, deep breath, she paused. The others waited in full support. Soon, as if lifted by the group, the petite woman rose.

"Cecilia Adhiambo, a new memba, " she announced. The syllables echoing like an African drumbeat the power and possibility of long silenced women.

In that moment, I knew my life's work would be in support of women claiming the transformational power held inside our new stories about ourselves.

After a time of sharing between the Western women and the African women, Mercy took up the narrative of what she called the merry-go-round concept.

"We started by paying a small fee each month," she said, sounding for all the world like a corporate CEO. "With this money we bought dishes for one member per month. In time, we said, 'Enough with dishes, we want pigs and cows.' But we were too poor even to afford a matchbox. By saving and not buying dishes, we purchased cows for six women. By selling their milk, the cow owners could contribute additional funds to purchase cows for more women. Our income generating project grew and grew. We now have three hundred paying members."

With a tall spine and a glowing presence, Mercy gazed at each woman in the circle before she continued. "As word of our project spread, more and more women have asked to join."

Mercy then raised a handful of compost from a bucket by her feet. "To improve poor soil, we make organic compost for our crops. It becomes like a mother's milk for a baby. Such knowledge of compost had been forgotten."

Lifting a section of rope from the ground, Mercy extended it to show knots tied every twelve inches. "A simple way for spacing corn seeds in rows rather than broadcasting them in the traditional way. We now use our rope to plant in rows producing more corn, using fewer seeds, less weeding and less water."

I gasped. Mary Marunga! She wanted me to photograph her rows of healthy corn. Ancient wisdom, rediscovered, had become sustainable agriculture. A process to increase yield like what I saw in Nepal with the rice producers. And I did not even realize what I was seeing.

I wished I could let Mary know my thoughts. "You're a grain goddess. You're like the Greek Goddess Demeter, who presided over corn and the earth, but I didn't understand. You reign over agriculture, like so many of your sisters gathered here. You renewed your plot using a new idea. You harvest. You compost. You try new ideas.

"I'm a city gal. I know about buying potting soil for begonias, but I know nothing about making organic compost. I'm from an agricultural part of my country, but I am more familiar with shopping malls than cornfields. However, I share a desire to grow and learn new things. Yes, our lives are different. I've never tried to grow corn. I've never worried about going hungry or worried my daughter might not have enough to eat. But I understand, if we use what we have, add new ideas, to nurture and compose with the support of a circle of women, we can make life better. It's what women do. We connect, we support each other, and we share what we know. You've discovered how to plant seeds of change. You want to share what you know. So inspiring! You and I both want to be seen and heard. What we know matters."

In my mind's eye, I pictured an invisible web weaving the world's women together from a common center. Connecting us to feminine power and potential. The power of the possible. Together with other women, I'd shift into a new story of what was possible. I moved inside my body to seek the clarity I could hold by trusting all of life was supporting our rising.

The need to work together, to cooperate rather than to compete were concepts our W.O.W. Network would uphold. Concepts, not abstractions, due to personal stories we were gathering to share as clear illustrations.

Cecilia approached. She held a white chicken by its yellow feet. As it squirmed, her excitement bounced off onto me. "We have never been meeting with white women before," she said. "We're glad you came to meet us."

With that, Cecilia handed her chicken to me. "Take it to your home."

I struggled to hold the chicken. "*Asante sana*," thank you very much.

I watched Cecilia walk away. What to do with a chicken? I pictured tomorrow's safari, and riding in an open-roof Range Rover with a chicken in my lap. I imagined the flight home to Oklahoma, me flying with a chicken in my lap.

Just then our driver returned with Sam, wearing a bandage where the leprosy clinic had stitched him back together. I needed to thank our driver. The chicken would be a perfect gift. Issue resolved!

The next day, we traveled along a narrow road bordering the Great Rift Valley, a rugged gorge extending 3,500 miles across the African continent. This massive birth canal, and the cradle of humankind. The place from which our human ancestors migrated during the early evolution of our species. We all came from Africa, I was reminded as we bounced along. I peered into this massive wound in the earth. Or was it a womb?

Peering into the valley below, I envisioned our ancestors. Some, like me, must have been seekers. Ever driven to find places other than the place where they were born. Humanity's earliest ancestors were wanderers, too. They trudged across history's greatest walk—a migration out of Africa to the Levant, to Asia, to Europe and to the Americas. Today, some two million years after that great migration, I arrived carrying fragments of their DNA. Perhaps I held their wounds too. And their yearnings and callings, especially those of ancient women.

Midday, the Range Rover parked while we walked along the rim. Holding my deeper thoughts, I said, "Over time male warriors emerged from our ancestral species born in this rift."

John rubbed his throat as if to say, "What's coming next?" Shelly sat up straight and cleared her voice. "And women became the warrior's chattel."

"Maybe it was no one's fault it happened," I said. "Along the way, males and females took on roles alienating us from our authentic selves. At least that's how I understand our evolutionary past. Peering into 25-million years of geological history makes me wonder if humankind will learn to cooperate rather than to control and conquer. Ever wanting nothing more than wealth and power enshrined in the masculine operating system. One good for some things, but not for all things. Many things require the connections and creativity feminine power can bring."

No one spoke, not even John. I sat contemplating how far we had come in our evolutionary journey. There seemed no limit to what we might yet become, though the forces of resistance would not yield easily to the change.

A night darker than any experience in my light-polluted world greeted us on arrival at the Maasai Mara lodge. A gaunt, long-legged Maasai tribesman stood guard at the gate—his face smeared with red pigment—his body wrapped in red fabric with a red and black plaid cape draped over one shoulder. A cow bone at the middle of his forehead decorated plaited hair. Beaded earrings bobbed below quarter-sized loops in both earlobes. Topping off his ensemble, the fellow held a sharp spear.

On the way into the game reserve, I saw numerous Maasai tribesmen carrying similar spears as they herded their cattle. But this spear seemed poised for action. The warrior bent to lift my duffel bag, lodging it onto his shoulder. He motioned for me to follow him. A cicada symphony accompanied us as I ushered my travelers into the lodge.

Soon, the Maasai warrior brought me to a wood-planked porch connected to a canvas tent. He lit a torch and unzipped the opening. "My name is Koyati," he said, pointing me inside. "Tonight, I will stand guard outside your tent to protect you from hyenas and lions."

Trying to maintain my composure, I said, "Oh my, I thought the hyenas and lions would sleep to be rested for us to see them tomorrow."

Koyati feigned a smile. I could hear a roar from the Mara River flowing in front of the tent. "Hippos," Koyati said, positioning his spear upright. "They're the most aggressive and dangerous of all the animals. They feed on crocodiles—or tourists if you venture too close."

Not a comforting thought, but I forced a laugh. Walking behind me into the tent, Koyati lit two lanterns. Since no one ever told me not to enter a tent in Africa with a man holding a spear, I ventured forward as if nothing were out of the ordinary. Standing in the lantern light, a space unfolded before me more inviting than any safari pictures shared with Charlie and Abby before the trip.

I noticed the white linen bedspread, the dark wood-planked floor, and an oriental rug. Up a step, behind the bed, stood a claw-foot porcelain tub, inviting me to a hot bath. In one corner, a writing desk and chair waited, ready for penning thoughts in my journal. A slice of paradise all to myself. A night of deep sleep awaited.

When I unzipped and opened my tent at sunrise, there stood Koyati with both the blade of his spear and his white teeth gleaming in the morning light. At the breakfast tent, I introduced him to the group, now gathered around a white-clothed table with a basket of freshly baked bread. A silver pot steaming with freshly roasted Kenyan coffee awaited.

"Join us," I said to Koyati, motioning him to a chair. Soon, he was entertaining us with stories about warrior training.

"I flunked," he said, "because I allowed one of my cattle to be killed by a lion. My father was so disappointed he sent me to a British missionary school."

Koyati told us he became Martin to the missionaries, who schooled him in Western ways. "But I struggled," he said. "I wanted to combine my traditional culture: oral traditions and ancestral songs, dancing, connection between people, land and wildlife. I wanted to connect these with what I learned about modernity: the written word, advanced mathematics and science."

Me too, I wanted to say. As a female from a traditional Western culture, I'd been challenged to find my place in a changing world. One where women faced different roles and expectations from those of our mothers and grandmothers and mixed messages about being a woman in a male dominated world. About how to honor ancient wisdom alongside modern science. How to connect the values of the feminine with the masculine.

Koyati left school to return to life with his family, sleeping in a hut called a boma, inside a compound fenced with thorny brush. Working at the safari lodge as a guard, guide, and naturalist, he added to his traditional life, providing an income while he shared the Maasai life with visitors.

After breakfast, Koyati led us on a footpath through the savannah. "The main diet of the Maasai is milk and blood," he told us for a start.

"Now I know why the Maasai have no weight problems," Shelly offered.

This warrior school dropout turned naturalist told us that they used mistletoe to treat parasites.

"We sophisticated Americans think we know what mistletoe is for—kissing—but we never imagined it might treat parasites," I announced.

Koyati chuckled, then pointed to a purple morning glory vine growing near the lodge. "We use this flower to cure low spirits. It's plant medicine."

"Morning glories, better than Prozac!" Ida Mae said.

Traveling inside an open top Range Rover, our group, minus Koyati who stayed behind to pursue his work, crossed the spacious, golden grasses of the savanna glowing under a pink and purple sky, the pastel tones my reminder of the feminine face of God blessing an adventure with travelers thirsty for an encounter in the wilds of Africa. Ahead appeared baby elephants playing with their mothers. Nearby, a lion cub yawned, cuddled by oat grass the color of her skin. A lilac-breasted roller garbed in pink, aqua and gold feathers sang at the dawn.

Before I knew what was happening, Patricia issued a bone-rattling shriek. A furry baboon with a beet-red rear jumped through the open roof of our Range Rover, hopping onto Patricia's lap. The baboon gaped open its mouth, displaying fangs sharper than Einstein's mind. It seized three granola bars stashed in Patricia's seat pocket. Mission accomplished; the baboon escaped. We had provided a fast-food stop. I saw how our fast-lived fast-food lives impacted even Africa's baboons.

Oddly, at that moment a different baboon popped into my mind, the mystical shaman Rafiki from the *Lion King*. "Oh, yes, the past can hurt," Rafiki told Simba. "But the way I see it you can either run from it or learn from it."

Once that was me, a baboon on the run from hurt. Now I understood that new worlds lie on the other side of loss.

I saw how shaken Patricia and the others were, so I brushed away Rafiki's words and instead offered my rendition of Elton's John's "Hakuna Matata." The "no worries" song shifted the mood.

We approached a grove of acacia trees where a 20-foot-tall giraffe gracefully fed from the treetops. Three elegant zebras cantered nearby. In the distance, two mighty African lions peacefully lazed in the morning sunlight.

As we dipped down toward the banks of the Mara River, I heard thunder. It was gathering strength. Our ranger pointed toward an embankment. The rumbling of hundreds of hooves gathered into a roar—wildebeest.

One calf slipped and fell into the gaping maw of a crocodile's waiting mouth. A furious tug of war ensued. The wildebeest wobbled free, swimming to safety across the river. Other wildebeest would not be so fortunate. Some would become breakfast for patient crocodiles lying in wait in the river. Others would become breakfast for a stealthy lion, cheetah, or hyena waiting on dry land. This year a million or more wildebeests would repeat a pattern some two million years old. In search of rain-soaked grasses, crossing 1,800 miles from Tanzania's Serengeti to Kenya's Maasai Mara, the herd would trek back along the same perilous journey following the instinctively understood rain patterns.

As the thundering subsided, vanishing into the distant horizon, Shelly put down her camera. "This wildebeest deal has me at a loss for words," she said. "And that does not happen often. Dang good thing I didn't head 'Out of Africa' that first day."

Profound stillness followed the thunder. I felt it in the deepest parts of myself while watching grazing wildebeest on the other side of the river. Mothers multi-tasked, nursing their calves while feeding themselves from the rich grasses.

I longed for Charlie and Abby to be here with me—the rhythms of nature and nature's creations covering the savanna as light set the day in motion. And for them to hear both the thunder of life, its wildness, as well as its stillness coming together without humanity's manipulation.

Deep purple bougainvillea and burning red shrubs delighted me at the foot of the Ngong Hills as we walked onto the shaded veranda of a stone farmhouse—not just any farmhouse, but the one that belonged to Baroness Karen von Blixen. This farmhouse had once been part of a 6,000-acre plantation with 600 acres of coffee, the setting for a book she'd had to write under a masculine pseudonym. *Out of Africa* had been nominated for a Nobel Prize. That year the prize went to Ernest Hemingway, who announced in his acceptance speech that he believed *Out of Africa* deserved the prize.

As I arrived, I pictured the woman I liked to call Tania. I pictured her coming to Africa with trunks containing Persian rugs and fine china. In my imagination, she was dressed in a cream-colored traveling suit and wearing a feathered hat and single pearl earrings. Here, she'd lived with a philandering husband before a divorce. In one part she returns to this porch after a big game hunt with her lover, Denys Finch-Hatton (he is Robert Redford in the movie, she is Meryl Streep). Then comes the day she realized Finch-Hatton's plane had crashed and he would never return.

I entered what struck me as classic European grace with lace curtains, wood floors, leather-bound books, crystal chandeliers, fine china, and oil paintings. A hand-carved brass-studded African chest, a gift from her faithful African steward, Farah, showed me how she blended her aristocratic European heritage with her acquired love of African culture and her admiration for those who lived within it.

"All sorrows can be borne if you put them into a story or tell a story about them," Tania's words echoed in my mind. I could almost see her sitting here in her favorite chair by the fire, a Somali shawl on her shoulders, wearing khaki pants and leather boots. "I think it will be truly glorious when women become real people and have the whole world open to them." I could almost hear her say these words.

"Yes," I thought to myself as if speaking to Tania. "What a glorious thought. Did you imagine all these years later how many women would continue struggling while dreaming a new future into being?"

My imaginary conversation continued, "Rather than living as a baroness in Europe and Africa, I've lived as a middle-class female, much of my life on the Oklahoma plains. Land that once belonged to Native Americans, in the way the land you lived on in colonial Kenya once belonged to indigenous Africans.

"Though much about our eras and our lives differ, our longing to escape containment and silencing and our need for love connect us. After you left Africa, you returned home to

Denmark to write about your life experiences. Someday, I'd like to do the same."

I turned to make my way to the gift shop. Inside, I saw a pair of rolled newspaper earrings painted a light lemon color. They reminded me how Florence worked to survive making earrings. I bought these as a special remembrance. Back outside, waiting on a bench, Ruth came and sat beside me.

"You know," she told me, "I came to Kenya to please John. My idea was Italy, but here I've come alive. I danced with the village women, inspired by their efforts to bring change. I felt my wildness growing as I watched thundering wildebeest herds." She paused, as if holding the experiences in her imagination.

"Ruth," I said touched by her words. "You amaze me and reaffirm the life-changing power of our trips."

John soon arrived. He pulled out a slip of paper and tucked it in my hand. It was a most generous check.

"For the honeybee project," he said. "We know what brings change. It's the women."

"It's the women and men who understand them," I said with huge gratitude on behalf of the women who had impressed John.

7

PEARL OF THE ANTILLES

Oklahoma to Haiti, 1998

"Has anyone seen the salt and pepper?" Daddy asked from his seat at the head of the dining room table. It was Thanksgiving afternoon. The family had gathered to enjoy our meal.

After Daddy's question, I watched my mother shake her head slightly, as if blaming herself for failing to assure the table was set to perfection. Before the clock hands touched a new minute, she jumped up to retrieve the salt and pepper shakers from the kitchen. After buying the food and preparing the meal, Mother felt obliged to scurry back to the kitchen. To a place as foreign to Daddy as his investment portfolio would be to Mother.

For my part, I shifted in my chair and stayed silent. My fingers rubbed my neck. I was the culprit. After arranging the sterling silver place settings, adding the cream-colored Franciscan Apple Pattern Pottery, the white linen napkins, and a cornucopia loaded with fall foliage; I forgot the salt and pepper shakers — the tall silver ones reserved for holidays. Normally, I would have relished satisfying the Martha Stewart in me by setting a beautiful Thanksgiving table, but today the excess of it all jarred me.

I sat without budging while Mother retrieved what I forgot. Savoring smells from roasted turkey and dressing, sweet potatoes with marshmallows, green beans with almonds, rice with giblet gravy, cranberry sauce and homemade rolls. My stomach quivered as I contemplated world inequality.

When Mother returned from the kitchen, the conversation stopped. We followed Daddy's lead and bowed our heads so he could recite his ritual blessing. "Heavenly Father," he prayed, "bless this food to the nourishment of our bodies, and bless us in thy service, keeping us ever mindful of the needs of others."

Charlie announced, "Amen, and dig in."

Would Daddy ever pray to a heavenly mother? Was he aware of my mother's needs? Would he ever be "mindful of the needs" of me? Of a little girl, now a grown woman, sitting at the table longing to be acknowledged and valued by her father. Was it possible for me to be close to this decent, hardworking, emotionally withdrawn man? And what could I do about a hidden hurt, the father wound that never went away. A hurt never intended, but one that lived with me always.

I had read about the ways in which the absence of a father's overt expressions of love and affection can affect many aspects of a person's life. My self-doubt and "not enoughness" were textbook characteristics. As an adult, I wanted to live a different story. Yet I wondered if I would forever seek approval from every male boss or authority figure who crossed my path. And why did I expect Charlie, my adoring husband, to forgive me for failing to appreciate him, while seeking approval from intimidating men?

As thoughts gnawed at me, I filled my plate from the passed serving bowls and platters loaded with Mother's home-cooked food. Before taking a first bite, Mother said, "Cindy, how was your trip?"

Her words reminded me how often Mother changed the subject to avoid potentially conflict-producing situations such as when she imagined Daddy might get upset. I reminded myself I did not want to live always changing the subject. Staying small.

To Mother's question, I replied, "My gosh, I could write a book." After pausing to lift a slice of turkey from the passed platter, I added, "But first I need to organize a trip to Haiti. We leave in three weeks."

"You're going to Haiti?" Mother replied with a gulp and a tight smile. I knew she would worry about my traveling there, but I also wanted her to understand I could not miss the opportunity. Surely Mother sensed I was not content to live my life forever attending to other's needs, giving little thought to my own aspirations and interests. Surely she grasped how travel allowed me to explore new places and to discover new parts of myself while attempting to make it possible for women to write new stories for their lives.

As our meal continued, nothing prepared me for what was about to happen. After Daddy swallowed the first taste of his pecan pie, he announced, "Sign me up for your Haiti trip."

Did I hear that right? Did Daddy just say he wanted to go to Haiti? Did he think I said Tahiti?

If an open, authentic, father-daughter connection had existed between my father and me, he might have explained why he wanted to go to Haiti. Daddy might have said, "I want an adventure before it's too late." Or, "I want to see the Change of Possibility programs I support." Or if Daddy had not been emotionally distant, he might have told me he wanted to join the Haiti trip to spend time with me. Instead, Daddy announced his intention in the same business-like voice employees heard during my father's forty years as a bank vice president, and the same matter-of-fact voice used to ask for the salt and pepper shakers this Thanksgiving day.

My mind flashed back to a story Mother told me about the day my father arrived home from the war.

I remember her saying she was with my grandfather on the front porch of his home. From that spot, he watched his decorated military officer son walk up the steps. Not an embrace, not even a burst of joy was shared between the two men that day after a full year of separation by war.

I was coming to understand how Daddy, the son of an alcoholic father, had become the man my grandmother wanted him to become though his own unmet needs prevented him from knowing how to meet the emotional connection of others.

It was painful, but I concluded that both of us shared the same wound—a father wound. Would it ever be possible for us to heal our wounds and enjoy an authentic, loving, father-daughter relationship? I could lead the way.

Three weeks later our driver revved the Toyota pickup truck and sped us away from the airport. Standing bolt upright in the pickup bed, Debbie alongside, I gripped the bars across the back window. Both our lives literally depended on our grip. Zooming along the coastal highway as we tried to balance ourselves, Daddy, Naomi, Rachel, and Donna bumped along inside.

Suddenly, the truck swerved to miss a massive pothole. Oh my God. "Highway to Hell." Only now did I remember reading this label for Haiti's Route Nationale No. 1. Never had I imagined traveling it. I should have studied the route.

Debbie, a recently hired Change of Possibility journalist, shot a tough-gal glare that penetrated my body like a dart. I had but one thing to be grateful for. Glares don't kill.

In no time, the sky filled with ominous, dark clouds. This could not be happening. But it was. The sky opened and a torrential downpour soaked us with nothing but our wet skin and hope to protect us.

Through the truck window glass, between the steel bars, I read Daddy's fear and concern written over his wrinkles. Donna, Naomi, and Rachel faced forward, sparing me from their glances.

Everything was my fault. Our driver, who met us at the airport, cautioned against driving to Ivwa after sunset. Especially with clouds gathering. Prepared to follow Jean-Claude Etienne's itinerary, the one agreed upon in the email before leaving Oklahoma City, our driver's warning missed my ears. As did Debbie reiterating the same concern.

Doing what Jean-Claude, the Haiti Change of Possibility program director, asked was as vital as pleasing Daddy and every other male authority figure on earth. Such was my modus operandi, whether at home or in Haiti. We had landed in Port Au Prince three hours late. It was imperative to proceed quickly. I had decided that with no phones to call Ivwa, Jean Claude would worry if we did not arrive soon.

Thunderclaps rattled the truck and my bones. When a zigzagging lightning bolt crossed the sky, Debbie's eyes narrowed. Most people, when frightened, look scared, but not Debbie. She looked threatening. "You should have listened," she shouted above the thunder.

I knew Debbie felt like shaking me. And I understood her urge. "Driving on this road in a dark storm is a suicide mission," she said. "And if this Jean-Claude guy expects us tonight, he must want to scare the hell out of a bunch of naïve 'blancs.'" No reply from me would be adequate.

The next moment, we both realized neither the headlights nor the taillights were working! No wonder everything was pitch dark. I felt a big bump. "We just hit a sleeping policeman," Debbie said. My heart stopped. "Sleeping policemen are what Haitians call speed bumps. They show up with no warning."

Laughter or even a grin escaped me. I recalled reading a U.S. State Department bulletin at home warning citizens to stay off Haitian roads after dark. What allowed my brain to forget the bulletin or the Tonton Macoute death squad that could rob, rape, or kill us in a blink? As guilt filled my body, we made a sharp turn. Surely Ivwa lay around the bend.

Wrong! Once off the main highway, we headed across a sand and gravel "road" with not one village in sight. Water rushed off denuded mountains, turning the road into a rising riverbed. Water covered the truck tires. Getting stuck in the mud seemed a certainty.

As the truck crept forward, for reasons as illogical as Haiti, our driver managed to steer up a deforested hillside. My mind wandered, disassociating from the present moment.

As a stewardess for Pan Am, I had landed in Port as Prince many times. In those days, I never traveled beyond the chain-link fence surrounding the airport. After passengers deplaned into the terminal, I would join other flight crew along a fence separating us from hand-carved, mahogany salad bowls, vodou drums and Haitian masks. Haitian craftsmen eagerly sold us their handicrafts for prices far below those sold to tourists inside the airport. I once saw a Pan Am pilot exchange an old pair of shoes for a salad bowl set.

After each Port Au Prince transit, I would return to my Coconut Grove life loaded with Haitian items. I still prized my Haitian mahogany salad bowls, though the mahogany trees had long since disappeared here. I had played a role in depleting Haitian forests. I allowed struggling Haitians to be poorly paid for their work.

At the hilltop, outlined by starlight, a cinder block community building, double-car-garage size, appeared. Brilliant red poinsettia blooms covered bushes on either side of the entrance. A struggling banana tree nearby reminded me of the huge banana tree I played under as a child in Casablanca. Life had shown me much since those days.

A crowd of Haitians circled us with enormous smiles. No concern for our now four-hour delay marred the moment. It seemed time was not of the essence here. A lesson that a clock-watching, time-obsessed American would do well to remember. Chirping birds soon replaced thunderclaps. In the dark, despite having arrived at an isolated Haitian village without electricity, running water, or indoor plumbing, I felt as comfortable as if approaching a Motel 6 with the lights on and with the equivalent of the local Chamber of Commerce to greet us.

Into this mix emerged Jean-Claude Etienne, the Change of Possibility Haiti program director, a tall, lean, self-possessed Haitian. His razor-thin, graying beard stretched from below both earlobes and met under his chin where it drew attention away from his balding head. I rushed to speak to him while trying to hush Debbie's comments about the terrifying truck ride.

Once inside the one-room cinderblock community building, lit by a kerosene lantern, we travelers sat around a rectangular, rough-hewn table where Daddy was given a seat of honor next to Jean Claude. The horrific truck-ride never came up. Instead, Daddy discussed how much he had wanted to visit Change of Possibility's Haiti programs. I admired Daddy's ease in connecting with Jean Claude, and I wondered why the two of us did not share the same ease.

While conversations ensued, my thoughts drifted to concern about where we would sleep. But food aromas wafted into the room, interrupting those concerns. Two Haitian women, resembling Kenyan village women, brought heaping bowls of carrot, cabbage and chicken stew. Jean Claude noted our meal was cooked outside using a pot balanced over a charcoal-fueled fire. As we ate, I stayed mindful that hunger and malnutrition raged around us, though our stomachs would be filled.

Jean Claude proposed a toast.

"Are there still people under the table?"

Villagers entered the room gathering behind us chanting: "Yes!"

"Are there still people on top of the table?"

"Yes!"

"With each passing day, we will reach our goal of sitting together at the table," Jean Claude replied.

I turned toward Daddy, surprised when our eyes met. I had never noticed him looking directly at me. Normally, I felt as if he looked over me or through me.

As I slid my chair a bit closer to Daddy, Jean-Claude began to speak about a powerful populist movement led by Jean-Bertrand Aristide, a former Catholic priest who rose to run for president. This followed a popular grassroots movement overthrowing 30 years of brutal and corrupt dictatorship under the Duvalier regime—one supported through the years by the American government believing the dictatorship of "Papa Doc" and continued by his inept son "Baby Doc" was both anti-Castro and anti-communist. The position was maintained by the U.S. while both father and son dictators assured death nor imprisonment to anyone who dared oppose them.

Into this oppression and pain for all but the elite, Aristide's "Lavalas Movement" emerged like a flood—the meaning of the word lavalas. "Aristide, against all odds became our Moses," Jean Claude said.

My mind wandered again. I thought of Daddy as a Moses figure. He led soldiers in the military, led employees at the bank. He was a church leader. A community leader. His family's leader. He supported Change of Possibility projects. I also saw Daddy like Moses in that his wife, Zipporah, received little recognition for aiding and supporting Moses in freeing the Israelites. Mother had received slim recognition for her aid and support to Daddy, to our family, our church, and our community.

"To the shock of the elites," Jean-Claude said as his arms rose, "Aristide won the 1991 election and became Haiti's first democratically elected president."

A freely elected president leading a popular democratic movement proved too much for the Haitian elite. Within eight months, a coup supported by U.S. interests toppled Aristide, labeling him a dangerous communist. More bloodshed, with a reign of terror aimed at Aristide's supporters followed.

With profound sadness in his down-turned eyes and anger heard in his voice, Jean Claude looked toward the wall behind the table. "This," he said, pointing to six holes in the wall, "is where Tonton Macoutes fired six gunshots to frighten Ivwa villagers for daring to vote for Aristide. Other local supporters were killed.

I swallowed hard. Gunshots fired at walls. Poor people killed for the audacious act of voting in a democratic election!

Jean-Claude put down his locally brewed beer and raised a Coca Cola bottle before pouring the contents onto the ground. "I waste this Coca Cola to remind myself how multinational corporations like Coke waste our people's energy by paying abysmal wages to factory workers who labor on land grabbed from owners without adequate compensation to build hugely profitable U.S.-owned sugar companies. Such situations leave my people, who can't afford a Coke, to struggle for their next meal. I join them in fighting back."

I took a deep breath. I watched Daddy grimace. He seemed to struggle believing the American government and American companies could do harm abroad. As a patriotic American, he had believed America was present in the world to assist and to support democracy, capitalism, and its benefits for all. My awareness of shortsighted thinking mounted. Maybe Daddy and I could discuss U.S. foreign policy and multinational corporations someday. My hope was that first we might at least tell each other it was good to be in Haiti together, despite differing perspectives.

The women who cooked and served our food returned with sheets and blankets to make floor pallets for us. Knowing we had places to sleep, I smiled and thanked them, though I spoke no Creole and they spoke no English.

The women directed us to the newly constructed latrine, and the offer was gratefully accepted. At that point, I led our group in applause—aware that both new sheets and blankets and indoor plumbing and running water were unimaginable luxuries in these hills.

When it was time for sleep, Daddy lowered his body onto his pallet. Despite exhaustion and the sparse accommodations, his eyes and smile suggested he was pleased, not only for a pallet, but for his presence in a Haitian village. And I assumed he was pleased to be with his daughter, as I was pleased to be with him.

Sunrise after sunset, a new day arrived. Standing outside the community building, through the thick morning dew, we watched six village women balancing large plastic water jugs on their heads. Each barefoot woman proceeded with graceful steps down a dusty path lined with banana trees and high grasses. To the accompaniment of roosters crowing and swallows warbling, the women made their way toward a watering hole at the foot of the mountain. Jean-Claude invited us to walk with the women. He explained the day's water had to be retrieved and hauled home for drinking, cooking, and for bathing, for both people and animals, and of course also for nourishing the crops. Women's lives existed around these tasks, continuing from adolescence until they could no longer carry a bucket. I felt painfully aware how the ritual happened each day in Nepal and Kenya, also aware much of the world's population relied on such women water carriers.

As we walked, Daddy kept up with us, while his water bottle bounced against his side and his safari hat protected his head from the scalding sun. When we approached Ivwa's open-hole main water source, we spoke with a woman dressed in a torn red blouse. One lacking buttons to keep her sagging breasts covered. She greeted us as she bent over the hole, using muscular arms to draw up a bucket of water.

On a Caribbean Island only seven hundred miles from Miami's luxury homes, swimming pools, fountains and waterways, poverty-stricken Haitian women pulled water from a hole. Why didn't Jean-Claude assist the community in securing a well? When I asked him, he looked in the direction of the mountains behind us and said, "As Haitians we know, behind mountains are more mountains. Step by step, we will climb them. Wells will come, but first we must work to secure the community's food supply. The struggles and choices here may seem impossible for you to comprehend."

As we silently walked away from the scene, Jean-Claude said, "I've heard it said Americans depend on pushing buttons while we depend on relationships and working together to solve problems."

"A profound thought. Depending on relationships. Working together. A feminine principle. So may it be the world over," I announced with strength in my voice.

With pleasant breezes to cut the sun, we gathered near another dusty path where Jean-Claude directed us to several rickety wooden benches. In front of us, a garden grew loaded with lettuce, cabbages, cauliflower, and rows of corn. Beside the garden, a barefoot woman grinned. Madame Sofana was her name. She appeared in a white cotton dress with a white headscarf around her hair, tied at the back of her neck. As erect as her corn plants, she greeted us. "Bonjou! Koman ou ye?"

After our Creole "Bonjou" responses, Sofana touched her healthy cabbage plants as if they were her children. A year ago, she had begun using new organic farming techniques like those I learned from Mary Marunga in Kenya.

Beaming with pride, Sofana pointed to the rock barriers she had built to keep her mulch enriched soil from rolling down the mountain. Lifting a sharp-bladed machete, loaned from the Change of Possibility funded tool bank, we saw what provided an alternative to the sticks thousands of Haitian peasant-farmers relied on for clearing and planting land. And I felt the urge to mulch and harvest the empowerment rising in me as in Sofana.

Known as *poto pitans*, the female pillars of society, farm women such as Sofana planted, weeded, harvested, and marketed most food grown in Haiti. Having witnessed the same phenomenon in Asia and Africa, I knew the reality, but I was unprepared to learn of the additional struggle Sofana and many other oppressed Haitian women faced.

After Aristide's forced exile, Ivwa villagers began whispering plans to organize for change. At times pretending to play checkers while discussing community organizing, such a process became ridiculous and unacceptable. Sofana and her husband were among those who vowed that neither bullet, death, or prison would stop the meetings or the training in Ivwa.

Raising her eyes and lifting her lean, sharp-boned shoulders, Sofana told us as Jean Claude translated, "Thanks to my cabbage, beans and corn, grown on rehabilitated land, and thanks to the tools from the tool bank, my five children, my imprisoned husband and I are still alive."

Silence fell over our group. Sofana's husband had been thrown into a primitive prison a year ago. His arrest without a trial occurred while he met to discuss forming the tool bank. Such a daring act cost Sofana's husband his freedom. And since Haitian prisons provide no food to prisoners, Sofana continued growing his food as well as food for her children and herself.

Tomorrow was market day and this week Sofana would have beautiful, big cabbages to sell. With her family's stomachs fed, with seeds to plant next season and with the hope of securing her husband's release through connections with human rights activists, Sofana would labor on.

Debbie, in her walking boots with a navy bandana around her forehead, settled onto the bench under a scrubby tree— one that somehow had escaped being cut down to make charcoal for cooking. Sofana took a seat beside Debbie and a connection happened. Soon the two women were communicating in a language beyond words, in the wondrous way women can do. After a bit, Debbie got up and picked up Sofana's hoe, turning over soil around the cabbages. Sofana could hardly contain her laughter or her obvious delight. She had never seen a white woman working a garden. I loved what was happening between Debbie and Sofana.

Later, after heartfelt hugs with the promise we would work to gain more support for women farmers and their husbands, our group returned to the community building. Daddy turned to me, saying, "Sofana must get help. We must do something."

As Debbie untied the bandana around her head with her dirty hands, she told me, "Ya know, I'm a Garber, Oklahoma gal, not some sweet, prissy princess, but a gal with fire and ice inside. I can throw a left hook, if need be, or make a cake or make crazy love, and when I have an opinion, you're gonna hear it."

My body tightened as I wondered what would come next. "Okay," Debbie said with her hair blowing in the wind. "This time your poor judgment paid off. If we had stayed in Port Au Prince that first night, we would have missed Sofana."

"Tomorrow Sofana would be in the market," Debbie said.

"I would have missed meeting one of the bravest women I've ever known." Straightening her spine, Debbie said, "Sofana understands staying alive is the ultimate resistance."

I felt an odd vindication for pushing us toward our nightmare storm travel as I listened for what else she would throw out.

Before another night sleeping on a floor pallet, feet away from Daddy's snoring, I wondered about women's lives. For Debbie, being a woman meant telling-it-like-it-is. It meant telling those she loves her thoughts and telling those who cause her problems how they must stop. For Madame Sofana, being a woman meant resisting oppression by growing food and vegetables and staying alive.

What about me? A woman born in one of the richest countries in the world, someone living in a country where poverty and oppression have an ugly hold, but where safety nets help address some problems. I'd never been a fighter like Sofana or a tell-it-like-it-is, no-holds-barred type like Debbie. The battle to combat the powers of out-of-control forces that oppress women and kill or imprison men for whispering plans to resist oppression is a battle that fires me up. And I wasn't the only one fired up. Donna, a no-nonsense businesswoman from Tennessee, told me because of this trip she intended to ask her women's group to support tool banks and organic gardening for Haitian women. Naomi and her friend Rachel wanted to return on another trip to Haiti, bringing friends able to support the cause. I saw and felt the possibility of women like us joining together with women around the world to create enormous change.

As we headed back to the community center, I walked close to Daddy. Speaking directly to him seemed intimidating. I pretended to talk to myself. "Haiti's absolute poverty," I said, "comes from brutality and oppression enforced within the country while supported from without."

Daddy did not interrupt. He nodded. I continued. "Despite the mind-boggling complexity here, I see hope. Small at one level yet huge at another. The Sofanas of the world make me believe change is coming."

"You're right," Daddy said, pausing for a drink of water. "I learned this from a strong woman. Your mother. She handled everything while I was at war and most everything at home still today."

I wondered if Daddy had ever spoken those words to her, but I resisted asking the question.

The community organized a farewell gathering for our last night in Haiti. Women, including Madame Sofana and the woman with the red blouse we saw near the water hole, joined gaunt men with goat-skinned covered drums and tambourines gathering outside the community center. The risks of assembling were well understood here.

I arrived in Haiti unaware of how much sacrifice and danger seeking change could require. But tonight, with greater awareness, I gathered with black and mulatto Haitians as well as our white American group. Freedom and dignity were imagined here.

Jean-Claude remarked, "In Haiti, powerful spirits aid us. As descendants of slaves stolen from Africa, we call our spirits *loas*. They link us to the strength of our African roots and to the strength of our Creator. The connections sustain us through oppression and toil."

Jean-Claude added, "Under torn clothes, despite hunger and oppression, Haitians conjure *loas*. The experience allows imagining beyond physical reality. It's called possession. Tonight, we invite you to share an experience of vodou dancing."

As the drumming and tambourine playing began, dancing followed. Debbie participated. Her body swayed with the steady drumbeats. A softer woman emerged to join the blunt, bold Debbie I'd gotten to know. I saw a friend and ally motivated for a mission—not simply a colleague working to earn a paycheck.

To my astonishment, Daddy got up to dance. All of us joined Daddy to dance with the Haitians. Drumbeats echoed my heartbeats. Something opened inside, freeing me and perhaps freeing Daddy, too. Call it *loas* or call it possession. Whatever it was, I liked the powerful feeling.

The smudged lenses on Daddy's glasses disguised a tear. He must have been touched, as I was by the strength of spirit we'd found here. Despite growing up in the segregated South and despite being told "colored boys" could not join his Boy Scout troop, my father believed in the dignity of all people. Perhaps the young boys in Ivwa remind Daddy of "colored boys" not allowed to become Boy Scouts in Aliceville, Alabama. Maybe the women of Ivwa remind Daddy of "colored" women in Aliceville who cooked, cleaned, and cared for white people's children, including Daddy and his brother, leaving little time for these women to care for their own children.

"I'm glad you're here, Daddy." The words jumped out of my mouth as we danced and while I looked up into my father's aging eyes.

My father looked back at me with wistful eyes. "I've spent my life working," he said, "I left your mother to handle you kids. I missed out."

I paused, then placed myself closer to Daddy. "You were a busy man," I said, as drumbeats brought the energy to a feverish pitch.

"Hmmm," Daddy said, pushing his glasses up the bridge of his nose. "Well, maybe so."

With that I hugged Daddy's neck. I felt his shoulders lower and heard his breath move deeper. My breathing slowed. I relaxed. The wounded masculine living inside my father, inside me, in Haiti and around the world must be healed. I would name this healing as one of the biggest challenges of our time, impacting humans, the planet and all living beings. I had an opening to tell Daddy I loved him and maybe I would have heard the words repeated back to me. That did not happen. No matter, I felt closer to my father than ever before.

Images from our Haitian experience flooded my mind: I thought about Daddy taking photos with his camera, his walking and talking to Haitian peasants—whether they understood him or not. Wearing a safari hat, with his water bottle and camera dangling from his waist, I saw Daddy no longer playing the role of an Air Force lieutenant colonel or a bank vice president. He was an 80-year-old adventurer and a seeker as well as my father.

It seemed Papa Legba, the vodou masculine intermediary at the crossroads, joined Loa Erzulie, the dark vodou feminine spirit, allowing communication across races, ages, genders, religions, social classes, world cultures, and between Daddy and me. Maybe Daddy represented Papa Legba dancing with his daughter. Maybe Sofana and her friends represented Erzulie's wild and resilient energies. Or maybe what I felt was because of the beer we were drinking. Anyway, whatever the cause, it was powerful.

Looking into the sky, I watched the moon and the stars beaming down on Ivwa. Tonight, Haitians and Americans, poor and middle-class and wealthy, men and women, a father and a daughter, joined by the rhythms of drums and seashell tambourines. Together, we shared something beyond words in a country where poverty and oppression, as well as resilience and healing were also beyond words. Dancing with Daddy, I hoped every daughter and her daddy shared moments as touching as mine.

Such were Haiti and Daddy's gifts to me. But would Charlie, not having met Sofana, or having experienced the oppression and pain at times made worse by our own government, and not having danced a vodou dance, be able to understand how I was moving forward on a transformational path both personal and social? One with old assumptions to challenge. New understandings to grasp. A different power to claim. Would Abby understand my growing passions?

PART TWO

8

POWER LUNCH AND W.O.W.!

Oklahoma City, 1998

On noon of hump day, I was back at the office and inside my cubicle world again. Tapping computer keys echoed around me as colleagues' emails flew from cubicle to cubicle. Their messages bemoaned our organization's faltering fund-raising efforts. Such old news forced me to shut down my computer. I closed my eyes and remembered John's words to me in Kenya: "It's the women, stupid. The women."

Every point in my brain lit up at once. Like John, I'd come to believe the greatest untapped resources on the planet could be found inside the hearts, minds, and hands of women, including marginalized, uneducated but resourceful, strong women like the many I'd met. The world must incorporate the unique talents, wisdom, and abilities women offer. I needed a friend to talk over what was bubbling up inside. I had an answer to what our organization needed, and what the world needed, too. Rolling my chair back from my computer and careening my neck into the cubicle beside me, I whispered, "Debbie?"

"Yes, Cindy," she said without looking up from her desk.

"While the bosses are locked into one of their male powwows, let's get out of here and go have a powwow of our own. A couple glasses of wine and some quiche, and there's no telling what could happen."

"Sounds great. Let me finish a donor solicitation letter. I wrote it for our boss to sign. It's full of numbers and graphs. Zero emotion. He'll like it."

Thirty minutes later, Debbie and I sat with chardonnay in hand at a corner table inside a neighborhood cafe. The aroma of garlic bread made me salivate, but maybe I needed to meditate to calm my mind before spouting out my ideas. I felt a sermon coming on as I said, "What if we told it like it is? What if we shared what we saw and felt in Haiti, especially with Madame Sofana? And if we told it in female talk without holding back our passion and feelings? And I have so many other stories. My whole body remembers sitting with Sushila's group in Nepal. And I remember sitting under the mango tree in Kenya with Wasiwasi Women's Group. I felt powerful and connected by an invisible filament, like a web, weaving women together from our common center. We must act on what we've seen and felt—do something more to support the changes women want to bring. And, if we do our job well, we'll secure huge support for enhanced programs to target women's issues within Change of Possibility. I can see it, feel it and sense the impact."

"Well," Debbie said.

I waited and wondered. I needed Debbie to work with me, but did she perceive me as too emotional, too intense?

"I'll drink to your plan," I heard her say, raising her wine glass with a smile. "Ramble on. Let's see where your estrogen-charged ideas lead."

"All right," I said, before pouring more chardonnay, "I have an idea, a concept forming. I want it heard, and something done with it. If we could get my ideas off the ground, maybe our organization could stop spending time on the same old ineffective fundraising campaigns used for the past fifty years. We could help enact more positive change for women like those we've met, and we would be players helping in a bigger way to support the emergence of women and of feminine possibilities for all."

As Debbie buttered her croissant, I interpreted her lack of interruption as a cue to continue. "The fundraising campaigns targeting an aging male population do not bring in big bucks anymore. But no one is addressing what will happen when the small pool of male donors departs for their next incarnation."

I poured more wine for both of us. "Women hold the key to the future. In the past, Change of Possibility invited interested men to visit the program areas. But our trips appeal to women. Fifty years ago, the men traveled, and the men ran the organization from the headquarters. Other men directed the programs in the field. The checks to support the programs came from men. It was a man's world. Women's voices were absent, and the repression of women continued."

Debbie looked at me without interrupting. I kept talking. Two women at the table next to me stopped talking. They turned their ears as if interested in what I had to say. "Strides have been made to address women's issues," I said. "But more must be done, and if more women served on our board and at the top levels of management, more would be done. The dynamic women we've traveled with have ideas that must not go unheard. We've seen how many American women respond to our 'off the beaten path' travel. They get inspired meeting women in rural villages. Look at the untapped source of new energy, leadership, and financial support. No one has linked such women together or thought of how to bring them inside our organization. And there are men like John and my father who want to support women's issues. Female leadership, female relationship building and female philanthropy, and understanding the vast wealth women control—these things are not understood around here. You and I know women like to connect with the beneficiaries of the causes they support. Women like to participate in decision-making. Women see things and solve problems in different ways than men do. Women connect."

Then I leaned toward Debbie. "If we stay connected to women after their trips. If we encourage them to invite other women into a network of common interest, imagine the possibilities."

I watched Debbie's eyes light up and a rush of adrenaline surged inside me. "You're feeling it, right? We've got to mold our ideas into 'male think' so our management will approve what we propose. We'll need a concept paper, a name for our women's network, a budget and clear fundraising goals along with charts and graphs men can understand."

At that point, I sensed Debbie's brain switching into high gear. She put down her wine, and I watched as she sat up tall.

"So," she responded, her eyes focused like lasers, "we need a women's membership network to invest in the power and potential of women around the world. Right?"

"Exactly!" I said. "And a perk will be traveling to see the work of women in action. Though I'll grant you, when in Haiti we should avoid riding at night through a thunderstorm in the back of a pickup without headlights."

Debbie spouted her ideas, apparently unconcerned about my comment. "We could call the network W.O.W., as an acronym for the work of women. We'd write it as W.O.W.@ Change of Possibility."

"That's it! What about this for our brochure?" I asked, forgetting my food or wine. "Women care for families, teach values, impart wisdom, and produce most of the world's food. Women work two thirds of the world's working hours. Yet women earn a fraction of the world's income, hold title to less than a tenth of the world's property, suffer disproportionately from violence and are kept out of leadership and decision-making. W.O.W. will work to change the equation by inviting members to invest in the power and potential of women in our grass roots development programs."

"That's our mission statement," Debbie noted, jotting the words on a napkin.

I suggested a Dream Team of women from our trip to work with us. About a dozen women to help launch W.O.W. Maybe Shelly would host the group at her place in Santa Fe.

"That works!" Debbie said, finishing her quiche. The women at the table next to us stopped by. "Best of luck with W.O.W." one of them said.

Debbie looked at me. "You know," she said, "I have meant to tell you, your dad said before we left Haiti, he was really proud of you. My dad would never say anything like that to me. Hell, my dad thinks the only thing that matters in life is making a lot of money, and neither he nor I have been successful at that. I'm better at raising money for causes than negotiating for a big salary for myself."

"Did he really say that? He's never said those words to me."

Overcome with feelings hard to describe, I celebrated Debbie as a perfect W.O.W. partner, while celebrating Daddy's comment she shared with me. A bigger, bolder belief in my transformational capabilities now seemed not only possible, but probable.

For all the things Oklahoma City may not have, it does have glorious sunsets—magnificent, brilliant orange and red sunsets like the spectacular one I was viewing from my patio. I'd read how the red dust in the Oklahoma atmosphere enhances colors in the evening sky. What a great use for the dust not stuck to my glass-top coffee table. Well, I was not sure if the dust tale was true or not, but I did know one thing for certain, the sunset excited me the way thinking about the W.O.W project excited me.

Since the power lunch with Debbie a week ago, I had no doubt we were onto something. We had completed a concept paper with a budget for expenses, and we'd outlined fundraising goals and had created a work timetable for launching the network. We'd also lined up special W.O.W. trips. Everything was looking good; I mean it looked great and glorious, like the sunset.

We needed Rick's approval to proceed. As CEO, he had the final say on new projects. How to approach him? How to ensure he would not squelch our plans? I could not even imagine how devastated I'd be if he were to turn thumbs down on W.O.W., but I knew the Change of Possibility 50th anniversary campaign had Rick's attention. He thought the celebration would bring in lots of money. He might balk at anything else on the drawing board. I saw few prospects for success from an old-style campaign. Our organization needed something different.

The W.O.W. "Work of Women" project would bring in new funds from new sources—from women excluded from Change of Possibility fundraising in the past.

But I had one problem. I was scared to ask Rick for anything. I did not have the guts. Really, I did not. I could not risk rejection. I felt my heart beat out of my chest just thinking about approaching him. However, sitting and watching a dusty Oklahoma sunset, I knew what to do. Debbie must take our W.O.W. concept to Rick and get his okay to proceed. I stopped to call her right then.

"Hi. Got a minute?"

"Sure, I'm only fixing tacos, watching my kid destroy the

kitchen with his tricycle and listening to the news. What's up?"

"Well, I've decided you're the one to take the W.O.W. concept paper to Rick. Get his buy-in for everything. The membership organization. The Dream Team retreat. Launching W.O.W trips. And especially approval for our budget!"

I paused, wondering if Debbie had put the phone down to chase her toddler.

"Hmmm. Sounds like a plan," she said. "Dump everything on me. Well, no problem. I'll talk to Rick tomorrow morning."

"You mean it doesn't bother you to ask Rick?"

"Heck no, the worst he can do is say no."

"Say no?" I hollered into the phone. "Don't you dare let that happen. If Rick says no, our plan goes down the drain. And think of the women who will never be in a literacy program, or the women who won't have a trained birth attendant with them, and the women who won't learn about child spacing, or who won't have micro-credit loans or a chance to find their voice or to get a machete. It's up to you. We can recruit the network members. Find women for the trips, and find big funders, but you must get the head honcho's approval. I think he likes you. He will say yes to you."

"Hey, remember one thing," Debbie insisted. "Rick likes me because I did drugs when I was young. I screwed up and survived, and he did too. That's our bond. We're both wounded. Let's see how far that takes me."

"Well, Ms. Garber, Oklahoma, I don't know anything about your bond with Rick, but I know you're our best hope."

I launched into a long spiel, aware Debbie had her tacos cooking, her son at her feet, her TV blaring, and her mind in high gear. But I could not stop myself any more than I could have stopped from heading to Ivwa the night we arrived in Haiti.

"We can't let one man close the door on a great idea, but you know we're dead in the water without Rick's buy-in."

For the first time in my life, I knew my "why." My purpose and the cause I wanted to support. But I needed a partner.

"So," I reiterated, "use whatever approach you want, but make sure you get Rick's name on the dotted line. I can't ask because if I get nervous and stressed, I'll flush. That happens around guys like him. If Rick sees me like that, it'll be easy to say no."

"Good speech, Cindy. How long have you been practicing that one?" She continued with her wry tone. "So to keep Rick from seeing you with a red neck, and to support emerging women, I'll argue the case."

I became quiet then spoke. "I'm brave enough to do a lot of things. Being brave enough to risk rejection by male authority, I cannot yet pull up that courage."

After getting a proposal together with the necessary research and documentation, at ten o'clock on a rainy Monday morning Debbie headed into Rick's office. I huddled inside my cubicle, chewing my nails. Before I could chew the last one, Debbie appeared. What's the deal? I could not decipher her look. My stomach flipped. Why was she back so soon?

"Green light!" Debbie announced, grinning and throwing the W.O.W. proposal into the air. "Rick said yes. I guess yes was the quickest way to get me out of his office."

Adrenaline rush! Debbie got the answer we needed. That's all that mattered. Why worry that our boss had no idea how transformative our work would prove to be. And there was more. Debbie got Rick to agree to a $12,000 budget, provided we committed to deliver, within six months, $65,000 in donations targeted for women's training programs in Nepal, Kenya or Haiti. A budget of only $12,000 for developing a website, printing brochures and other marketing fell woefully short of what we needed, and six months gave us precious little time to see a return on our efforts. However, using what we had, in the way Mary Marunga did with her string and compost in Kenya, and the way Madame Sofana used her tool bank machete, we would succeed beyond anyone's expectations. So now it was my turn to call Shelly.

"Sure, y'all come," Shelly told me in her fiery few-word-manner. "But remember, I don't do food."

"No worries. We gotcha covered for food."

Wahoo! A dozen women cleared their calendars, booked flights, and arrived to join Shelly, Debbie, and me in Santa Fe at Shelly's adobe hacienda style house, a perfect place to meet. But would they each write the requested $1,000 check before leaving? We needed those funds to match our small budget.

We greeted Margaret from Virginia and her friend Marilyn, a sharp Yale graduate and strategic planning consultant who volunteered to be our team's facilitator. What's more, Margaret had already tapped into Marilyn's philanthropic interest in girls' and women's education, and Marilyn had become an enthusiastic W.O.W. supporter.

As our time together began, Marilyn kept us focused on specific goals, while the women's ideas flowed. Shelly mentioned involving her family foundation. The women insisted we needed more W.O.W. trips. They were excited about recruiting their friends. We discussed arranging W.O.W. trips to Mexico, Guatemala, India, and Indonesia. Shelly suggested a trip to the programs in West Africa. Marilyn got excited and said she would join a Mali trip. I watched Margaret beam as she offered to take photographs on each trip. Her artist's eye and ability to capture women's dignity and ingenuity meant her photography would be an invaluable gift.

Then came time for the "ask." I invited each woman to become a W.O.W Founding Partner by writing a check for

$1,000. I didn't know how many would respond.

Within moments, each dream team member had signed a check for $1,000 and had become a W.O.W. Founding Partner. It was hard to contain the enthusiasm.

Here I was, an ordinary woman with a plan brewed over glasses of wine with a colleague. Now I was connecting with other women invested in the power and potential of women and the feminine. Together, we would become the heart, soul, spirit, and strength of something growing and grand. I knew such words sounded huge and grandiose, but to me they were not an exaggeration. Much energy, much to organize and to implement; it was a big task, and I loved it. Tomorrow I'd begin organizing a Mali trip by contacting Thalia, the Change of Possibility country director. First, I had to locate Mali on a map because I knew for certain women's voices and stories were there waiting to be heard and amplified.

9

GOLLY MALI

Mali, West Africa, 2001

A dozen wide-eyed W.O.W. women joined me as we wandered inside an arid, mud-constructed, subsistence-farming village called Kakamu. The sparse number of living and non-living things on the landscape boggled my mind. Hot, dry whirlwinds, known as the Harmattan, blew yellow and red Saharan sand over everything and everyone in this land known as the Sahel. My face felt like a dustpan, my hair as if a blow dryer were blowing over it. My mouth, like I'd swallowed a bucket of sand. In the midst of it all, great expectations filled me. By golly, we were in Mali!

As I straightened my sun hat, I realized my feet had once again touched the African continent. When flying over Northwestern Africa en route here, I'd glimpsed Morocco below. Reminded I'd not become a goddess or a queen like my six-year-old-self once imagined, I took pride in having become a respected leader of the Work of Women Network.

I remembered my Northeastern African visit to Egypt. How as a single twenty-something I'd feared deciding to be with the man I loved might mean abandoning world travel and the quest for my purpose.

Three years ago, leaving Charlie at home, and our twenty-something daughter just finishing college, I'd traveled to East Africa, to Kenya. The voices and visions of the women I met there enhanced my passion for the empowerment of women.

As I stepped into an unfolding journey to Mali in West Africa, Abby would be dating a special guy while pursuing her career in Dallas. Charlie would again prove his willingness to keep our homelife running smoothly. Debbie would be in the Oklahoma City office handling details related to W.O.W. memberships, newsletters and arrangements for more trips.

I arrived in Africa on this journey as a "sage stager," surrounded by my wise, accomplished, bright travel companions. We were unwilling to watch the world pass us by— unwilling to stay isolated, silent or unaware when the empowerment of women and our own awakenings remained on the line.

Tameka, a first time W.O.W. traveler, wiped her hot, sweaty forehead with a tissue before she quipped, "I was supposed to come to Africa for my honeymoon, but that was ten years and two husbands ago."

Cora, Tameka's proud "Mama," stood next to her daughter. She seemed to ignore the sweat and dust, as she must have ignored both while picking cotton as a sharecropper's daughter in rural Alabama. Rubbing the joints between her fingers, Cora said, "Sweetie, I don't know about you, but I've come to Africa for something far more valuable than a honeymoon."

Tameka, a successful entrepreneur from Atlanta, nodded and stretched her arm around her mother's shoulders. I grinned in total agreement with Cora.

"Balimamusos," our group called ourselves, using the Bambara word for sisters. The Mali mother tongue and the language spoken in Kakamu, Bambara contained many fun-to-pronounce words. French, with its more difficult-to-pronounce words, served as the national language spoken by the educated elite—an indication of Mali's French colonial legacy.

Thalia, the dynamic Change of Possibility country director, who had given much time to arranging details for our visit, had joined us earlier in the day. Draped in her multi-colored, geometric-patterned long skirt and matching puffed sleeved blouse, her hair lay hidden beneath a wide-winged head-wrap. She swayed with grace beside us as we marched forward in khaki pants, t-shirts and sun hats. Our destination, what the villagers called their health hut, was a mudbrick building the size of a single-car garage.

In front of the hut door, painted a brighter blue than the hazy sky above, the village women waited to greet us. Our shared excitement filled the vast spaces of an otherwise sparse landscape.

"I ni sogoma!" These were the words we used to greet the women. The expression means "my power to you and the morning!" The Bambara greeting I'd taught to our group—one of a few Bambara expressions I had mastered. It pleased me to see our hosts smile at our attempt to greet them in their language.

With fabric head wraps, wrapped skirts and cotton blouses, the addition of bead necklaces and dangling earrings added adornment. Despite their dearth of material possessions, I liked the fact the women had created jewelry using their local kola nuts. I'd read about the nut before coming here, discovering that eating it quenched thirst in the desert. The irony that the inventors of Coca Cola added kola nut flavor to their soft drink as a thirst-quencher did not escape me. A bit of trivia, but evidence of how much I'd tried to educate myself about Mali before coming here.

Turning towards me, Thalia interjected, "The day you contacted me about bringing a group of women here, I wondered if you would pull it off. But I should not have doubted your determination."

"Determination is a strength I can acknowledge about myself," I said smiling. "It seems the same for you." I reminded Thalia, that while born in a village much like this one, she had earned her M.A. in community development plus a Ph.D. in public health—one of the few Ph.D.'s in Mali.

Simone, the gray-haired elder and group leader and Kaka-mu's midwife, told us, with the help of Thalia's translation, about the local women's empowerment circle. Through their hard work, they had organized both men and women to get the building completed. Looks of pride could not have been greater if we had been standing outside a new Mayo Clinic building.

Inhaling the smell of pounded millet, I attempted to record details of this moment in my memory bank. I considered the privilege of being with women mostly unknown in my world. Their faces, their hopes, their struggles, and strengths, it would fall to me to capture and share these after my return home.

When one woman asked if we arrived on a bicycle ridden across the sky, I knew it would be as difficult for those back home to imagine the life of a Bambara woman as for the woman asking the question to imagine the jet plane flight that brought us here. When another woman touched my arm ever so gently, and then looked into my freckled face, I understood how odd my skin must have appeared to her. But our smiles and our curiosity about each other bridged our other differences.

Simone spoke to us about how their new health hut provided an alternative to a lonely dirt floor as a safe place for mothers to deliver their babies. She told how during the first year, five hundred women from across the district had visited for a prenatal visit or a delivery.

Our applause rippled through the group, interrupted by a donkey braying. Thalia turned toward us and said, "The new donkey cart ambulance is here. It delivers women diagnosed with problem pregnancies to the district clinic, a site better equipped to handle complicated deliveries."

As we watched, a pregnant woman climbed into the ambulance and stretched out to show how she could ride to the clinic.

"At least this ambulance won't run out of gas," Shelly said as she asked permission to climb into the cart. It was a treat to have Shelly with me. Since our time in Kenya and Ecaudor, we had become close friends and W.O.W. allies.

Observing a long-legged, tall, blond-haired, fair-skinned woman climbing into the cart caused uproarious laughter. I watched, realizing how much Shelly's life had changed through connection with the lives and work of women in our programs. I took credit for my part in the transformational process.

The donkey-cart ambulance driver directed the donkey to stop beside the hut where both donkey and driver watched our group as we were invited to be seated on benches outside the hut. Shade provided by white fabric attached to the roof and draped across to a scrub tree brought relief from the intense heat.

Simone, with her back held erect and her sun-wrinkled face looking like a well-worn map, told us she had "caught" hundreds of babies in her lifetime. Marianne, an accomplished Oklahoma City obstetrician-gynecologist told Simone, "I'm a baby catcher too."

Simone's eyes widened, and she nodded to acknowledge Marianne before she replied, "I came to Kakamu at age thirteen. My father sent me here to be married to a village man."

We heard how Simone got pregnant and delivered a child,

a stillborn baby boy. Later, three more stillborn children. I ached for her losses.

Simone, with stoic words that failed to hide the pain and struggle her eyes revealed, lifted her chin to the sky. "My husband blamed me for not providing children."

Because of her history, Simone wanted to work as a midwife, "catching" healthy babies. Now she educates women about having babies too young, too close together and without adequate nutrition or birth assistance.

After a long pause, as if remembering what she could never forget, Simone said, "Things are better now."

"Thalia," Simone said, glancing at her mentor, "works with me and with other 'baby catchers' in nearby villages. One day soon, Mali will no longer be one of the worst places in the world to be a woman."

I could feel the power of women working together.

"Before, we had no idea how to organize or how to access more resources for family planning or for other needs," Simone told us as the women around her indicated agreement, "but we persisted and now have some resources long promised by our local government."

I watched as Simone's eyes squinted and her head lowered. She covered one side of her face with her scarf, causing me to wonder what made her look so serious.

Simone straightened her back before gesturing for us to move closer. Settling onto her space on the bench, she folded her hands in her lap and cleared her throat.

I felt a sense of dread as I prepared to listen.

"You must know," Simone declared, pausing as Thalia translated, "secrets lurk beneath our colored garments."

Simone rubbed her palms over the cloth wrapped around her body. "Ritual cutting of women's genitals," she said, looking at the ground, "has been a way of life in our villages for generations. It's been part of our religious beliefs and cultural traditions. No one knows for sure when the practice began."

My body contracted. Were we about to discover that, despite Thalia's presence and the accomplishments of the local women's group, female genital mutilation of young girls continued as usual.

My reactivity to a young girl's bodily trauma, to possible infection, to wounding that could cause infertility or death, made my stomach twist into knots.

"Cutting away the clitoris has long been the norm for young girls in my country, whether Muslim, Christian or animist, and whether rich or poor," Simone added in a direct tone of voice.

I watched Cora shaking her head and whispering to herself.

Simone admitted she had cut girls for many years, accepting the work as her duty and a way to earn small sums of money from grateful families.

I quivered.

"We were told," Simone explained in a hushed voice, "that no man would consider marrying an uncut girl."

I shifted my weight on the bench, not knowing what else to do as adrenaline rushed through my body.

"Men have been taught to believe uncut women poison them," Simone told us. "I was taught by other midwives how young girls' genital cutting would protect them from evil female impulses. I'd been taught that without cutting, it would be impossible for a girl to have a husband.

Stunned, I considered the irony of men having sex with multiple wives while denying women sexual pleasure due to cutting. But it was not only the men who followed such cultural beliefs, but women like Simone followed them too.

"Before puberty, or as young as three years of age, girls' clitorises or other parts of their genitals I cut."

Thalia made certain we understood that ninety percent of

women in Mali undergo cutting. The practice was not illegal.

How was it I'd not heard mention of FGM in reports from our programs? Were they hiding the fact? After looking into the faces of little girls in Kakamu and now imagining what they most likely had endured, my body quaked.

I noted the color had drained from the faces of others in my group. Would we be forced to hear Simone or Thalia defend FGM as part of their cultural and religious beliefs? Had I brought a group of women to Mali to hear of this horror?

"We cut using knives, sharp glass or even razor blades."

Oh, my God.

After what seemed like an endless pause, Simone added, "Or it used to be that way before Sister Thalia opened our eyes."

As Simone shared that her community now knew that nothing in their religion or culture required cutting and that "only false understandings could condone the practice," my heart began to beat normally again. I dropped down into my body as if every physically abused girl, every emotionally wounded female around the world had gathered to acknowledge and heal their body trauma and pain.

Simone continued, "Before, we lacked an understanding of the relationship between genital cutting, infection, and discomfort in sexual relationships or problems with having babies; we assumed such things came with being female. I now see my problems having babies could have been because of having been cut."

From the look on Thalia's face, I could sense her support of Simone's vulnerability.

Speaking in a clear, firm voice, Simone announced, "I no longer cut. Together, our women's group urges mothers to sign promises not to allow cutting. We bring men into our meeting so they may be educated as well. Change is difficult for some, but the baby girl born in our health hut yesterday will not be cut. Both parents signed a pledge against cutting now that they understand the dangers."

Simone's frankness astounded me. An archetype of female power, she embraced the courage to risk alienation from her community, not to mention the loss of income from the cutting ritual.

I sensed inseverable Sacred Feminine power and possibility encircling us. When Simone's eyes came in contact with mine, we shared a resonance in our knowing that women's wounds matter.

In the silence that followed, I motioned for Simone to stand. African and American, we stood in a circle of support. I felt midwife power. I held faith that together we would midwife a better world.

On a landscape covered by blazing sun that transformed red-brown sandy soil and the ever-present dust into shades of orange and gold, with straight backs bent forward, the women joined to dance. The air filled with the high-pitched, clicking sounds of their voices, called ululation. I was reminded of West African influenced vodou dancing in Haiti and wished Debbie were here so we could share the experience together.

Shaved-headed giggling girls in sky-blue school uniform dresses poked their heads outside their huts. When one young girl spotted Tameka, she sprang forward and clutched her hand. The two connected the way mothers and daughters do. Soon other children joined. Together we proceeded down a narrow, zigzagging, dirt alley. Chickens, goats, and a donkey paraded alongside us.

In a tone resembling a black preacher, Cora declared, "I'm proud to be here with women who know what I know. Only women who've been down—way down—could rise up with such voices."

"Aw ni sogoma," Thalia said. "While facing this day; you will be a winner."

I heard one woman reply, *"NSe."* Pronounced "nee say," meaning "my power," or "I'm winning the fight because my female power wins against time."

"NSe," I replied with goosebumps.

Unless it was a mirage, on a sun-splashed desert morning a day after our time in Kakamu, my travel companions, Thali and I had arrived somewhere beyond nowhere. The Kakamu revelations accompanied us. A sand-colored camel with a peacock-blue robed driver ambled down a dusty, almost empty road in stark contrast to the vast camel caravans that once carried gold, salt, and slaves from here across Trans-Saharan trade routes.

Into this Timbuktu scene appeared a tall, thin, nomadic Fulani woman with traditional dark tattoos around her mouth. What she wore in her ears brought our group to a halt. Two shiny gold earrings. Not any earrings, but voluminous, crescent shaped ones, the size of salad plates. Half-inch wide, hammered gold plates with posts wound with red cord hung from the woman's ears. The woman, like other Fulani women, carried her bank account in her ears. I'd seen photos and read about the women and their earrings. Since most of Mali's gold is gone, this woman's earrings might have been made of copper with thin sheets of gold covering them. But no matter, the earrings represented her wealth.

I decided that not only do Fulani golden earrings, but my earrings also, whatever they might be made of, represent my worth and the collective worth of women—a symbol for me of our divine worth.

My mind turned to imagine this once fabulously wealthy desert oasis that today appeared a faded, bone-dry, ecological disaster, sliding into shifting sand. The wealth from gold, long gone. And evidence of Mali as an ancient Islamic hub of wisdom and learning seemed to have faded as well. Holding these thoughts, I watched from a distance while a white-robed gentleman wearing a white skull cap and white chin beard approached. Under the skimpy shade of a forlorn acacia tree, the figure raised his right hand, palm faced towards us. Perhaps a blessing sign, or a polite greeting.

Behind the man, earthen architecture sprawled over the sand, covered by a flat roof. A pyramid shaped tower stood beside the structure. Protruding in numerous spaced rows, tree trunk poles, vertically embedded into the dried mud, added to the unique architecture of both the building and the tower.

"It's a mosque with a minaret!" Shelly announced, as she focused her camera. After Shelly spoke, the white-robed fellow approached us, his head lowered.

"It's a Sufi Mosque. I'm a Sufi Iman," he said in cultured English with a French accent, his robe billowing in the breeze.

"Our sacred Sufi Mosque is a place of high regard for us," the Iman added.

As our group perused the mosque, the Iman suggested he could direct us to a nearby library. "You can see rare ancient manuscripts and sacred Sufi texts there," he said, pointing the way.

I was amazed by the gracious though tentative way in which the Muslim man had spoken to Western women.

A robed guard sat on a stool outside the open door of the one-room library. The Iman greeted him before the guard motioned us inside. Mildew and dust filled the dimly lit, windowless, one-room library laden with shelves and a metal table stacked high with parchments.

"Centuries old sacred manuscripts," the Iman announced, carefully lifting one of them. "And manuscripts with ancient knowledge of mathematics and astronomy. More are held in private homes. And some are buried in caves for protection."

I moved closer to the magnificent manuscripts, peering at them with awe.

"More precious than the gold long ago traded away," the Iman noted.

I struggled to fathom how such treasures could be housed in such a humble, unprotected setting.

From a rotting sheet of papyrus, with faded purple and grass-green hand-inscribed calligraphy, the Iman translated an Arabic text, "Tragedies are caused by differences and by a lack of tolerance. Glory be to Allah who creates greatness out of differences."

Before I could respond to the profound beauty and value of the words, the Iman continued,

"Our Muslim faith is a tolerant one. You must remember this if you meet those who express our faith in illegitimate ways."

"What was he suggesting?" I asked myself, leaning in to listen.

"Sufi Islam honors the Divine Feminine. She's the compassionate, loving heart of our faith. And perhaps for this reason, Sufism," the Iman continued, "respects the Koran's attitudes about the equality of both women and men before the eyes of God."

The Iman paused. He cleared his throat and looked around the room.

"But you must know," he said in rapid fire, "Muslim fanatics want Sufi teachings destroyed. They want our women covered and veiled in a way uncommon in Mali."

With his shoulders pulled inward, the Iman said, "I fear what might happen soon."

The Iman explained that fundamentalist interpretation of Sharia law could destroy how the world sees Islam. Elements or sects within Sufism might even become radicalized, with those like himself killed or tortured. "I fear especially for women and children," he told us.

"Our storytellers and musicians share my concern. The fanatics want music banned without acknowledging how we praise Allah and allow others to praise their God."

"Music is Mali's heartbeat," Thalia said as she looked away. "Yet, it's the threat of Sharia law to women and children I fear most."

Even Shelly remained silent. We looked at each other. Extremists not unlike those Wariko warned of in Kenya and Somali could threaten Kakamu and the rest of the country, especially the females. Memories surfaced from long ago when Ameera expressed the same fears about Egypt.

We settled into a Timbuktu hotel that evening. We "balimamusos" shared dinner with Thalia to mark our last night in Mali. Bluesy guitar rhythms and heart-stirring sounds from a soaring female vocalist moved me like a *duende* moment.

Quiet reflections rose through conversations among us. I felt how the music and our experiences veered between hope, melancholy and commentary.

With the music lifting us, Thalia opened up about her fervent belief in allowing women to identify their most urgent needs, as they chose their group intention for their empowerment circles. She assured us she had never forced the "cutting" conversation until the women were ready.

From a private conversation shared while walking near the hotel, I knew the painful story Thalia wanted us to hear. The one whose emotion overwhelmed her when she shared it with me.

With Thalia's permission, I mentioned to our group that before issues about FGM emerged in the Kakamu women's circle, food security had been identified as an obvious need. The introduction of improved crop growing techniques resulted. Later the importance of literacy rose as a topic. And, of course, the health needs of the community that resulted in the building and supplying of the health hut were identified.

"Not until the six-year-old daughter of one of the members bled to death after an FGM procedure," I said, gazing at Thalia as her head dropped, "did the Kakamu group open themselves to a discussion about the dangers of cutting. The safety and trust among the members had allowed their shared grief and pain to lead to positive change."

It was a powerful time for us to show our support for Thalia. A commitment to the expansion of the W.O.W. Network emerged without further prompting.

"I'll donate proceeds from the sale of my Alabama pine forestland," Cora said, pulling a shawl over her shoulders as the night desert air brought a chill, or perhaps as a chill arose from sensing the stakes.

Shelly announced she would designate funds from her family's foundation for W.O.W. programs. "Grass root development combined with women's empowerment. That's worth my money."

Marianne pledged an additional $10,000 dollars to our work and shared her intention to connect with a friend she thought might have interest in producing a documentary about the Kakamu program.

Tameka offered to speak to women's groups and to raise funds in Atlanta and elsewhere. "And count me in for the next W.O.W. trip, so I'll have more to share."

About to leave Mali, I felt a deep, ignited certainty as to my purpose and destiny pathway. I felt aligned with deep values and was prepared to join arms to expand The Work of Women Network and its greater possibilities. Women's circles and women's connection would grow. The number of W.O.W. trips would continue as a way to disrupt our fixed mindsets and beliefs. Contributions to W.O.W. programs would increase from the inspiration of meeting women in the programs. Our Network would join the movement of women supporting each other to become unstoppable mid-wives for positive change in the world.

The next morning we said goodbye to Thalia, who was staying for an upcoming meeting. After a short flight from Timbuktu to Mopti, another flight to Bamako would follow before our scheduled homeward bound leg late in the night. Excessive hours of travel to get home, but it was doable. That is, it seemed so until we arrived at the modest Aeroport de Tombouctou only to discover an unannounced three-hour flight delay. We could miss our connections. Since the next flight out of Timbuktu was three days later, I panicked. Something was not right. No one spoke English. Why the massive crowds waiting to board one small prop plane?

More than three hours later, when the boarding process finally began, we were swept inside a pushing throng of passengers rushing toward the gate. When at last we each somehow managed to get inside the plane, we grabbed unassigned seats while other passengers continued to board. In no time, the 1950s Russian prop plane door closed.

I noticed the seats were filled, but the aisle overflowed with more passengers. Just then, the flight attendant directed an older woman to crawl over and take a seat with me. Not next to me, but with me, forced to sit on my lap. Astounded, I heard the engines roar. I did not know what to do as the plane proceeded down the runway. Other passengers fell into the laps of those already seated.

I saw a young mother with a baby bundled in her arms gently lower herself down onto Marianne's lap. A force smiled covered both women's faces. Next, the stewardess came down the aisle placing a toddler over Tameka's fastened seat belt. Good natured, but shocked, Tameka hugged the child before closing her eyes.

While seats were filled with a second layer of passengers, I got more and more nervous. None of us wanted to wait three days for the next flight. Should I force the pilot to stop and take our group off the flight?

Without an announcement, defying every law of aerodynamics, the aging, overloaded Russian turbo prop labeled "Air Maybe" attempted to lift off. I had never felt more frightened or out of control. Why had I not jumped up and insisted we exit the plane before the door was shut? Would my old fear of speaking up to male authority cost us our lives? Would we not make it home to share our revelations about FGM and about radical Islamist threats? It was too late to berate myself and also too late for the flight to be aborted. A strange, loud noise sounded as the plane began to take off.

10

WHAT ONCE WAS

Oklahoma City, 2001

"Cindy," Rick's voice sounded into my phone, "please come to the conference room. I'd like to visit."

Certain that Rick had heard about our harrowing flight out of Timbuktu, and that he would congratulate me on the success of the first all-female trip his organization had sponsored, I raced to his office and knocked. He opened the door, motioning for me to take a seat, before he shut the door and stepped back toward his chair. Rick's somber appearance was not what I expected.

I sat in silence. Rick gazed down before he spoke. "I've decided to discontinue the W.O.W. trips," he announced. "I'm concerned that your W.O.W. program dilutes the Change of Possibility brand."

What? My insides shook. At that moment, if the man across from me had slapped me in the face, I would not have been more shocked, hurt or dismayed. Rick's appalling statements sank into me like swallowed rat poison.

Was this a joke? Or a rerun of the fateful Donald Douglas scene? My neck felt hot. I flushed. I heard words in my head.

Words I could not make myself speak aloud. "You idiot," I wanted to tell Rick. "Why are you doing this? The W.OW. network and trips offer a tremendous benefit to fundraising efforts. We're attracting women donors to replace the aging male ones. The travel impacts both the lives of the women who travel and the lives of those visited. I have powerful new donor prospects ready to join other trips. Without the trips, the W.O.W. initiative is challenged or doomed."

My thoughts remained thoughts, not spoken words. I wanted to reply in a focused, calm way. Instead, something seized me. Words stuck in my throat. An invisible force compelled me to go along with a man who had crushed my vision and purpose, one now shared by many.

I remained stone silent. Stunned. Sickened. Not only for myself but also for the women in our programs. For women like Simone. And for those on our trip whose eyes had been opened to conditions women in other countries face. For conscious men like Gopal and Dale and John and Jean-Claude who grasp the problems caused by devaluing women and disregarding what women bring to the world.

The room remained quiet. I blinked to fan away tears. Rick would not see me cry. My boss, a tired leader who held power over me, despite the fact he lacked ideas to revive his organization.

Change was threatening. Did I represent insult, hurt, or anger Rick may have suffered from other women? Whatever his problem, I was devastated. I turned my head and gazed at a pathetic, contorted clay statue sitting on the console near where Rick and I sat. A woman hunched in a defeated posture. A figure trapped, unable to seek help.

I watched Rick shift his weight in his chair. With a strange grin, I sensed he was about to change the subject. "I'm a new grandpa," he announced. "My daughter had a baby girl this week. Isn't that terrific?"

I swallowed hard and said, "Great, Rick," pushing my pain and grief deep inside. "You must be thrilled."

As the words left my mouth, I wanted to stick my tongue out, Kali style. Didn't Rick want a more equitable world for his granddaughter? And didn't he see Change of Possibility would die without new support?

I lifted my wounded spirit and somehow walked back to my cubicle, where I dropped into my chair and cradled my head in my arms. Rick's black and white, chart-and-graph, dominating approach to management had seized power over my passionate, creative, intuitive, connecting, and relationship-building leadership. The old masculine operating system had collided with the rising feminine system of power and possibility.

The familiar tapping sounds from my colleagues' computer keyboards echoed like a funeral dirge. My work. My passion. My grand purpose in life had been squelched. Treasured photographs of women met around the world gazed at me from photos on my cubicle walls. It hurt to see their faces. The face of one woman especially touched me and took me back to an earlier Change of Possibility trip.

Doña Esmeralda Lopez Velázquez, the indigenous Mixtec woman I met in Oaxaca, Mexico. Standing near Esmeralda's home—a small stone hut in a village reached on foot or by burro—our W.O.W. group had completed a treacherous climb over denuded hillsides to meet her. The devastating effects of overgrazing, slash and burn and single-crop planting shocked us, despite forewarning. Heavy use of U.S. manufactured pesticides added to the problem. The barren land could no longer feed families.

Esmeralda expected us and welcomed us to her farm—one less than an acre. She stood tall despite her short stature.

Shoulders pulled back. Head held high. Dressed in a traditional hand-woven tunic-blouse called a "huipil." Her hair was braided in two thick salt and pepper braids. When we greeted and shook hands, Esmeralda's calloused palms connected with mine.

We conversed as I spoke Spanish— a language Esmeralda understood but did not speak— and she replied speaking her native Mixtec, a language I did not understand or speak. Ample body language and the feminine desire for relationship and connection guided our communication.

Esmeralda showed me her organically enriched soil lined with rows of enormous cabbage and dark green spinach. When she plucked a plump red tomato, she did so examining it with a mother's love.

"I also grow maize," she said, "and avocados, squash and beans. Sweet potatoes and jicama. The plants grow together."

Esmeralda called the system "milpa," a farming practice incorporating her ancestors' wisdom. "They knew not to plant single crops that rob nutrients and create arid land like a barren mother—unable to produce."

We walked toward Esmeralda's flower garden. Purple flowering licorice, golden asters, and snow-white lemon verbena scented the air. "I make medicines from plants," Esmeralda explained, lifting a vial of oil from her pocket.

"Oil from the foxglove cures irregular heartbeats. Verbena leaves make tea for stomach problems. Asters in herbal teas bring relaxation. Hyssops treat bronchitis and sore throats."

"You're a wise herbalist!" I told Esmeralda, with my heart filled with respect.

She placed her knotted fingers over her heart. "I know many things. I know how to kill a squirrel with a slingshot to provide protein meals. And I also know about saying goodbye. Goodbye to my husband who labors in California fields. Goodbye to my sons with dreams in El Norte. Goodbye to my daughters. They work in the city for wealthy families. My grandbabies will be born far from me. If they fall ill, I can't give them healing medicines."

I bit my lip. Esmeralda's pain and longings sank into my soul.

"I must remain on my land," she said as she handed each of our group a purple aster. "My mother and aunts have no one to care for them. And I must preserve this fertile plot for future generations."

The chasms between our realities evaporated. Esmeralda's despair was mine. We both wanted to share what we know. We both wanted a better tomorrow.

"Esmeralda," I said, holding my eyes on her photo today as I had when looking at her in person. "I can't kill a squirrel. I don't have a garden to grow chilies, avocados, or squash. But I, too, know many things. To share them, I need a voice. I can't shut down when masculine authorities challenge me."

As I spoke the words, I felt the strength and wisdom that grounded Esmeralda's life. The memory of Esmeralda when she lifted from under her embroidered "huipil" an image of the brown-skinned Virgin of Guadalupe, the Virgin Mary who legend says once appeared in Mexico. How Esmeralda listened to the Virgin's whispers. How they guided her in the darkest moments.

I understood Esmeralda's connection to the Virgin Mary as more than a connection to a "humble servant" and "hand-maiden" of the Lord. Why had I forgotten her and her Divine Feminine presence in my time of need?

I called Debbie. "It's over. Rick figured out how to destroy what we built."

"I felt it coming," Debbie told me over the phone line. "I'll resign in protest."

We hung up. If only I could find a way to speak my protest Debbie style, I could carry my despair but leave my work without shame.

At this point, Charlie, my tough and tender husband, had seen all my moods and emotions. He accepted much about me. However, my complaining he could not tolerate, even if he knew it was justified. Charlie believed in bucking up to whatever life dished out.

For Charlie every problem was simple and easy to fix. To him, everything had an answer. To me, everything was complex and complicated and difficult and time-consuming. "Don't make a big deal out of it." "Why don't you....?" Charlie would declare before issuing a solution. If I protested, he would come back with, "Don't worry, I'll fix it."

I know how much Charlie prided himself on his capacity to fix things, even though he could not fix his biggest problem—a faulty heart valve. While I focused on the loss of my grand vision for the women of the world, Charlie focused on fixing my gloom and not on his inevitable open-heart surgery.

A middle-aged woman caught in the middle of yet another confidence crisis. I was doing a good job on my path until I got slammed. Now I could not figure out my life, and I didn't know how to help Charlie either.

Living through the sixties with Age of Aquarius thinking, I righteously assumed my life would be special, and I would make a difference and live a purposeful, impactful life. With new possibilities for females rising, I had high aspirations and great expectations. With the growth of W.O.W., I thought I just might change the world. Instead, I was stuck with a seeping sore inside. Had I not learned how to move on? Why was I repeating a pattern of bosses not liking what I was creating?

To boost my spirits, Charlie suggested a trip to see Abby in Dallas. I took him up on the idea. Despite my gloom, being in Dallas on a magnificent spring morning, sharing time with our daughter, made me forget, for a while, what ailed me.

Abby sat behind the wheel of her car, the first one she had purchased for herself. She was driving Charlie and me across Highland Park, a stately, affluent residential area of Dallas. A sense of the world's inequality invaded me during my enjoyment of the drive.

Outside Highland Park, we arrived at a wooded, more modest street where Abby showed us her condo. One complete with her first mortgage payments. Pink crepe myrtle trees surrounded the front of the building. Inside showed potential, but it needed Abby's eye to make it a cozy home. When time came to leave for home, I hugged Abby with gratitude that she was not suffering my devastating loss.

As Charlie drove us back to Oklahoma City, the car radio provided a distracting noise, but it could not quell my concerns. I stared out the window, watching golden prairie grasses blowing in the wind. I heard the anthem of my generation playing on a golden oldies' station. "The answer my friend, is blowing in the wind. The answer is blowing in the wind." Bob Dylan's words worked their way through me like earthworms working through the earth. However, it was tough to trust the possibility that answers were blowing in the wind.

As we rode along in silence, I saw the flat, dry plains that joined Texas and Oklahoma. Inside, I felt flat like the plains, no passion rushing through me. Off-balance, dissatisfied. After my journeys and discoveries, why couldn't I figure out the next act?

While listening to my inner monologue, I watched an orange and brown monarch butterfly land on the front windshield. Was she hitching a ride? No, she was stuck. Her leg wedged into the trim of the windshield. I rolled down the window, reached my hand around the metal frame surrounding the windshield. A gentle tap on the frame provided the help the butterfly required to free herself. She took off with wings flapping in the breeze. Wouldn't it be great to be as free as this butterfly? How could I find the strength to get unstuck and to soar again? What blocked me?

Charlie interrupted my silent musing to suggest something as casually as if suggesting we stop for pizza. "Why don't we sell our house. Quit our jobs and sell one car. And take our SUV on the road. For six months or so. We'll camp. Sleep in a tent."

In the same breath, he added, "Without a house or the second car payment, we could afford to travel without using our savings."

I gulped and took an enormous breath. No doubt Charlie expected me to say, "Get real. We must work. Have you lost your marbles? We have obligations; we have commitments. Besides, you're as practical as an Eveready battery. You aren't serious about a crazy travel idea."

But something else happened. I did not say any of those things. My heart opened wide. My gut told me Charlie was right, and my mind prepared for the ride. The dreamer and the seeker inside me knew Charlie's proposal was not what we could do; it was what we must do. As we drove in cruise control, my mind cruised down the road. My adrenaline rushed. "Okay, let's do it. Let's go explore in our Explorer," I announced.

Charlie twisted his head toward me, as if not believing my words. "Done deal! Let's do it," he said, looking pleased and happy for me to focus on something other than donuts and gloom.

Mapping out a plan could happen later. Charlie's call to adventure was my answer blowing in the wind, and maybe blowing in the wind were answers to questions Charlie never asked himself.

Sometimes the pieces fit together. Five days after the drive home from Dallas, our Oklahoma City home sold for our asking price. The buyers wanted possession in three weeks. The following day, Charlie resigned from his work. With my W.O.W. dreams destroyed, I left Change of Possibility with a two-week notice.

Because our wild ride idea got rolling after we left Abby in Dallas, she had no idea about our plans. When Charlie called her, he asked about the new job. Her first after college graduation. Abby sounded happy and pleased with her new work.

In his next breath, Charlie spewed these words, "Guess what? Mom and I sold the house. We quit our jobs. We're getting rid of lots of stuff. Then we're heading out for a half-a-year lap around the country. We're gonna buy a tent and camp. Take each day as it comes."

Silence. Then a flabbergasted voice barreled back. "You did what? Why would you sell our house? What do you mean you're going to travel and sleep in a tent? What am I supposed to say when someone asks me where you live? Where am I supposed to stay when I come home?"

More silence followed before sobbing sounds. I experienced my daughter's pain the way I felt her birth pangs twenty-some years ago. I got it. Abby had the rug pulled from under her the way I had it pulled out when I lost my dream job. We both got robbed. It hurt worse than dropping a hammer on my toe to think of upsetting my daughter.

I was done. Done trying to figure out my life. Done with the idea of adventure. Done wanting to save the world. I wanted to tell Abby, "Just kidding. You know we wouldn't do anything so wild and crazy."

From somewhere within, a new soft voice announced in my ear, "Trust Abby to move forward with her life while you and Charlie do the same."

Jarred to my senses by the voice, I heard myself say, "Abby, we love you. We trust you to follow your path as we follow ours. We will be just a phone call away." Our conversation ended. I could only hope our loving relationship was not harmed.

Sending shock waves to people I love was not over. I had to tell Mother and Daddy, my eighty-something parents, about our trip, despite my concern for their multiple health issues. We would be leaving in two weeks. Dread stuck to me. I stepped tentatively onto the front walkway of the house where I had grown up. Where Charlie and I had gathered for many holidays and special occasions. How many times had I come and gone through that front door? Blurting out our great escape scheme scared me more than telling my parents I had wrecked their car in front of the Charcoal Oven when I was sixteen.

Mother's mental capacities amazed us all, but her physical problems would take a full page to list, and Daddy showed hints his mind was slipping. As the oldest of their four children, I was the one my parents had relied on as their front line of support. Walking into the house, something gripped me like a binding belt.

I had to tell Charlie the game was over. Even though the house sold, we'd have to find another place to live. We'd have to find new jobs. I could not upset my parent's life after already upsetting Abby's.

As my heart dropped to my stomach, the whispering voice came to me again. It was as if something inside me shifted once again. I focused on connecting to my wisdom and courage. I found a way to trust the unknown—the unknown for my parents and the unknown for Abby, for Charlie and me. Our trip would proceed. Charlie and I would keep in close touch with my parents. My sister would be a few miles away. No more questioning our decision.

On a cloudy, windy evening, heavy with emotion, I walked with Charlie into my parents' home. I sat on the antique camel-back sofa stuffed with family memories. Daddy was seated in his gray-blue leather lounge chair. He looked distant and detached, saying almost nothing.

As usual, Mother, seated in her rocking chair, opened the conversation. "How's Abby? How's work? And what's your latest house decorating project?"

That was my cue to announce our unplanned plans to leave for an extended adventure with a tent and our Explorer. I watched Mother's face as I waited for her response. My pulse raced and my breath came from high in my chest. Mother sat in silence. She twisted her wedding ring as if watching her life reflected in her diamond.

After what seemed longer than it took to sell our house, Mother's head rose. "After raising four children," she said, looking straight at me, "I've gotten used to shocks. But camping... I can't imagine you two camping. And how could you give up your home? You've worked so hard to make it just right."

Mother's two points stung me. No doubt the camping gene was recessive on my side of the family—not one family member camping dominant. The genes on Charlie's side didn't help. As to the point about loving our home, Mother nailed that one too. We had worked long and hard to make our house a home. Without a thought, we sold it.

Charlie looked stunned. I don't think he imagined how hard this moment would be. He loved my parents as much as I did. And would never want to hurt them.

Before either Charlie or I spoke a word, I heard Mother clear her throat. "I know one thing for sure," she said. "Life is short. If you want to do something, go do it. Don't ever look back."

I felt a lump in my throat and pushed back tears. As

always, Mother unselfishly supported me and had given us her blessing, though I knew she hated our leaving.

I watched Daddy for signs of approval or disapproval, without detecting either. I couldn't help but remember the Thanksgiving when Daddy, age seventy-nine, cast caution to the Oklahoma wind as he announced his desire to go with me to Haiti. Maybe inside Daddy wanted to encourage our trip, though conflicted because he relied on Charlie's support as well as mine. That's when I realized I did not need to continue trying to guess what was on my father's mind. I could simply ask him, "Daddy," I said. "Are you comfortable with Charlie and me heading out for an unplanned adventure? Will you and Mother be okay?"

"I think you should go," he said, though I could not decode his feelings.

Looking at my parents, I concluded they had enjoyed a good marriage and were living a comfortable life, though they had health challenges. Their life was not everything I desired, but my parents had provided me with many blessings. I imagined Mother may have wished for more emotional openness from Daddy, but perhaps in their private moments she had found it, or she had accepted the lack.

Charlie and I had announced our intention and both parents signaled acceptance. I was grateful. The next steps were up to the two of us.

11

LEAVING MINUS DIRECTION

USA, 2001

"Where are you going?" "How will you get your mail?" "Who will color your hair?" "Where are you keeping your sterling silver?" "What's your plan after you return?" "Aren't you afraid of bears?" And one friend added, "I wish I had the guts to do what you're doing." Such were the questions and a comment from the going-away party our friends threw for us the night before our departure.

On Friday, April 13, 2001, exactly twenty-one days after Charlie issued a call to adventure, our home was sold, jobs quit, stuff sold, stored or given away, and twelve plastic boxes of essentials were loaded into our maroon Ford Explorer. Time to wave goodbye to the world I'd known for much of my life. Every emotion I'd ever felt circled within me, but pure excitement topped the list.

Out the rear-view mirror flashed a windy city on the plains. Scenes of Abby, Charlie, and me living our suburban lives played on the screen of my mind. I pictured the three homes we'd owned, how we'd celebrated birthdays and holidays. Hopes, dreams, and joys were housed in those homes, not to mention the chunks of our paychecks deposited to pay the mortgage and living expenses.

Glancing at my chariot driver, I announced, "We're writing a new chapter. Let's get going."

During the first miles along Interstate 35, Walt Whitman's words from *Song of the Open Road* came to me. "I think whatever I shall meet on the road I shall like, and whoever beholds me shall like me."

Grand Canyon, Arizona

On day two of the odyssey, our maroon Ford Explorer stood stranded somewhere inside a dense, dark forest while blinding sleet pounded our windshield with riveting ice bullets. A chilling change from the thrill of how we began. I had imagined heading west along the back roads of Arizona, taking in never-before-seen sights, driving until we found a campground to pitch the blue and yellow K-Mart tent. Then, like Thoreau, we'd enjoy the great outdoors. Positive forces driving us forward had departed, leaving us alone at night, inside a freezing utility vehicle where stomach-wrenching worry made me as nauseous as a first-trimester pregnant woman.

What a fiasco! Why didn't I stop to consider the dangers and risks? Incidentals like food, water, staying warm and keeping dry had slipped my mind. At nine o'clock at night, Charlie and I were stuck in darkness as black as newly poured asphalt. Freezing rain continued to hammer the windshield of our Ford Explorer, the model some call the "Exploder" because of its propensity for bursting into flames. Perched on bucket seats, wrapped in black sleeping bags, parked off a winding road in the first clearing to appear for twenty-six miles, if we died out here, our sleeping bags would double as body bags.

Stranded somewhere inside the Coconino National Forest in Arizona, along Highway 64, Desert View Drive, the dashboard temperature flashed a freezing thirty-two degrees. The ice covering our tin can vehicle made it look like an igloo, and our new cell phone picked up no signal out here. We had no food or a place to get food, and but one half-empty bottle of water. And no one in the world knew we were in this crazy predicament.

Adding stomach-churning anxiety to a dismal scenario, I remembered we had no home or jobs to return to, even if we made it out of here alive. Charlie, the Prince of Optimism, seated on the driver's side of the frozen Explorer, sat like an erect bowling pin determined to ward off forces trying to topple us both. He knew I was scared and needed someone to blame.

"Why didn't we get supplies and directions? I told you to stop miles back," I grumbled to Charlie, the one person, other than myself, I could blame.

Charlie snarled. My single-minded husband, determined to get to a campground, saw no need to stop for supplies or directions. Charlie's motto: one thing at a time. Arrive to a campground, worry about supplies later. Linear thinking and singleness of purpose proved inadequate tonight. I would have pestered him to listen to me earlier, except I was immersed in landscape wonders. As the sun set, it hit me like running into a parked car; we had no food, almost no water and no place to stay.

Thrusting his chin forward, Charlie, a Pennsylvania steel mill town kid, who never, not once in his life had camped or slept in a car, morphed into Mr. Outdoor World. "Just hang tight! Don't panic! Relax! There's no reason to get upset," he barked. "We can sleep right here in the Explorer and figure out where we are tomorrow. You won't starve before morning."

Knowing we'd be forced to sleep sitting upright, Charlie's "Don't worry, be happy" routine irked me. The space behind our bucket seats, all the way to the rear window, was crammed with what I thought necessary when packing for our adventure. Sleeping in the Explorer or reclining our seats didn't occur to me until now. What mattered was a hair dryer, make-up bag, folding mirror and a fishing pole for Charlie—who hadn't fished in 30 years. We would want our battery-powered massager in case we developed stiff backs, and of course our tent for two, along with a toolbox and bath towels. I also needed six pairs of shoes, with three pairs for Charlie, plus our t-shirts, shorts, cargo pants and underwear. A travel journal and the *Rand McNally Road Atlas,* given to us by friends. Other essentials included our first-aid kit, a wine opener, Charlie's navy dress suit, and my black cocktail dress, in case we decided to attend a party or eat in a fancy restaurant. Oh, and glasses, lots of reading glasses, because I was famous for losing my glasses, and I could not read without them.

None of these "essentials" would help us now, and the far-away look in Charlie's eyes told me he was weary and worried too. But his self-sufficient stoicism covered his inner worry. Not a word of despair left this man's lips.

Even while ignoring my need to play the "woe is me" game, I knew Charlie hated to see me or another living thing suffer. The man detested bugs and all insects, but he would not think of harming one. His need to protect living things was so strong that he once tried to protect a family of skunks that made a nest underneath our deck.

Charlie had convinced himself this trip was a winning lottery ticket for us both. An answer to everything—an escape from my depression and workaholic devotion to a project now derailed, and a much-needed escape from routine for Charlie. Maybe a reminder of his days as a young Navy officer seeing the world aboard the USS Miller. His memories of the Navy, like all his memories, suppressed the tough stuff and savored the good. While paused, I wondered about other reasons for his idea.

Understanding Charlie's desire to make my life perfect, and his personal excitement about our trip, I resisted more gloom and doom. Instead, I allowed my mind to reel back to another terrifying night. A time I could not control my panic, and Charlie was not with me to say, "Don't worry!"

On that night, I had nothing to hold on to except the airplane armrest as I sat gnarled-knuckled and buckled into the middle seat of an American Airlines flight circling above ice-covered Andean peaks, among the tallest in the world. I looked out the window, saw zigzagging lightning flash above volcanic fire-pits surrounding a 1960s airport in the middle of a sprawling, skyscraper-covered city. I'd heard the airport earned the title of among the most dangerous in the world. Planes had crashed into mountains, slammed into buildings, and careened off runways.

On the first day of a Change of Possibility trip to Ecuador, I was enduring a terrifying hour circling above Quito, waiting for clouds, wind, turbulence, lightning, and fog to clear. With my nerves fried, I glanced around to see other's reactions. Shelly, the same zany one I first met in Kenya, was bending the ear of the passenger seated next to her. I heard her announce, as if wanting everyone to hear, "Never take life too seriously; it isn't permanent, ya know."

Some passengers giggled, others burst into laughter, most did not understand English. Yet tension appeared to disperse, as had happened in Kenya when Shelly leveled John after his squat toilet fit.

"I don't think it's ever too soon to panic, do you?" Shelly

asked the baffled fellow beside her. The next moment, the captain's voice boomed over the microphone.

"Ladies and gentlemen, we're in a holding pattern waiting for the weather to clear. It is 11:20 pm local time. We must land before midnight when runway lights are shut off. If we can't make our approach in the next ten minutes, we'll head to an alternate destination for the night."

Shelly got it right. It was never too soon to panic. Where would our group stay if we landed in a strange city in the middle of the night? What about Juan, the Change of Possibility country director, waiting to meet us in Quito? "Wait, hold on," I told myself. "Put on your calm, collected mask so the others won't see you freak."

There I sat in silence as we bumped through a sea of black clouds. Even loquacious Shelly stayed quiet for what might have been the first time in her life. After about five minutes, a thrusting sound made my heart leap to my throat. I heard the reverse thrust of the engines. Without another word from the captain, a jarring descent through the dark began. The plane shook and quaked. The movement made me crazy.

Not a bit too soon, despite the turbulence, the steel shell separating a hundred passengers from meeting our maker hit the slippery black tarmac. I heard a thud. The brakes held. We were safe in Quito. We would not careen into Hotel Colón, where we should have arrived hours ago. The Quito flight, like the horrific flight out of Timbuktu, would be hard to forget.

Despite the turbulent beginning, Ecuador provided gifts to cherish. A needed reminder, while it may never be too soon to panic, perhaps it's never too late to calm oneself.

Bringing my thoughts back inside the Explorer, I leaned toward Charlie's side of the SUV. "Have you seen my rose-colored glasses?" Silence reigned. I changed the subject. "I need a bathroom," I said.

"Well...," Charlie replied, watching to see what I'd do next.

I climbed from the Explorer like an astronaut walking on the moon. The sleet had stopped. My feet hit loose dirt and rock. Inhaling the sweet scent of Ponderosa pine, I listened and heard a wolf howling. She ignited my almost forgotten wildness.

Squatting my body above the dirt, lowering my cargo pants and panties, I clung to my tissue while moving my chin toward the sky. The light from a new crescent moon greeted me. The beams from the Big She in the sky penetrated the mantle of cold surrounding my body. A familiar, far away presence brought me light. As warm pee dribbled from my body, a flood of pent-up emotion rushed through my body. My eyes flooded before tears rolled down my cheeks, surprising me as their warmth touched my cold skin. The still beauty and the wild wolf howling combined in a magnificent, compelling way.

I remembered Pachamama from Ecuador, the Andean Mother Goddess, and her feminine, guiding, protecting energy. She spoke through the moon, the stars, the earth, wind, mountains, rivers, volcanoes and through living beings to reveal resources needed to live, love, and find our way. Maybe I could trust the moon and Pachamama to help us through the night.

Moving back inside the Explorer, I slipped into my sleeping bag like a caterpillar entering a cocoon. Looking at Charlie with his back and neck pushed against an upright leather bucket seat, I saw his eyes close and listened to his breath grow deeper and slower. Other than the upright position and his sleeping bag cover, my husband looked the same as when asleep on our queen-sized, pillow-top mattress with soft cotton sheets inside the bedroom of the home we used to own. Seeing Charlie, as if oblivious to our situation, caused me to whisper as I closed eyes, "This night could make a good story someday."

And that's when an idea seized me, a vision aligned with the one I'd left behind. I would visit with women met along the way, share a bit of my story and invite them to share theirs. Yes, that was it. I'd explain about being homeless and unemployed, traveling the country, camping with my husband, and gathering women's stories for a book.

Tom Brokaw wrote *The Greatest Generation*, with stories about men from my father's era. My book would tell women's stories from my era, woven together with my own story.

No one could stop me from penning these stories. Our voices would not be silenced. Renewed and enthused, I closed the Explorer door and reached my hand over the console to rest on Charlie's chest. Containing myself until I could share my idea would not come easy.

"Wake up! It's getting light," I announced to Charlie at sunrise the next morning. "Look outside. No more frost. See the orange, pink and purple covering the sky?"

Once outside the Explorer, through the trees, I saw a sign: Mather Campground, South Rim of Grand Canyon National Park. That's when I heard Charlie's confident voice boom. "You panicked for nothing. I drove us right where we needed to be."

Jumping back into the car, we both laughed as we drove to the small office adjoining the camp entrance. A smiling park ranger greeted us. "Good morning. How can we help you?"

"We need a campsite," Charlie replied, with no hint that we had driven here in pitch dark unaware we were at the Grand Canyon. It seemed impossible, but that is what hap- pened.

"This is your lucky day," the attendant announced. "Usually, we're booked."

I glanced at the brochure he handed me and read aloud the park rules. Number one: "Be aware it is illegal to sleep in your car inside the park. Heavy fines will be imposed."

"Glad we stayed under the radar on that one," I announced before spilling my book idea.

"I'm not surprised," I heard Charlie say. "I always thought you'd write a book."

His support seeped into those crevices that doubt might otherwise have filled. I'd grown accustomed to his accepting my dreams and the fact he felt no need to ruminate about details. Parked in our camping space, tent-pitching 101 commenced. First, Charlie opened the tent package and read the instructions, something he rarely did. Still, we were both clueless as to the purpose of the bag full of pieces. Where were the Sherpas who pitched my tent in Nepal or the outfitters who handled the task in Mali?

In what must have been at least twice the normal tent assembly time, Charlie and I teamed up to raise a fully upright and tied down tiny two-person tent. Our navy blue and yellow sleeping place looked as wonderful as a five-star hotel, or it did so compared to sleeping upright in the Explorer.

Time for breakfast alongside tourists at the Grand Canyon Village. Most of these folks had spent the night in the lodge. They missed peeing on the ground and inhaling sweet pine scents in the process. During breakfast, we imagined ourselves ready to explore the canyon, a little less the newbie campers we were last night.

"Aren't you glad I thought of this trip?" Charlie asked as he downed a second cup of coffee.

"I wouldn't have missed it for all the gold found in the gold rush," I said, as my smile stretched to my ears.

Excitement fused with awe as I glimpsed the giant canyon for the first time. A more spectacular chasm or a more sacred space would be hard to imagine. The sun glowed on a vast rainbow of colored rock formations. I moved to a place inside myself as deep as the canyon. My body became as light as a feather. My heart wanted to sing. Inhaling and exhaling deep breaths, I repeated the process again and again.

As my lungs filled with crisp, fresh air, it dawned on me. I was praying a breath prayer as described by Thich Nhat Hanh, the noted Vietnamese Buddhist monk, in his book, *Present Moment, Wonderful Moment.* When I first read his book, I was too busy and preoccupied to practice the mindfulness he described. But now was different. Before a brief mindful breathing practice, I allowed myself to imagine joining the writers of the world club.

When I could no longer stay centered in mindful breathing, I blurted out, "Charlie, do we have enough water? It's dry in this desert. And did you put on your sunscreen?"

Ignoring my annoying questions, Charlie pushed ahead as if on a quest as real to him as the cattle drive was to Billy Crystal's character, Mitch, in *City Slickers.* That's when I noticed Charlie was out of breath. I'd never known him to get out of breath from a little exercise. It seemed odd. It bothered me, but I dismissed the thought.

I slipped back to my wonder and awe space. How marvelous to be free, to be out of doors, to be surrounded by Mother Nature's spectacular creation—a living desert sculpture painted in terracotta, purple, blue and beige, with hints of every shade in a crayon box. Granite and limestone walls, seven miles wide and two miles deep, with peaks and crags, beauty, and grandeur everywhere. Charlie and I, climbing down the rock trails of a giant abyss, taking in wonders formed, not by human hands, but by water and wind wearing the rock away over millions of years. Mother Nature's power at work.

On this glorious April morning, I would not be attending

meetings, or preparing reports, or listening to office gossip. Instead, I was descending below the south rim of the Grand Canyon. Straining to see the bottom, I noticed what looked like a tiny ribbon of water winding along the canyon floor. The mighty Colorado River. From my perspective, the river looked like a piece of grosgrain ribbon laid out in a meandering pattern, exposing billions of years of history. I remember reading about John Wesley Powell's 1869 exploration of this river. Of course, mostly men did the exploring back then. I was fortunate to live in an era where women were explorers too. It was about time!

This year alone, millions would visit the canyon, gratefully not all on this day. Some would take a quick glance before heading to buy a baseball cap, or a t-shirt and a burger. For others, today would be the day for a long-awaited mule ride down the canyon, like the one about to pass us. They say reservations must be made a year in advance. We committed to our road trip only three-and-a-half weeks ago and never discussed coming to the Grand Canyon, much less planning a mule ride for today at eight o'clock in the morning. Anyway, I preferred walking the trail.

I realized, on this carefree day, I'd shifted my mood to a much more life-positive stance. Moving into the canyon was like moving deeper into some place new, different, and exciting. The great unknown lay before me.

Walking step by step into the canyon, I heard the crunch of my boots on the rocky path. I looked down at my dusty, worn hiking boots. Bam! Mind travel! Off I went, remembering another time I wore these boots, thousands of miles away on another continent while trekking into Nepal's Himalayas. That trip, another unexpected adventure with little time to prepare.

In those mountains, I first began gathering stories about women's work. My passion to support women's empowerment grew as I trekked. Looking at the same trekking boots worn while hearing Nepalese women's stories and while discovering Nepalese goddesses made me wonder about my story and my purpose. I was once again on a journey, with a purpose. I was not running away, but traveling to find a way to move past barriers blocking women's growth, including my own.

I recalled something Gail Sheehy wrote in *New Passages*. "Women who start over in mid-life seem exhilarated by the idea that on the other side they will be something else, without having any idea what."

In my mid-life, I was seeking that new "what." An impulse I felt but could not easily name. I was certain the manifestation of my longing would require bringing forward the flow of feminine energy. Along with many others, I'd found that relying solely on the push of masculine energy and the masculine operating system, useful for building things like roads and bridges, could not alone create what growth-mindset women and men longed for. While there seemed little agreement in the culture about the definition of masculine and feminine, there was no doubt in my mind the two concepts belonged balanced together. No doubt, the words masculine and feminine needed to be understood as more than names for two genders. The challenge was to bring about the balance before we destroyed the planet and ourselves.

12

"THE WICKEDEST CITY IN THE WEST"

Jerome, Arizona, 2001

Approaching Jerome on State Highway 89A, Charlie drove up a 5,000-foot mountain, zigzagging across a treacherous two-lane road with a twenty-five mile-an-hour speed limit. Cars approached within inches of our back bumper. A Harley rider dashed around us, crossing the double yellow lines. Suddenly, I felt woozy. I thought I might throw up.

"I'm dizzy!" I told Charlie as he made his way around the next hairpin curve, one of 127 on the 15-mile road.

Reddish boulders, some the size of refrigerators, clung to the mountain side, taunting us as to when they might catapult on top of us. The radio station blasted synthesizer-enhanced chanting with 1980s Sly Fox lyrics declaring "Let's Go all the Way," followed by a deadpan "Yeah, yeah, yeah." The lyrics or the beat or something caught my fancy, and I clapped and sang along. My dizziness receded. Charlie joined me singing as he swayed with his steering wheel. Doing so on the curved road was a bit frightening, but fun. Charlie winked, something I'd not seen him do for years.

Somehow, the sorority blackballing comment about my

appearing I wanted to "go all the way" flashed across my mind. In reply, I simply sang, "Yeah, yeah, yeah."

We'd made it to Jerome. It was difficult to believe that an unplanned, extended getaway had brought us to mile-high Jerome, Arizona, a city I had never heard of until I saw the sign. Population: small. A funky hippie enclave, the town clung to a dynamited mountainside with the same fierceness required by the residents who dubbed the place "The Wickedest City in the West." A stop at the visitor's center gave us the backstory. In the early 1900s, Jerome served as an opium den populated with rough and rowdy gold, copper, and silver miners. A tourist brochure explained that "in 1953, after seventy years of belching copper and iron ore, more than $800 million worth, Jerome's 1,900-foot-deep shaft closed, leaving a scarred patch of earth. A few got rich—the rest got shafted."

As we pulled into town, I belted out, "Well, I don't know about getting rich, but I sure know about getting shafted."

Charlie's shoulders rose to meet his earlobes as he looked for a parking place in the middle of town. I'd pushed his buttons, and he was going off. "That's your trouble. You won't let go. Move on! Focus on your book project."

Round one of an all-too-familiar boxing match between the victim in me and the rescuer in Charlie began. On one side, Charlie hunkered down, waiting for a fired back verbal punch to defend myself. Instead, I stepped out of the ring. Maybe the clear mountain air had brought me to my senses. I did not admit it to Charlie, but he got it right. Yes, I got shafted like Jerome, and like this reinvented city, it was time for me to reinvent myself with a future free of victim stories. I thought I'd let go of old pain, but my loss still plagued me. It popped up in unexpected ways, and in unexpected places, like here and now.

Charlie parked the car and our discussion stopped as we strolled in front of quaint shops that had brought a new future to Jerome. Looking in the window of *Magdalena's Bazaar,* an assortment of creations from all parts of the world enticed me. In a corner, a mannequin stood, wearing a floppy straw hat over a red wig while holding a pink felt purse with multi-colored felt flowers sewn across the top.

I remembered that among the boxes stored in Oklahoma City, I had packed a similar felt purse purchased at the *Abhaya* boutique in Nepal. I wondered if they now exported their felt purses to shops like this.

Pulling Charlie's shopping-resistant arm through the door, we made our way inside, where we were welcomed, like best friends, by the woman behind the counter. Striking up a conversation seemed natural. In no time, I was telling this total stranger how I lost a dream job that took me to meet women who create treasures like the ones in her shop. I explained how passionate I was to support the powers and possibilities women hold, but I ran away rather than confront a force opposing my mission. Next, I told her about my book idea.

Melanie, the manager, found a break in my storytelling to launch into her own. She pushed her hair back off her face, suggesting she had nothing to hide, not her face, her feelings or her story.

"I love traveling. I go a lot to Mexico with my kids," Melanie told me. "We take wild bus rides and sleep in hammocks at small guesthouses. Along the way, I find treasures for the shop. And ya know what? I've never lived with a husband in all my life, but I have three kids I love to death, two boys and a girl. They're happy kids. The other day my son came home and told me, 'Mom, I've got my skateboard and my guitar. School is fine. And I don't know why, but I'm really happy.' His words mean the world to me."

I learned Melanie had four brothers, two junkies, and two in prison. She loved her brothers, but they were messed up by "violence and meanness" imposed by their father.

"In my family we were expected to do whatever my dad said," Melanie added, looking down as if remembering pain and torment from her past. "The cardinal family rule allowed my father to get what he wanted, no matter what. So, I learned how looking to male authority for approval and validation creates alcoholics, addicts, depression, and low self-esteem. Well, I don't like living by those rules. So, I've changed the rules in the way I live and parent. What happened in my childhood," Melanie declared, "won't happen to anybody I can protect!" She continued as if holding the same need to tell her story I held when coming into her shop.

"My mother," Melanie told me as shoppers browsed, "was taught that a woman must pretend to be content and must spout off whatever the man wants to hear." Melanie continued telling how her grandfather became a college professor while her grandmother was forced to leave school in eighth grade to help raise her younger siblings. Later her mother was forced to leave school for the same reason. "My grandmother and then my mother were expected to convince people they were well educated when forced to show up at college professor events." Later Melanie was expected to pretend by keeping secrets too. "The whole deal was about looking good and pleasing male authority and oh, my God."

After Melanie crossed her shop to help a customer, she picked up her conversation, telling me how she grieved that her grandmother and mother never came into their power. I was reminded of similar concerns for my mother, and at other times for myself. Though neither of us had lived the same horrors. The era of secrecy Melanie blamed for maintaining a status quo that held men at the top assured of their superiority no matter how they behaved.

"But things are changing, baby," she said, straightening items on a display shelf. "Now I say who I am to anybody who comes through the door. That's huge for me."

I was drawn into Melanie's words, especially the idea of women coming into our power.

"Women need to share instead of hiding and pretending to look good," she announced. "Anyway, I'm saying fear and not love is the prevalent thing. If we could break down fear, we could get somewhere."

I heard myself say, "Yes, let's!" At the same time, I wondered if I would ever possess Melanie's courage to speak my truth to whomever. To do so, I would need to disrupt a worn-out pattern of dimming down and feeling invisible in certain situations.

That's when Melanie spoke out. "Did you know the *Oxford Dictionary* defined the word feminine as 'weak' until 1994?

Was it any wonder I had found it difficult to claim my feminine power? I stood in the aisle and tried to feel the place in my body where my power might be stuck—where I often felt tight or anxious. Around my solar plexus, that was where I held it. I breathed deeply and noticed some release. I could bring tender love to the parts of me that lived in an old story. It was time for my mature self to give new meaning to those old limitations. Dislodging all my "stuckness" might take time, but the process had begun. Melanie's story gave me the impetus for new awareness.

About that time, a busload of tourists poured into the shop. Charlie looked happy to see I had gotten a story for my book. With mission accomplished in his mind, he motioned his readiness to move on. I turned toward the door. After offering my thanks to Melanie for her story and her contact information, I watched a disgruntled old man enter the shop shouting, "What sort of music ya got blasting?"

Melanie boomed back before reaching to turn up the music. "It's reggae. Listen up! It might be good for you."

We left as the upbeat, repetitive reggae lyrics conveyed rhythms of a world freed from oppression or containment of our potentials.

Next stop, the New Spin Laundromat a few blocks from Magdalena's Bazaar. After digging out a box of detergent and a bag of dirty clothes from the back of the Explorer, I marched with Charlie into the aging laundromat. We needed two washers and dryers because we both insisted on separating whites from darks. It was a ritual as sacrosanct as flossing and using deodorant or filing taxes

As I loaded whites into one washer and Charlie loaded darks in the other, something came over me. Thinking about Melanie's words sent a powerful zap to the center of my chest. "It's the same damn thing," I announced to Charlie. "Women are still victims of a plague, if we allow ourselves to tell ourselves we are not worthy or not enough rather than claiming our feminine power." Putting detergent in the washer, I watched a woman next to me. After throwing her clothes in the washer, she declared, "That's right, sister."

I nodded to the woman. "We require more than equal rights," I shouted as if standing behind a podium. "we need to use our voice. To stop listening to the demeaning voices in our heads. It's about compassion, connecting, relating, creating, listening, and intuiting, rather than always relying on logic, linear, scientific, black-and-white thinking and trusting only what can be seen and touched."

"Why are you making your speech in a laundromat? The world needs your voice on a big stage," Charlie demanded, while shuffling clothes. "Let's just get the clothes washed and get something to eat. I'm hungry. We can talk over a meal."

"You know how important women's empowerment is to me. This is not some 'stuff' I'm talking about. I'm talking about women and what we can accomplish for ourselves and for the world. It's huge. I must become more confident so I can join in the rise of the feminine."

"I agree," Charlie said. "Don't let anybody stop you."

My husband's reassuring voice and the sound of our jeans, towels and underwear spinning in the dryer echoed thoughts spinning in my head. I imagined myself as a woman who would not back down to forces holding me or any other woman down. At the same time, I could be kinder and gentler with myself and others. We each carry challenges and outdated stories.

Folding towels, I announced, "I vow to get braver and bolder and not just older."

"Let's get a beer and toast that thought," Charlie said.

13

THE SPADEFOOT TOAD

Organ Pipe National Park, Arizona 2001

I rode beside Charlie this morning as the Explorer glided on cruise control across the Sonoran Desert inside Organ Pipe National Park in southern Arizona. The last time I crossed a desert it was the barren, bone dry Sahara Desert outside Timbuktu. This time I was crossing the most lush and diverse desert in the world, one with rain and wet monsoons in summer and early fall. The moisture of this desert fed some of the most eerily beautiful and bizarre plant life imaginable, including the gigantic organ pipe cacti that gave the park its name.

Charlie and I spotted the National Park Service Visitor Center. Once inside, we met Laurie, a national park ranger, standing tall and welcoming with her olive-green slacks, khaki-colored shirt, and a wide, flat-brimmed hat. After introductions, Laurie asked why we happened to be here today.

"We're wandering around the country looking for our next act," I told her.

We heard how she and her husband felt stalled in life until they left their former careers when their kids left for college.

Working as Park Service rangers let them live close to nature. "We live in a trailer inside the park rather than in our big house in Houston. We like the life we've created. A time to discover new parts of ourselves and to leave other parts in the dust."

Laurie's passion about her work and her new life was contagious, and I resonated with "leaving old parts in the dust." I explained about gathering women's stories for a book and asked if she would like to be included. I heard a resounding positive answer which pleased but did not amaze me. As women we like to share our experiences and we especially like to be heard.

I embraced her passion about work and life. Charlie and I enjoyed having Laurie share more about herself while guiding us through the park. At one point she bent to dig her hands into the sandy soil, honoring it like sacred ground.

"I've discovered," she said, "how every rock, cactus, creature and even the desert soil holds a hidden world revealed through mindful presence. And let me tell you about one ancient amphibian—a bumpy, lumpy creature with exceptional survival skills. Searing heat in the desert brings the threat of death to the Spadefoot toad," Laurie told us.

The story continued as Laurie explained how the toad must descend deep into the darkness using spade-like projections on her hind feet to dig down into the earth. Once submerged in cool, moist desert soil, she remains buried and inactive for a year, or even two years. Down deep she stays, waiting for the right moment to emerge from darkness to light.

The call to surface comes after thunder and lightning signals the rains are arriving. Once pools of water have formed on the surface, the Spadefoot senses it is her time to emerge, to mate and to make tadpoles. This is how the Spadefoot toad legacy has continued for so long.

In our short time with Laurie, I'd collected another story as well as insight about following intuition regarding the right time to emerge. A book launch would be my moment to emerge. That process would take time and require moving past old mindsets. For now, I had another thought—waiting a year or two to mate sounded unacceptable.

Before leaving Laurie, I had a question, "What, what would you do if you had only one day to spend in the Sonoran Desert?" I watched Laurie's face. "I would cry," she said.

Back in the Explorer I took out my journal and wrote notes from my time with Laurie. At one point, I felt myself struggling with how I would connect the stories from this trip with my stories from other parts of the world. I had to trust. Somehow, I could discover how to create what my longing was telling me I desired and needed to do.

14

MOUNTAIN HIGHS

Jackson Hole, Wyoming August 2001

Weeks later, Charlie and I crossed the Rocky Mountain glacier-formed valley around Jackson Hole, Wyoming. We marveled at the majesty of the Grand Tetons. We watched a cobalt-blue sky peering at us through shimmering gold aspen leaves. Jagged, saw-toothed, snow-covered peaks presented their faces at 14,000-feet. Log pole pine forests added another element of beauty. I had the sense Mother Nature was pleased to have our company.

We proceeded along the road toward Jenny Lake Campground. By arriving in the early morning, we hoped to find a campsite the guidebooks said would set us back a mere six dollars a night. When we got to the camp, we had the luxury of selecting from many available sites. As we searched for our perfect spot, we waved at campers cooking breakfast or sitting back to enjoy the morning.

"What day is it?" I asked Charlie as I looked at the sky. He looked up, as if to think.

Who would have imagined a few months ago, when our lives were scheduled to the minute, that we'd be in a place like this, unaware of the date? Though unsure of the date, my rapid expansion from the person I had been to a rather unfamiliar new identity was for sure.

With a site chosen, our now tried and true camping skills allowed us to set up our campsite in no time. Next stop, Peterson Hole Mountain Resort to ride the aerial tram. From there we would catch a bird's eye view of the Tetons.

With tickets in hand, Charlie and I took the fifteen-minute ride to the top of breath-taking Rendezvous Mountain. As we stepped off the tram, we watched prospective paragliders haul their gear in preparation for gliding off the cliff. The process would happen in tandem with a trained instructor. It looked exciting. I thought Charlie would want to jump, but he passed. "Too expensive," he said without even knowing the cost. He held another concern. The one neither of us allowed entry into our consciousness.

An instructor modeled how to run with him to the edge of the cliff. After the jump, they would both sit back in the glider seat for a 4,139-foot flight to the valley floor.

There was one woman in the group. A brunette with her hair color likely coming from the same source as mine. Dressed in a navy warm-up suit with a sweatshirt that read "Grandma," she stepped into the jumpsuit provided.

The young instructor told her to practice running without hesitation. The grandmother practiced as told. I could sense her confidence.

I watched two men attempt the same practice run. In both cases the instructor asked them not to jump, out of concern they might hesitate at the edge.

To me, the men seemed humiliated. I had known what humiliation felt like. I suppose men feel it too when they're afraid or intimidated.

"Let's meet the grandmother," I said to Charlie. In the next breath, I approached her to ask if we could visit after her jump.

"Sure! I'm Kathleen. Let's meet down at the lodge."

I felt nervous watching Kathleen strap her harness to her instructor's.

"Ya gotta run to the edge without a thought of turning back," the instructor reiterated. "If you run and put your feet down to abort, you could abort both your life and mine."

It looked and sounded scary, but Kathleen nodded her head with assurance. The soon-to-glide grandma then took a breath.

A countdown began. They ran. They jumped. Off the edge they flew. Kathleen and her instructor flew in tandem as if both had grown wings.

I saw two become a single flying dot in a vast open sky. My stomach flipped at first, before my spirit soared. I enjoyed the beauty and wonder of the open parachute against the cloudless sky.

I picked up my camera and caught an image of the parachute descending through the air.

As I did so, an eagle soared above the canyon walls. My "mountain high" reminded me of another one.

It happened while I climbed with a Change of Possibility group onto the black rock incline of Mt. Chimborazo, a volcanic peak located within the Valley of Volcanoes, high in the Andean Mountains of Ecuador. Because of the bulge of the equator at the spot where Chimborazo rises, this volcanic mountain reaches closer to the heavens than any other place on earth, including the top of Mt. Everest.

Looking into the heavens from the side of Chimborazo, I watched in amazement as a huge bird spread its wings across the sky, lifted by warm thermal currents. What I witnessed was the majestic sight of a condor in flight.

Mesmerized, my eyes followed the graceful, powerful movement of the ten-foot condor's wingspan. The mighty bird put on a show for us as we listened to Juan Beingolea, the

Change of Possibility Ecuador country director, share an ancient Andean prophecy of two divergent paths taken by humans across eons of time.

"One path is the condor's," Juan announced, "representing intuition, heart, spirit, we call the feminine. The other path, the eagle's, represents the rational, the mind, the material, or the masculine."

Juan explained that the eagle would reign supreme for a very long time, becoming puffed up with false pride. The ways of the condor would be almost forgotten. However, in time, the prophecy says, the condor will rise, inviting the eagle and the condor to share the sky flying side by side. "Because the prophecy mentions only the potential for such an event, it's up to each of us to work for these mighty forces to fly together."

Forgetting about condors and eagles for a while, with Charlie by my side, I took the tram down to the lodge. Gathered at a table alongside Kathleen and her husband, we introduced ourselves to her husband as he beamed with pride, resting his arm around his wife's shoulders. It was beautiful to watch the two of them together. No competition, only connection. Maybe like two condors, Kathleen and I had, in our own ways, encouraged our eagles to share space with us.

As with Melanie and Laurie, I explained my idea for a book. Kathleen immediately said she wanted her story included.

"Jumping off a cliff is nothing compared to living life with its challenges," Kathleen said. "The unexpected is what challenges us. Like being with our daughter and her husband when their infant son, our grandson, underwent life-saving heart surgery."

I looked at Charlie and noticed how he looked away.

Kathleen continued. "Years ago," she said, "I served as a Catholic nun at a hospital in Zambia. Those women taught me true courage. Each day presented enormous challenges for them. It was a struggle to survive poverty and oppression while keeping their children alive."

"Yes, I've met many such African women and more in Asia and Latin America," I said. "My work in international development is where my belief in women's power was ignited."

I pictured Wariko, Florence, the mid-wife in Mali and... Suddenly, I pictured myself standing on the edge of something new and different. Doing so with confidence and feminine power. I would make it over my edge. I could leap and fly in tandem with my interest in supporting women to grow and evolve. Until time for another leap, I could stay curious and open to what might appear.

"By the way," I told Kathleen when it came time to say goodbye, "it was great to watch a woman pass the tandem test. So inspiring."

She grinned with a tall spine. As we prepared to leave, I said, "Kathleen, when I get my book written, the story of a former nun, wife, mother and grandmother who leaped over the edge will be included."

Later, in the Explorer, I took out my journal, put it on my lap with pen in hand to reflect on this glorious day and the time with Kathleen. Before words got onto paper, I stopped myself. In the past it had seemed easy to write in my journal. The words flowed because I never expected anyone to read them, but as I imagined putting them into a book, the all too familiar self-doubt crippled me. Who was I kidding? How could I become an author? Why had this old doubting narrative popped up again?

I pictured Cindy, the child in Morocco who felt shut out of her father's world, the one she imagined filled with big words and actions. This time, I stopped myself to disrupt negative self-talk and crippling "I'm not enough" feelings.

Out of the blue, my mind moved to another thought. I felt

the need to make a mental checklist of my must haves. My purse. My glasses. Did I leave them in the tent last night? My cell phone and phone charger. The camera. Are these things in my purse? What about my journal and a pen, my water bottle, sunscreen, and the map? Going through the irritating accounting of my stuff, I broke into a rush of heat, a big Yellowstone hot flash. "Quick, open the window. It's hot in here."

"What are you talking about? It's sixty-three degrees, for God's sake," Charlie retorted.

"I don't care. Roll down the windows, quick. I'm burning up. It's a hot flash. You have no idea."

Charlie submitted to my demand, hitting the window opener to lower the windows. A cool Yellowstone breeze blew over my face. I completed my mental checklist of essentials. Relief! Miracle of miracles, nothing was lost or left behind so far today. Now I could settle down for the ride. A couple of minutes later, I hit a button to close the window. I was cold. This hot, cold deal was as regular for me as the search for my stuff and my search for my true self.

Charlie looked over at me, shaking his head. I replied, "Another day with 24/7 blissful togetherness. We're gonna love it."

I pictured Kathleen and her instructor flying together in balance and harmony. I loved the feeling of Charlie and me also in harmony and balance. And I was reminded how much we must work for these forces to come into balance every-where.

15

FOAMING FUMAROLES

Yellowstone National Park, Montana 2001

Among the most extreme landscapes on earth, here lived a disproportionate number of the world's geysers, fumaroles, mud-holes, and hot springs. Norris Geyser Basin in Yellowstone National Park welcomed Charlie and me that morning.

While hissing hot springs, gushing geysers, foamy fumaroles and a faint mist rose from multi-colored geothermal formations, my feet touched the earth's crust. Standing at the place on the planet closest to the earth's melted magma core, forces under my feet had caused rocks to break up, releasing pressures that melted magma and created steam shooting into the sky. Here we could witness geyser power surging from earth's deep center.

All around at Morris Geyser Basin turquoise water hit mustard and chocolate-colored mud banks ringed with cream-colored mineral deposits. My lungs filled with spewing sulfur dioxide. The pungent sulfur odor fused with a sweet pine scent. An eerie, bizarre, beautiful sight. The shifts and changes and breaking apart inside geysers and fumaroles reflected similar forces operating inside me. Maybe I was cracking up, or maybe I was waking up and finding ways to release my feminine powers from entrapment in old stories. In either case, I was reminded of another waking up moment in a place where I inhaled pine tree aromas wafting through the air.

My W.O.W. group and I had come to a tiny mist and cloud-covered community called Bramadero Chico, located high in the Andean Mountains of Ecuador. Quichua villagers, young and old, welcomed us as they prepared for a long-awaited tree distribution ceremony. We waited, privileged to witness what was about to unfold.

Before the ceremony, a young schoolteacher showed us the nursery where hundreds of tree seedlings had been planted inside reclaimed plastic soda bottles. Growing healthy and strong, the seedling had benefited from the organically enriched local volcanic soil. Her students had planted, monitored, mulched and watered their seedling as a school activity. The impressive collection, placed on shelves outside a one-room, mud-brick schoolhouse, allowed the teacher to share a concept known as "spiritual ecology." Children planted native trees rather than imported pine and eucalyptus trees that depleted the soil and required much water. The seeds and trees were recognized as sacred gifts from Mother Nature, to be revered and cared for so they could restore damaged lands.

Dressed in red ponchos and tall rubber boots, the dark eyed, dark-haired Quichua children had waited months for the first signs of growth to appear. At long last, the children's native tree seedlings had sprouted leaves and were ready for distribution to their mothers, who would replant and care for the life-giving gifts.

On the grassy hillside where the tree distribution ceremony began, men with felt fedora hats and sky-blue ponchos produced hauntingly beautiful music. Some played flutes.

Others strummed their charangos—small Andean guitars made from armadillo backs. Tomato-red, poncho-draped young boys, sporting black felt wide-brimmed hats, performed a traditional circle dance. Their mothers, draped in turquoise ponchos and brown felt fedora hats, showed their beaming faces.

The Andean music and dancing connected my heart and mind to wonders and blessings from Pachamama, the Andean Mother Goddess. Breathing the mountain air allowed me to sense her Sacred Feminine presence.

After the festivities, the ritual distribution of the seedlings to the mothers began. I watched as Rosita Llumionono waited to receive her precious gift. Her sun-parched face and deepset eyes looked toward the ground and then up to the sky as she spoke in Kichua, the language of her Incan ancestors. (A separate people from the indigenous Andean group who speak Kechua). An English speaker translated how grateful Rosita was for the seedlings she was about to receive.

"They will grow tall," Rosita said, "returning oxygen to the lungs of the land. They will protect my soil from the wind. Someday, the tree roots will keep the soil from spilling to the bottom."

After breathing the Andean air into her lungs, the same way in which the lungs of the land must do, Rosita continued, "I labor each day so my land will produce for my children. If I care for my small plot and my trees, one day I will have shade over my land. I'll provide the necessary labor, and Pachamama will bless my efforts."

Rosita said she dreamed of land filled with green, fertile, mature trees, replacing those long ago cut for fuel. As she spoke, this mother glanced toward the child on her back. "My daughter must go to school to learn the things I never had a chance to learn. I struggle," Rosita declared with a determined voice, "for my infant daughter and for my other children. I now have three children who have grown up on this land. Also, two children in heaven."

Rosita's tender voice, powerful words, and strong composure touched me deeply. Her challenging life, her joy in the moment, her openness gave me wider appreciation for the gift of life. I sensed seeds of hope for a new day for us and for the planet. Goals encompassed in the work W.O.W. members supported, I looked down to appreciate the dark, rich soil that fiery volcanic flames had enriched for those like Rosita to preserve and use to nourish new trees for the community.

Rosita explained how she learned to plant and grow trees and crops without using poisonous chemicals. "Next time you visit, life will be better," Rosita promised. "Fewer children will die from curable diseases. When they grow up, they will not migrate to the cities. This is my hope. I want my children to stay here on our land and in our mountains."

Rosita's words mirrored a life-positive posture I wanted to live from. I was reminded of my hope that Abby would remain close—if not near in proximity, then close in love and affection.

A local leader gently placed half-a-dozen seedlings, each nestled inside a soda bottle, into the folds of the bright turquoise poncho draped around Rosita's body. I would cherish forever watching the grateful look on this mother's face. Underneath the gratitude, I could appreciate the concerns and conflicts that must plague her. Similar ones plagued me and our world. How to balance modernity with ancient wisdom? How to care for land and people? How to love and to let go? How to change and to preserve?

Bramadero Chico meant little-resting place, or tethering post, a name that beautifully described the community's gift to me. When centered, connected and tethered like now, I could remain calm, collected, and optimistic. At the same time, I was painfully aware of something missing from the frantic, satiated, materialistic world I had left at home. Affluence invaded our atmosphere, creating more dangers than ozone as our egos tried to rule.

Juan said we needed more "sumak kawsay," meaning good living in balance and harmony with ourselves and with the natural world. And he was right. High in the Andes I absorbed "sumak kawsay" while surrounded by long oppressed Quichua people who possessed a depth of knowledge and awareness about living in harmony with nature that I wished were more abundant in my country and in my life. The tree planting ceremony provided a ritual of connection with the sacredness of the earth, with the need to care for Mother Earth, to care for women, for the feminine and to heal the divide between nature and humanity and between men and women, between masculine and feminine energies. The story of Rosita and my Andean experiences would also become part of my book.

Today, years after traveling in Ecuador, I again experienced "sumak kawsay." This time I enjoyed Mother Nature's wonders—not in the Andes—but inside a basin where I watched living, spewing geysers, and bubbling fumaroles, ones surrounded by mountains, waterfalls, and Yellowstone's magnificent wildlife. Everything around me looked challenged like the Andes hillsides. Both the strength and the fragility of nature came to mind along with our responsibility to care for our earth home. Living in suburbia, I did not feel as connected to nature and to the necessity to preserve the wonders as I'd felt each day on this journey.

With Charlie beside me, I watched and contemplated. We had come far. Experienced much, seen much. I wondered what lay ahead. I was anxious to have time and space to reflect in my journal. Over the past six months I'd gathered twenty-five women's stories. I'd only invited one woman to share a story who refused, the others willingly wanted to add their story to my book.

16

CROSSING OVER

Canon City, Colorado, 2001

"There are lots of things we don't have control over, things like taxes, the weather and our relatives, but when it comes to pizza, we can each demand the very best." That's what it said on the back of the menu from Pizza Madness in Canon City, Colorado. Reading the menu made me laugh. I decided what applies to pizza applies to life. It's important to go after the best life can offer. The trick comes in deciding what the best is.

Charlie and I sat this afternoon inside a funky pizza shop on Main Street of an economically depressed town in the foothills of the Rockies. We were about to devour a mozzarella cheese pizza with a crispy crust. According to the menu, this place served the best pizza on the planet, and my first bite made me a believer.

Along with the pizza, I swallowed the notion that tomorrow we would bid farewell to the Rockies to enter the flat, open Kansas cornfields. It would be the path back to the Oklahoma plains, a place we left behind half a year ago. We'd lived without a home or jobs, without agendas or obligations.

We'd enjoyed laid-back living and exciting adventures as we looped back and forth around the country. It seemed hard to believe average, hardworking mid-lifers like us had pulled off such a magnificent getaway. I relived the delight of meandering without a plan while I looked at our Atlas and traced the thread connecting the random back roads we'd traveled. While reminiscing, I was struck by a song on the radio. Nellie Furtado's lyrics resonated, "I'm like a bird... I don't know where my home is, I don't know where my soul is..."

Nellie was singing about me. Despite discoveries on the road, despite new awakenings and soul stirrings, Charlie and I were living without a home or a plan for the rest of our lives. For a moment, the thought scared me as much as riding through a Haitian thunderstorm in the back of a pickup truck with no headlights. Or it did so until a soulful trust in life and in myself began to wedge its way up through my body to disrupt my limited thinking.

Crossing over Colorado's Royal Gorge Suspension Bridge, the tallest suspension bridge in the country, we were suspended over a mammoth hole in the earth's surface. Also suspended between the world of adventure and routine life at home. And we were suspended between the dominant masculine, linear, scientific way and the awakening feminine, circular, intuitive way with a chasm between the two. A plan for bridging and balancing the different worlds and ways hung suspended in the air. I recalled what Gail Sheehy wrote in *Silent Passages*: "On the other side we will be something different, but we have no idea what."

Could I dare imagine something different? How would Charlie and I create a new life and with a new consciousness? I wanted to live in balance and harmony with the natural world, using my voice to advocate for the changes that must come, but how? What work could I find? We had bills coming due. I had better get a resume ready to send to someone, somewhere. Words for my resume came to me. I jotted them in my journal as we drove.

Wild and crazy fifty-something. Absentminded. Impatient. People-oriented. Creative and curious wife and mother desires a great paying job allowing time to write what will surely be a best-selling book. Other benefits requested:

- *Flexible hours*

- *Health insurance, paid vacation and a pleasing work environment*

- *Work experience includes reporting to male bosses who failed to grasp my brilliance or to accept my imperfections.*

- *Kindly call to arrange an interview.*

With a resume rewritten for my new self, it occurred to me I wanted to respect the wonder of the life I was living. Alexander Pope's words came to mind. "Act well your part; there all the honor lies."

I'd found the feminine rising around the world and close at home too. One day I'd finish and launch my book with the same hope felt at the launch of the W.O.W. initiative.

After crossing the southeastern corner of Colorado, we headed down America's Highway, old U.S. Route 40, an east-west highway that would take us from Kansas to Oklahoma. The thought of heading back to Oklahoma City and ending our free-spirited journey tied my stomach in knots. Charlie said we were returning for the first University of Oklahoma football game of the season. But we both realized concerns for my parents' wellbeing added another reason to return home. And I longed to be closer to Abby in Dallas. Many days we could not even call her for lack of wireless service. But was I actually ready to return?

My practical side knew it was time to find a place to live. We were not dedicated to wandering into eternity, but why head back today? A little more time on the road wouldn't hurt. Or was I simply putting off the inevitable? With conflicting thoughts battling in my mind, a non-judgmental, inner voice I was learning to trust whispered, "Don't rush, be still."

The voice had it right, I decided. My parents had managed without us so far. I trusted they could do the same a bit longer. My sister was nearby in case of an emergency. And the first football game was two weeks away.

Without another thought, I shouted to Charlie, "Head east, not south. Don't go home. I'm not ready." My determination trumped my uncertainties as the words left my mouth. "I don't know where we're going, but don't drive to Oklahoma City, at least not yet."

Charlie turned his head toward me with a glare. As he did so, his frustrated energy bounced onto me. "Why can't you make up your mind? One minute you are freaking crazy with worry about your parents, about money and about wanting a job, a purpose, and a house. You're worried about Abby. Is she happy with her job? The next minute you're off on another tangent. It doesn't make sense."

"Life doesn't make sense in the logical way you are talking about," I interjected. "Logic needs to listen to intuition at times. Today is one of those times. Just turn off this road."

"Well," Charlie said with a calmer, but still annoyed tone. "Where do you suggest we go?"

"I have no idea. Just keep driving until I come up with an answer. I'm looking at the map now."

Charlie shook his head, turned the radio volume up, and drove east with no notion of where we were headed.

My body relaxed. I watched Charlie's shoulders drop before his lips turned up to form a slight grin.

Once again, we were on our way to who knows where. It felt good, or at least it didn't feel bad. From somewhere inside my scattered brain a quote memorized long ago surfaced. I repeated it to Charlie. "It's good to have an end to journey toward, but it is the journey that matters in the end."

I felt lighter basking in the freedom to roam, something I had less of an idea how to do before the start of our adventure. With the Atlas in my lap, I looked at it as if the roads on the pages were arteries and veins providing nourishing blood to my body.

Fort Dodge RV and Camping Resort near Dodge City, Kansas might not rank as a five-star resort, but it offered a cheap place to pitch a tent for the night.

"Honestly," I told Charlie, "I'd rather be at the Ritz Carlton rather than camping, but at least we're still on our journey."

"Why do you always want to be somewhere other than where you are? This is a good spot," Charlie said as he steered through the entrance of the "Camping Resort."

I imagined the owner built a tongue-in-cheek tribute to campers like us. Or perhaps the owner was serious about calling his business a resort. My camping negativity, intended somewhat in humor, showed I had not fully abandoned my City Slicker self. It also showed Charlie had nailed one thing for sure. For far too long, I had not been able to enjoy living in the moment. As we drove toward the entrance, I read aloud from a brochure describing nearby Dodge City as "a resting point for weary travelers, vagabonds, and unsavory characters."

"Sounds like a city after our hearts," Charlie replied as he stopped the Explorer in front of the registration area. I knew he also saw the humor in our circumstances. He would have enjoyed a five-star resort had it been in our budget.

While Charlie registered, I sat in the Explorer, imagining Matt Dillon from *Gunsmoke* inside at the counter with his rifle aimed horizontally, commanding unsavory dudes to "Get the heck out of Dodge." I also wondered if Charlie, after almost six months on the road, would appear to the guy at the registration desk, like one of the unsavory vagabonds Dillon wanted out of Dodge. Charlie returned in a few moments with a tent space assignment. I was anxious to pitch our tent.

After the sun went to sleep, I looked up to the sky. The waning moon meant the night was dark, allowing an unimaginable number of stars to show their brilliance. I felt connected to the web of stars that reminded me of an ever-expanding web of women bringing light to the world. I thought I had fallen out of that connection, but the connection with women and their stories had followed me across the USA. So many new stories I'd added. The strength of feminine connection had followed me as surely as the stars above had followed us.

I crawled into our tent and stretched out inside my sleeping bag. My eyelids closed as I snuggled close to Charlie before he slipped his body over mine. Great sex in a tent was not something I'd seen in any romance novel, but something worth experiencing.

About midnight, the winds began to hit the sides of the tent in a way we had not heard before. The tent shook. The next thing we knew, the whole thing collapsed on top of us. For some reason, Charlie and I looked at each other and laughed at our ridiculous situation.

Exiting the tent, we heard what sounded like a railroad train, or we thought it was a railroad train. Then the mood shifted from laughter to horror.

"Look," Charlie shouted, "a big funnel cloud headed our way." Grabbing what we could from the tent we hustled, not to a bar from "Gunsmoke," but into the registration center filled with anxious campers. We hovered near the TV listening to Dodge City tornado warnings. An employee with a cigarette dangling from the corner of his mouth and a tan cowboy hat cocked on his head told us to, "Find a table. Get under it. Wait to see if the damn thing touches down near here."

"Well, mighty fine," I told Charlie, my heart pounding. I put the stuff from the tent on the floor beside a table. It looked like we were caught in a real predicament, and I was the cause of it. Or should I say, as a woman, I assumed I was responsible for everything, even a tornado.

Part of me felt crazy scared, but part of me imagined my book with this story and many others, each with a life-positive outcome. For Charlie's part, he wrinkled his forehead as he spread our sleeping bags under a protective inside table-for-two.

I looked up from under the table. I saw a woman. She looked exactly like Miss Kitty from Gunsmoke. Same red hair. Same walk. Same sassy smile.

"Just checking. Everybody okay?" the Dodge City Camp Resort employee said.

"As women, we see ourselves as good caretakers of others," I told myself.

"I'm taking cover," Miss Kitty announced. "You're on your own now."

"And we must remember to 'take cover' ourselves," I said.

I loved this Miss Kitty's spunk. If it weren't for a possible tornado, I'd get her story. And that's when I recalled the woman Miss Kitty's character was based on was a real-life brothel owner. A role that must disappear from the work of women.

Gratefully, the funnel cloud did not touch down at the Fort Dodge Resort that night. We survived the threat as we had others. The next morning, once again, we loaded our gear into the Explorer. I examined the map, pressing my right index finger east across US-50. I envisioned flat, repetitive plains filled with water towers, gas stations and tired Americana. I announced, looking over at Charlie, "Guess what? I kinda have a plan. Let's head to Missouri on US-50."

"Okay," he said without hesitation. "Sounds good to me."

The familiar glow in his eyes suggested my unplanned plan worked for him. That moment, I realized how much I could learn from this man who took life as it came. At least he did so most of the time. It was only when I seemed out of sorts that he got irritated and befuddled, ever determined to fix whatever he imagined was bugging me. If I was fine, Charlie was fine.

As the day and the miles wore on, I looked out the window. What we passed bored me, but I kept quiet, trusting something interesting would appear.

To break up the monotony, I suggested we make a stop to walk beside an old Santa Fe railroad track. It was a strange thing to do, but I thought the exercise would do us good. I thought so until we had walked for a while, and I noticed Charlie struggling to keep pace.

My mind was jarred to a suppressed thought from a day about a year ago when Charlie returned from an annual cardiologist visit. In reporting the visit to me, Charlie said, "one of these days" surgery would be necessary to repair his heart valve. Having surgery too soon would not be good, putting it off too long would risk a heart attack or stroke. I felt his fear, but somehow after the shock of that day, Charlie and I placed the "one of these days" as a far-off day. Six-month checkups would be scheduled, but in between visits our lives would not be affected.

Now, as I watched my husband walking by the railroad tracks, I noted his heavy breathing. I could not push the doctor's warning from my mind. I had to admit I'd noted signs of his struggling to breathe at other times during our trip.

I dared not bring up the subject of surgery right now. Neither of us wanted to think about it. As if reading my mind Charlie interjected, saying, "I don't like this walk. Let's drive on down the road."

After a few minutes driving, Charlie leaned over from the driver's seat to read the map on my lap. "Pay attention," he announced, snarling. "And turn the map in the direction where we're going."

"Back off, buddy," I said. When I did so, I realized this time Charlie was not bothered by me. He was worried about himself, and I had reacted poorly.

"Well, you're supposed to be watching the map," Charlie continued.

"There's nothing to watch," I said. "Just one nothing after another. It makes it easy to slip into the map of my interiority where things are more interesting."

Ignoring my digression, Charlie added, "Don't forget you were the one who wanted to head this way," Charlie said.

"I know."

PART THREE

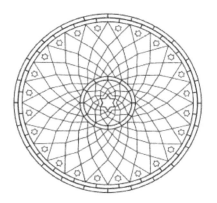

17
EUREKA!

Eureka, Missouri, 2001

A sign popped up near Eureka, Missouri. "Black Madonna of Czestochowa, Shrine and Grotto to the right."

"See that sign," I said. "Turn right! I wanna see the Black Madonna."

"That's ridiculous. The Madonna is in Poland, not Missouri," Charlie said, still out of sorts.

"Just turn at the next right," I insisted.

"Okay, okay. Since I'm driving Miss Daisy..." Charlie grumbled.

As we drove toward the Black Madonna, I wondered what pulled me toward her.

With the Explorer parked, we sauntered across a tree-lined, grass-covered path. No other people appeared. A stone wall caught my eye, one embedded with an amalgamation of seashells, marbles, costume jewelry and concrete-filled tin cans. Overall impression: we had come upon a tranquil folk-art grotto with shrines honoring various saints.

A steady mist covered us as we continued to wander. The sky turned dark.

"We're about to get trapped in a downpour," Charlie said.

Ignoring the possibility of rain, I read aloud from a faded wooden sign with letters of varying sizes. "Beware, the place you are entering is holy."

I giggled. So far nothing seemed holy to me, instead the place seemed quirky, but I had a feeling we needed to be here.

At the end of the trail, nestled among the trees, an outdoor chapel greeted us. An altar had been built in front of a mosaic wall that suggested flowing water. Above the altar hung a sorrowful, dark Madonna with scars, or perhaps tears, on both cheeks. She held her son with one arm.

A brochure on the altar told us this Black Madonna was a copy of a Byzantine icon displayed in the Jasna Gora Monastery in Czestochowa, Poland. The Eureka Black Madonna, like the Jasna Gora one, was covered with bronze and silver filigree metal called a riza that covered the painting, leaving only the hands and face of the Madonna and child exposed.

Since the site had been built years ago by a Franciscan monk from Poland, I wondered if he had carried the Madonna icon with him. The brochure did not explain.

"I told you she was Polish," Charlie announced. "I remember. My mother had a book about a Black Madonna in Poland."

Charlie paused to take a photo. He then stood as if transfixed by the Madonna's face.

I also connected to the somber, dark face of this mother as I watched tears fill Charlie's eyes. I took his hand. He began to weep. I'd never seen him like this. Almost unable to speak, he held back no emotion.

"What is it?" I asked, putting my face against his.

"My mother. She never knew you. She never knew Abby."

"Charlie," I said, holding him and the visceral threads that connected our lives. I felt his hurting heart. The depth of his grief, buried for so long. His long- repressed sorrow and grief had come to light. I gazed back toward the Madonna. When we enter pain, we touch what our hidden suffering reveals. I wrapped my arms around my husband and held him close.

In a moment, Charlie raised his chin.

"Is she speaking to you?" I asked, meaning both his mother and the Black Madonna.

Charlie lowered his head. His weeping lessened before he nodded without saying a word.

"Do you feel your mother's love? Her gift to you. She gave you the capacity to love. Abby and I are the recipients."

Charlie wiped his eyes. "Just seven years with her..." he said.

In a world filled with unspeakable loss, in a remote grotto off a rural highway, a painting of a Black Madonna, of Mother Mary from the Russian Orthodox tradition of Charlie's ancestry, connected him to his mother and to her love.

The dark face on the altar connected me to the strong, compassionate, dark feminine of Kali, to the Virgin of Guadalupe, to The Queen of Peace and Mercy, each image freed for me from religious dogma or attachment to any single religious tradition. I felt trauma and pain transformed. And I connected to my mother holding love for us in Oklahoma.

Had a divine guiding force brought us to the grotto? Or did we stumble upon it? Either way, we'd found renewal for the road ahead.

No more words were necessary as we drove towards home. Along the way, I reflected on the growth I felt we both had found. I was not the same woman of six months ago. The anger, the bitterness toward a boss I did not know how to speak up to had faded. I felt more emotionally, psychologically and spiritually mature, allowing myself more space to speak, to think, to feel and to be. I had realized self-validation that did not rely on others' opinions of me or of my work. I could confirm from experience that the Divine Feminine was present as a guide, wherever I roamed. Now onward toward what lay ahead.

18

SHOCK!

Oklahoma City, 2001

Charlie and I had situated ourselves on stools at my parents' kitchen counter, where we dipped our spoons into bowls of granola. It was about 8 a.m. on September 11, 2001, in suburban Oklahoma City. After a quest to discover a new significant life, I had landed in my parents' house, eating their food, and sharing with Charlie the bedroom and bath I had shared with my sister while growing up. This was not the script I intended for my new and expanded life; though, I had to admit, it was wonderful to have an indoor shower and toilet! And I was happy to see my parents in rather good health and I trusted new possibilities to express my gifts and talents existed.

In a few hours, Charlie and I were to sign a contract on a new home. I called the place "Casa Caca," a 1950s house in serious need of a facelift. Maybe somewhere inside the bones of the house, a cute cottage lay hidden. We both had assured ourselves we could create a "Casa Bonita." We planned to live in the house as we remodeled. Later we'd flip the place to buy another, repeating the process. The house remodeling idea occurred one day on our trip. Along a remote road, we came upon a dilapidated, abandoned shack with the roof caved in.

Charlie stopped to take a picture. He grabbed a hammer from his tool bag and posed as if knocking down the shack's front door.

"We'll put this photo in our trip album," Charlie said. "Call it, 'hammering out a new place and a new way to live.' That's what I'd wanna do."

We'd buy an inexpensive house in need of remodeling. Charlie would employ his engineering and project coordination skills. I'd handle design elements and write my book. We'd live in the house while the work was done. Later, we'd flip it and repeat the process with another house. As I thought about our plans, I smiled, picturing Abby situated in her Dallas condo, probably ready to start a workday at her lucrative sales job.

Now back at home, preparing for Abby to visit soon, I knew one of us needed a real job to pay for hammering out a home renovation and to pay for health insurance. Charlie's commitment to complete a remodel placed me in the position to land a paying job. My mind swirled with job possibilities when I heard the phone rang. It was Debbie. I missed her a bunch. I began to chat. In a shocked voice, she interrupted to ask, "Are you watching TV? A jet just flew into the World Trade Center."

What? I rushed to the television, shocked to see an American Airlines aircraft heading toward New York's Twin Towers. Our call ended.

While struggling over the next few weeks to comprehend the 9-11 events, I heard a chilling response from Jerry Falwell. From his pulpit, he declared the terrorist attacks were a punishment from God, with blame belonging to feminists, lesbians, and homosexuals. Pat Robertson echoed the thought, applauded by thousands.

While heartsick from the unconscionable 9-11 terrorist

acts committed in the name of a religion, my reactions intensified hearing the inflammatory words expressing other certainties from a different religion. Both ideas relied on blaming and shaming others. I wondered if on top of the religious, economic, cultural and political divisions, there lay a reaction to the rise of women?

And how had we arrived at this anger, hatred and demonology so opposite from the Christian mysticism of Saint Teresa of Ávila? Different from the Christian wisdom of Sophia I first gleaned inside the Hagia Sophia—a basilica that later served as a Muslim Mosque. Different from Muslim beliefs shared by the Sufi Iman in Timbuktu, or from the compassion and love Charlie and I experienced when present with the Black Madonna in Eureka.

I thought about Votna, a Muslim. Did she have a son or daughter she feared would be radicalized by Islamic fundamentalism? And I felt the intense pain of the LGBT community included in Falwell's blame for the terrorist killing of innocent people.

I placed my hands over my heart in remembrance of the tragic loss of human lives. I realized in that moment that my travels had helped shape my perspectives, ones different from those shared by many Americans. The tensions inside me from this realization I would have to endure along with the gifts of awareness.

As time passed, both the 9-11 atrocities and U.S. threats of war and revenge had become a new reality. Through our shock and pain, Charlie and I had made the move from my parent's house to the house we named "Casa Bonita." I admired the look of the master bathroom with bright, white tile rather than the cracked and faded 1950s pink tile. No longer would there be a nonfunctioning wall-mounted heater.

A new sink, toilet, tub, and lighting made me imagine our bathroom in a magazine showcasing cottage makeovers.

Tonight, after much struggle and disappointment about jobs, I felt certain I would be offered a position with *Women Unlimited*, an organization dedicated to professional training and empowerment for women. The work hours were flexible. I would have time to write, and they offered health insurance. After a second interview, I knew the committee would appreciate my skills and abilities and would offer me the position. The Chairman of the Board assured me he would call the winning candidate soon. I was about to end my job-hunting hassle. I heard the phone ring and imagined my new workplace. I prepared to thank the caller for offering me the position.

The deep voice of the Chairman of the Board sounded in my ear. "Hello, Cindy. We appreciate your interest in our organization, but we're sorry to inform you we've decided to hire another person for the director's position. I wanted to thank you for.... blah, blah, blah."

The words crushed my spirit. I hung up. In my mind's eye, I saw thirteen job rejections standing in a pile beside gobs of resumes forwarded without any response. My battleship had sunk. I had value, but I couldn't prove it. Nothing was working. All the guides and aids had disappeared. I was scared and numb. How could running away for a wonderful quest land me without a job or an encore act? It was frightening to be unable to find a job at the point when I was becoming my most powerful and capable shelf. Had I aged out? Was I used up? Should I plead for a job, declaring if hired I wouldn't get pregnant? A tidal wave of worthless feelings overwhelmed me as in the past. All optimism and illusions were gone. I couldn't pick myself up this time.

I thought about the 9-11 widows and widowers, and the mothers and fathers who lost husbands or sons or daughters

---

in the 9-11 bombing. My issues were nothing in comparison to theirs. Maybe I was not as strong as they were or as determined as Gopal and Saraswati in Nepal, Mary Marunga and Koyati in Kenya, or as resilient as Madame Sofana and Jean-Claude in Haiti, or as assertive as Melanie in Jerome, Arizona or....

Suddenly, the voice of a woman I met in a little shop in Andes, New York, came to me. The voice was Brooke's. Charlie and I wandered into her shop, Brooke's Variety, on our drive through upstate New York. Brooke spoke to me as soon as we entered. "What brings you to Andes?" she asked, our wandering hippie status obviously on full display.

"We ran away to see the country about six months ago," I said.

Brooke, the owner, looked surprised and said, "Really? I ran away too. Not long ago. Brought my husband along. I was overwhelmed. Depressed."

"Seriously?" I said. "I'm gathering women's stories for a book. I'd love to add yours."

"Well, here's mine," Brooke told me as she arranged items on a shelf. "I'd struggled to maintain a diminishing career as a Hollywood actress. The stress and depression became unbearable. That's when I took a decisive step. I called my agent. Quit my work as an actress. Left New York City for this small, economically challenged town of Andes."

"Interesting," I said, lit up by her story. "We quit our jobs too. And sold our house. We have no idea what's next."

Brooke nodded, as if she knew the feeling. I heard how she and a friend, another former actress, had gone to work reinventing themselves as female entrepreneurs. Each opened a shop along Main Street in what was once a prosperous farming community. Others had followed their lead. Andes had taken on a new life.

"The second you take the first step; you cannot believe

how fear blocks you... It's the identity crisis that's hard. It's a public persona that you work at maintaining. For me, success included a good seat in a restaurant. And giving that up was hard, very hard."

Now with my challenged feelings oozing from my body despite a comfortable "Casa Bonita," I repeated the words. "Identity crisis." Brooke named it. I never imagined it would be such a challenge to let go of my public persona. The notion did not occur while we prepared to hit the road back on that Friday the 13th. Before we both quit our jobs, I had relied on my work, a nice home, the security of health insurance and money in the bank. I envisioned making the world a better place for women. I had not realized how much my ego wanted recognition in the process.

During months on the road, without the trappings of our former life, I had relished the adventure. Life felt sexy and exciting, full of endless possibilities most days. But after months sleeping in tents and roaming like gypsies, I expected we would magically create a new life with the same amenities enjoyed before running away. Living without my equivalent of "a good seat at a restaurant" was never my intent. I had lost my identity. Without a job or health insurance or evidence that I had a purpose waiting to be manifested, how could I cross the scary line Brooke talked about? What was my equivalent of Brooke's Variety? What was my new story?

Almost as if Brooke were standing beside me, I imagined her voice encouraging me, "Cross the scary line. We've all got to face our fears. Trust your deep inner knowing. Shift how you tell your story to yourself. Take the next step."

19

A CALL GIRL

Oklahoma City, 2002

As I drove this morning through the lower level of the Oklahoma Health Science Center parking garage, I searched for a parking place. With the launch of the war on terror, the radio blasted an orange alert, warning all Americans to be on the highest state of awareness for suspicious-looking characters. Remembering Timothy McVeigh's 1995 Oklahoma City Murrah Building bombing reminded me a bomber could look like the kid next door.

Despite the high-alert government warnings with instructions to screen mail for suspicious letters, I tried to take a step forward without adding anxiety about my career to the political and cultural anxiety of a post 9-11 world. At least, I had landed a job with a small salary and insurance. Since I was working in the Health Science Center's call center, I secretly called myself a call girl, though I knew what a disrespectful label this was for the hardworking women earning an honest day's pay in the call center. I also realized the term "call girl" was an awful term for the victims of trafficking.

Josephine, my boss, had planned her staff meeting for later

this day and expected each of us to attend. Before the meeting, some twenty-five female employees would begin completing random computer-generated calls to collect information from Oklahoma citizens about their health.

Despite pep talks to myself, I felt of no value in this job. The work embarrassed me. It proved I had not lived up to my potential. Once situated inside my cubicle, I forced myself to push the computer button to bring up yet another random phone number. When the person I called answered, I read the text from the screen beginning with, "Good morning, my name is Cindy. I'm calling from the University of Oklahoma Health Science Center. I'm gathering information about your family's health...."

I heard from the other end of the line the easy to recognize voice of Mary, from my Bunco group. I hadn't told her about my new job. I hung up and vowed never to mention the random call to her. False pride maybe, a crazy response for sure, but the unempowered mindset I had fallen back into held me hostage. It was pathetic.

I should have appreciated working for my boss. Josephine Gibson was one sharp fifty-something woman. Firm, fair, intelligent, dedicated, and caring, she listened to her staff. When she directed us to the conference room, she did so dressed in a professional gray suit, silver earrings and high heels. While we found our seats, Josephine adjusted a TV monitor and VCR as if to assure every detail had been attended to before our meeting began.

Standing at the front of the room, after sipping water and clearing her throat, Josephine began the meeting. None of us knew what to expect.

"Good morning to each of you," she said. "Thank you for being here and for arriving on time. Thank you also for your dedication..."

Josephine further explained we would begin a different

survey next month and would be expected to complete the required number of surveys each week. Longer and more involved, the new survey would gather data indicating how many Oklahomans had communicable sexual diseases, like herpes or HIV.

Oh my gosh, I could not possibly ask people if they had herpes or HIV.

With a softer tone to her voice, Josephine moved to another topic as she acknowledged we each might have personal challenges at home. No matter, it was imperative that we meet our department's survey goals. To that end, she wanted to ensure we had ample encouragement and support.

Josephine reached over to turn on the TV monitor and VCR. I wondered what she was about to show us. Drums, cymbals, and brass instruments sounded. On the screen appeared Egyptian pyramids and hieroglyphics. A voice boomed. It repeated words spoken by the ancient pharaoh sorceress Hatshepsut speaking to Isis, the Egyptian Goddess of a Thousand Names. My imagination flew back to Egypt. What I saw was most unexpected in a staff meeting.

"Oh, Mighty Queen," Hatshepsut's words declared on the video, "with this amulet you and your descendants are now endowed with the mighty powers of the animals and the elements. You will soar as the eagle soars and you will be a mighty foe of evil, the champion of truth and justice."

I was watching a 1970s TV series, starring Andrea Thomas as the super-heroine. Wearing go-go boots and a mini skirt, she could save lives and stop crime. In this episode, Andrea, an American school teacher, had arrived in Egypt for an archeological dig where she discovered a magic amulet once worn by the Goddess Isis.

We watched Andrea lift the amulet, attached to a chain. When she placed it around her neck, she became a dual person, Andrea Thomas, and the Mighty Goddess.

How pathetic that today the name of the Islamic State, abbreviated and known to the world as ISIS, could in any way be equated with the Goddess Isis. Her strength, her feminine energy and power represented that which is most despised by fanatic fundamentalists. Isis, the goddess, must be remembered and honored.

With the amulet glowing on the screen, a teacher raised her arms to the sky and declared, "O Zephyr winds that blow on high; lift me now, so I can fly...."

Right there, Andrea seized the full power and glory of the ancient, revered Egyptian goddess. An ordinary woman transformed into an heir to long-lost feminine secrets, powers, and abilities.

Sitting in a staff meeting facing a TV monitor, something magical happened to me as it happened to Andrea. I watched the schoolteacher with her arms raised. My eyes opened wide. My spirit soared, lifting me from my black leather chair while also lifting me from my black despair. Me, Cindy Hollingsworth, also an ordinary woman. Right here, right now, while working in a call center, I was in touch with extraordinary secrets of the universe, including ancient goddess wisdom. I felt the power, potential and strength of each woman in the center and of each woman whose story I had collected. My co-workers' faces appeared as ignited as mine.

I vaguely remembered watching the 1970s TV series with Andrea Thomas as I left for college, but I didn't know how to call up such powers and energies back then. Today, as my spirit lifted, I claimed ancient secrets as *my* secrets. I could fly above negativity and limitation and disappointment. Today, ancient wisdom had been revealed to me as it was revealed to a schoolteacher on an archeological dig. I'd been living inside a setback, a time of falling into negativity and discounting my capabilities, but today I moved forward. My setback did not equal the impossibility of getting back on my path.

I was no longer looking at an archetype of the sacred feminine that dwelled outside of me. I held feminine power inside me. I held a spark of the divine, the light, the power given to me and to all of us, if we will claim it as our truth.

The staff meeting became a blur, but when it concluded, I thanked Josephine for what was shared. I pictured her as an embodiment of the Black Goddess Isis standing in her power, modeling the same for us all. Another moment never to forget.

When I moved back to my cubicle, I imagined donning a lost amulet. Something magical, like the magical earrings I wore for one moment as a child in Casablanca, and like ones I wore today.

Before making calls, I stood and raised my arms with my palms turned toward the sky. "Oh, Mighty Goddess," I announced without hesitation or dimming down, "here we are ready to rise, women telephone interviewers, heirs to hidden powers. We have energy, intuition, creativity, inner strength and wisdom to share."

Women seated at their desks, preparing to make calls, looked at me. A woman named Destiny grinned before clapping wildly. In a few minutes, the room burst into hoots and hollers. Our team looked psyched and ready to go. No more dimming down or putting ourselves down. Josephine cheered us on.

I took my seat, ready to push the computer key to dial the random phone numbers. During this ritual, I heard footsteps. I looked around to see Josephine standing behind my cubicle. "I like your style," she told me with a pat on the back. "Now, how 'bout sharing what you know with a new employee. I need you to train Marisol Velazquez so she will be as proficient at her job as you are."

Until today, Josephine telling me I was proficient at my job would have been about as pleasing as learning I had eczema. That's because I viewed working here as beneath me. I would have scoffed at being asked to train someone for this job. However, owning my dual role as a call center employee and an heir to the secrets of the Goddess of a Thousand Names, I accepted Josephine's request. Today I would take pride in doing a common job uncommonly well. I did have something to share. The Oklahoma Health Science Center would serve my needs and training a new employee would be a chance to champion a new employee.

"I'd be pleased to support Marisol," I said. "I'll give my best to help her become her best."

"Good," Josephine said before revealing that Marisol and her two-year-old daughter lived in a battered women's shelter where they had fled after Marisol had endured beatings and abuse from her husband. The shelter director had recognized a bright, capable woman who needed a job with a chance for a better life. She called Josephine to see if there might be an opening in her department. Needing additional callers for her team and touched by the young woman's situation, Josephine decided to give Marisol a chance.

But Marisol failed to appear for her first day of work. She returned to the shelter when fear caused her to leave the line to catch the bus. Marisol later called, asking Josephine for a second chance. She confessed her fright about leaving her daughter behind combined with a fear of failing to complete the training.

I imagined the courage it must have taken Marisol to call after not showing up. Josephine agreed, telling me she empathized with Marisol because years ago she had to leave an abusive husband and raise a child on her own. Understanding the fear of failing at a desperately needed job, Josephine allowed Marisol a second chance, with the understanding that no employee could become a permanent hire without completing the training.

Marisol's story tugged at my heart. I'd seen women around

the world and their burdened lives. I could not forget how fortunate I was to live my privileged life.

I met Marisol Velazquez, her upper lip quivering. Her dark eyes likely filled with horrors I preferred not to imagine. Wanting to connect, I said, "So, tell me about your home."

"I'm from Oaxaca, Mexico," she said in a monotone.

"I've been to Oaxaca! I can picture your homeland." As I spoke, I sensed a strong, bright woman as well as a young woman who had endured much trauma.

Marisol replied with a tight smile while speaking with a hushed voice describing how a couple brought her to the United States, claiming her as their daughter. How she was forced to live with the couple. To work as their unpaid maid.

How could this have happened to this lovely woman?

After suffering three years in a deplorable situation, Marisol fled with nothing but the clothes she wore. Soon she met the man who became her partner and the father of her daughter. Before Marisol's daughter was born, this partner began abusing her. The abuse escalated when he drank and became worse after the baby was born.

"A month ago, after three years of torment," Marisol told me, "I declared no more and fled with my daughter. We walked miles to a women's shelter, the one I saw on a flyer at the drugstore."

"And now you have come here for a job and safety. No one can enter this space without approval. Here we care about each other," I said, filled with such intense emotion that I had a hard time speaking.

My mind drifted for a moment. When I had slumped in the stairwell this morning, feeling sorry for myself, I would never have imagined meeting Marisol and feeling a connection and desire to sponsor her success.

Wanting to see Marisol relax, I said, "I have a daughter. Tell me about yours."

The softening of Marisol's face assured me a connection between two mothers with daughters had begun.

"Would you like to start the training again?"

Marisol listened, but showed little reaction. I forged ahead. "If a person answers a call, you will read questions from the health survey." I acknowledged she could expect reluctance by some to complete the process. "To encourage participation, we note the information is critical to improve Oklahoma's health care delivery."

Marisol stared as if inside an executive suite and told to run a business or be fired. I noticed her shoulders slump. The wounded woman's somber expression seemed to reflect the fears that sent her back to the shelter from the bus stop before her first day of work. How could I assist this wounded soul?

"I struggled to learn the system," I told Marisol. "I didn't believe I could do what I heard other callers do. I felt incompetent. Embarrassed. I wanted to quit. To run away. But it got easier."

Hours passed as the training process proceeded. Marisol floundered. She hesitated to speak. I wondered if her English fluency was sufficient for her to learn the script. Maybe she had taken on too much, but without a job, her future looked grim. Tension was etched in creases across Marisol's face, like what I felt when doubting myself.

Time to change tactics. "Enough for today," I said.

I told her about the 1970s TV series showing a schoolteacher transforming herself into the Mighty Goddess Isis and claiming her power to rise high.

I showed Marisol how I had closed my eyes and imagined claiming the same power. Marisol looked at me in a way difficult to interpret. Maybe I was talking too much and maybe she wished I would stop.

"Marisol, go be with your daughter," I said. "We'll start again Monday."

The moment the clock above Josephine's desk showed five o'clock, Marisol and I parted ways. I wondered if I would ever see this struggling young woman again.

Back at work Monday morning, I did not expect to see Marisol. I wondered what more I could have done to help her. Perhaps it was all too much. If she lacked the ability to read English with ease, how could she learn the script well enough to read it convincingly?

However, when I looked over my shoulder, I saw Marisol sitting at her desk. I was shocked. She looked rested and calm, with different presence than on Friday.

"Good morning," I said. Not knowing what else to say, I asked, "Do you want to continue the training?"

"Yes," she replied, " but I'm nervous."

"I understand. The process scared me too. But you can do it," I said.

"Hello, my name is Marisol," I heard her say tentatively after opening her computer and making a call. Marisol's voice trailed off. She paused, then spoke again. "I'm calling on behalf of the Oklahoma Health Science Center to help establish Oklahomans' health needs..."

With a soft voice, Marisol continued. The person on the other end responded, indicating Marisol had conveyed the importance she gave the call. A breakthrough. A magical moment.

Marisol completed a second interview with another caller. This time she completed the survey in Spanish. Josephine needed a caller with Spanish fluency. Another call followed in English. When that caller hung up, Marisol simply noted this on her sheet and placed another call.

"Your confidence, and your voice..." I said. "You've got this. You can do this!"

I thought how I was a woman who calls myself and all women to claim our best selves. My purpose was not out there somewhere. It was here with me now. I could reveal my purpose by how I show up each day.

During our morning break, Marisol came to my cubicle. She placed a hand-written note on my desk. "Thank you," the words read above her signature.

Tears collected in my eyes. Something wonderful was happening to Marisol and to me. I could imagine zephyr winds blowing, allowing us to fly high. I hugged Marisol and paused before we continued our work—the work of women on our way.

20

THIS CAN'T HAPPEN

Oklahoma City, October 2005

This can't happen. A visit to the cardiologist for an echocardiogram brought the shock that Charlie needed immediate open-heart surgery to replace his faulty aortic valve. Without surgery, he was at high risk of a stroke, heart attack, or death. Reaching deep to access my newly claimed wisdom and power, I remained focused. Charlie resisted what he was told. I understood. A surgeon would be required to break open Charlie's ribs, remove his heart, hook it up to a machine and make repairs as if his heart were a part of an old car. My husband, averse to self-pity, looked at me with searching eyes.

With Charlie facing a heart condition like the one that took his mother's life, I could sense how much he wished he could stay inside his male stoicism story, but that story was not his to live anymore. Today fear and uncertainty covered his face.

As we held each other in a surgeon's office, I realized it fell to me to muster the courage to tell my husband his surgery must happen. This strong rock, optimistic, charging forward and believing he could fix anything, a tough, self-reliant soul had to allow a surgeon to fix what he himself could not fix.

There was not a do-it-yourself kit for heart valve replacement. Charlie's resistance continued in the hospital even while he waited stretched out on a gurney with his blue and white stripped cotton hospital gown tied down his back. Moments before being wheeled away, he had a chance to refuse the surgery.

Glancing at his down-turned eyes, I rubbed Charlie's forehead. "Lie down, Honey. Close your eyes. Let's trust the surgeon. Soon you will have a heart as good as new."

In a minute, Charlie shut his eyes. I watched as he was moved down a sterile hall past the surgical area doors.

Eight months ago, Abby and Blake, her boyfriend of three years, had announced they wanted to get married

"You both have good heads on your shoulders. This is great news, and it's time," Charlie told them as he shook Blake's hand that exciting day. I nodded and hugged them both.

The past months had been a whirl of wedding planning with their wedding day set in our own backyard six weeks from today, surgery day.

I sat in the waiting room with Abby and Blake for a couple of hours before something strange happened. Before we expected the surgery would be over, Charlie's surgeon walked into the waiting room. He pulled off his cap. As he stepped toward, I lowered my eyes to avoid meeting his eyes. I saw blood splattered blue "baggies" covering the surgeon's feet. Why was he back so soon? What happened? Was Charlie all right?

21
MAGICAL

Oklahoma City, November 2005

"Everything was perfect!" Charlie said.

Alone, side by side, Charlie and I stood together inside a flower-filled tent in our own backyard. We sent Abby and Blake off on their honeymoon before saying goodnight to about a hundred family and friends gathered to celebrate a beautiful wedding inside a tent in the backyard of our newly renovated home.

On a magical November night, Charlie and I could celebrate on our own. We stood under the light of a wrought iron chandelier hung from the top of a wedding tent that rose over our grassy, tree-lined backyard, behind the home we called "Chateau in the Woods." Abby and Blake had insisted our backyard would be perfect for their wedding. It turned out to be a wonderful place to celebrate, exactly six weeks after Charlie's successful open-heart surgery.

After the ceremony, the reception, the toasts, the dancing, after the guests had departed, slices of the bride and groom wedding cakes remained on the table where Abby and Blake had cut into them earlier. I never tasted one morsel of cake. Everything happened so fast, only now could I relive and savor the evening.

Holding Charlie's hand, I felt the love we'd shared all these years. "Watching you and Abby dance," I said. "That moment I'd describe as about the happiest of my life." Charlie beamed ear to ear.

I relived the energy, the tenderness and the fun of dancing tonight with Blake, with Charlie and a dance with Daddy, too.

"I love you, Daddy," I told my father as we danced together for the first time since Haiti. Daddy replied, "I love you too." It seemed so natural to hear the magnificent words I'd waited until my sage years to hear. Why had I waited these many years to say three words that encouraged Daddy to say what I needed to hear?

Mother looked radiant, wearing her pearls and a soft beige silk dress. I thought of how much she had poured herself into the life of our family. I had been fortunate to have the parents I was born to. Though it had taken years for me to feel close to Daddy, a connection was happening along with a deep level of appreciation for my mother.

Crickets and rustling leaves echoed outside the tent. Along with these sounds, I heard slow blues, jazz, and folk-infused guitar echoes around the empty tent. Norah Jones's sultry voice sang, "Come fly away with me." The song was a gift on the CD Abby and Blake gave their guests.

I thought about how far and wide Norah's combo of sounds had traveled. How they combined Western folk rhythms with the powerful South Asian and North American heritage of Nora's voice and lyrics. The magic of Charlie having been part of our daughter's wedding and now with me sank in as Norah sang. Charlie put his arms around me the way he did the first time we hugged and kissed.

"Let's dance," he said.

As our feet moved over the grassy tent floor, I rested my head on Charlie's chest. His rhythmic heartbeats sounded in my ear, igniting an unimaginably beautiful feeling inside my heart.

"I was thinking..." I said.

"What were you thinking?" Charlie asked without waiting for a reply. Instead he jumped in to say, "I was thinking that I never asked what this affair cost, but whatever. It was worth it!"

My thoughts flowed past thoughts of money. "Abby and Blake were married tonight, and it felt like we were married all over again. A sacred marriage," I said.

"Hmm," Charlie said, bending down to pick up a linen napkin left on the ground.

I talked about the sacred marriage between the King and the Goddess Inanna. With their union came renewal. The Isis and Osiris myths in Egypt told the same story. How I experienced our own version of a sacred marriage with the mature masculine and mature feminine uniting. Shiva and Shakti joining. God and Goddess. Yin and Yang.

"Is that like Jack Sprat and his wife who could eat no fat? Together they licked the platter clean?"

"Oh, come on! You understand," I said. "I'm talking about uniting not only as male and female partners but uniting the gifts of the masculine and feminine principles and energies."

"I get it," Charlie said as he led me from the tent to our bedroom.

As we walked into the house, for some reason, a completely different thought jumped into my mind. "Where should we go next?"

"How about Mumbai? Or Dubai? Or Shanghai?" Charlie said with no hesitation and with a glee I had not seen in his eyes for a long while.

22

WITHOUT WORDS

Dallas, Texas, 2015

I called Abby. "You should come soon." That's all I said.

It wasn't long before Abby, Blake, and our six-year-old grandson Stanton arrived at our home. The downsized house on Ivygate Circle we bought after a move to Dallas from Oklahoma City. It had been a good decision to move here. New friends and being close to Abby, Blake, and Stanton.

Together, the four of us made our way into the bedroom where Charlie lay asleep. The hospice nurse stood close by. For several hours Charlie had not changed position or spoken a word. I assumed my husband was resting in a liminal space. Perhaps the space comforted a body worn-out from a long heart disease battle. Everyone knew how much Charlie loved life. He wanted to watch Stanton grow up. To share the future with us. But he'd come to accept that was not to be his future.

I could not imagine life without Charlie, though I had not allowed myself to dwell on that reality. Yes, end-of-life issues had been addressed. A practical man, Charlie wanted his affairs handled. No funeral. He preferred a going away party, he told me. "A Party for Pops," he said, using his granddad's name.

A daughter about to lose her father, a son-in-law about to lose the man who was like a second father to him. A six-year-old grandson about to lose his Pops. The adored and much-loved grandfather who fixed everything. Everything from Stanton's pancakes to his bicycle.

Always excited to see Stanton, Charlie now lay still and silent as we gathered to touch his face and rub his arms. The nurse broke the heavy mood circling the bedroom. "Charlie," she said. "Who is this little boy who came to see you?"

Charlie lifted his head. He gazed at Stanton and the corners of his lips tuned up. His eyes glistened. Maybe with tears and surely with joy.

"That's my grandson, Stanton," Charlie said in a clear, tender voice.

With that, Charlie lowered his head onto the pillow. We had heard his last words.

A bit after midnight, Charlie breathed his last breath. It was November 14th, my birthday. At first, I wondered why Charlie left us on that day. It could not have been coincidental. The reason came to me. I was bad at remembering dates. Charlie knew that. He chose his death date as an easy date for me to remember. I could not help but smile through tears and unimaginable grief.

A desire to make my life and our family's life easy. That's what drove the man whose love and devotion had accompanied me through forty-five years of marriage. My husband valued being a husband, father, father-in-law, and grandfather above all else.

"Bebe," Stanton had asked the next day, while cuddled on my lap, "Since Pops died, who will cook for you? And who will make pancakes when I come over?

Lacking an adequate answer to my grandson's questions or to mine, I looked out the window to assure myself the world was still there. The trees lacked leaves. My begonia plants had shriveled. I sat in silence beside Stanton, wishing for a place to park my mind.

A quiet presence came to join my aching heart. Spring would come. I'd learn to cook, to make pancakes for Stanton. Soon I'd travel again, adding stories to my book. The one I'd dreamed of completing all these years.

23

ALONG THE NILE

Egypt, 2019

On a November evening, I found myself sailing the timeless Nile River aboard *The Sanctuary Adventurer*, a luxurious sailing vessel carrying me and nineteen other passengers. As a solo traveler, I'd looked bold and brave to my friends back home. Rather than bold and brave, I saw myself as an escape artist fleeing the unresolved challenges of living as a woman on my own. After my first visit to Egypt with Emily half a century ago, I knew I must return to visit the Temple of Isis at Philae, which I could not visit on the first trip.

Welcomed aboard by a delightful crew, I had settled into my cabin with its contemporary styling and Egyptian touches. I was actually in a beautiful sanctuary removed from the hassles of the outside world. Time to dress for dinner. Standing in front of the closet, I lifted out my golden-yellow silk suit jacket. I watched how it draped over the hanger as if it were a hand-woven ancient garment. The couture jacket belonged to a dear friend who gave it to me saying, "Take this to Egypt. Wear it as you cruise down the Nile."

I admired the delicate gold-leaf threads, sewn into horizontal quilted rows covering both the jacket's front and back. I noted how the thread sparkled under the moonlight that streamed into my cabin window. Two white doves, symbols of love, adorned my jacket. I touched them, trying to touch the love I'd known with Charlie, while forcing myself not to go too deeply into the pain of what I'd lost.

I looked at the golden bark painted below the doves and imagined the Goddess Isis floating down the Nile inside such a bark. How amazing it was for me to be floating along the same river.

I pictured myself at dinner, meeting adventurous, curious travelers like myself. I could feel the ship gently float toward Luxor as I slipped on gold-sequined shoes. As a final touch, I added dangling gold earrings. Wearing gold and holding golden nuggets of wisdom from many journeys, I was dressed not to impress, but to honor the magnitude of a reunion with Egypt and in anticipation of tomorrow's visit to the Temple of the Goddess Isis. For me, the temple visit would be the crown jewel.

Before walking out the door, I drew my fingers over the painted images on the jacket. Egyptian hieroglyphics, papyrus stalks and two doves painted not white, but lapis blue and moss green. The richness of the detail enthralled me. The couture jacket was a work of art. As I slipped my arms through the sleeves, I noted how the soft silk fabric hugged my body. A perfect fit. Ideal for a cool night on the Nile. The jacket images matched the rich seven-thousand-year Egyptian history also reflected by the ship's artifacts and décor.

The irony did not escape me that I wore a t-shirt and jeans during my first visit to Egypt half-a-century ago, nor did the fact I traveled back then from Cairo to Luxor on board a third-class train.

I'd done much living since that trip. Despite the changes in my life and in the world, the Egyptian ruins remained as if waiting to impart more wisdom to me.

I proceeded toward a wide wooden staircase winding down to the ship's dining room, where I looked forward to meeting other passengers.

When I stepped into the candlelit dining room, the maître d' greeted me with a tip of his head. "You look radiant," he said. "Like an Egyptian princess."

His kind compliment pleased me. Despite my upcoming 72nd birthday, I felt like Cleopatra on the Nile.

When directed to my table, I was surprised I had been assigned a small table by myself. I accepted my spot and sat down. My chair pressed against the back wall while I faced an empty chair in front of me. None of the other passengers sat alone. I supposed they thought I was an odd person who lacked friends or family. Or worse, the other passengers thought nothing about me at all. I never imagined being seated alone with no one to share dinner with.

I lifted a glass of wine. I pictured Charlie. We had shared a marriage with Khalil Gibran's poetic wisdom that reminded us to, "Let there be spaces between your togetherness." The space widowhood brought included an expanse of emptiness and questions to consider as I moved along the Nile. Maybe creating and living within my personal space and sense of myself had helped me move through the past years. Alone was fine, I told myself, gulping rather than sipping wine.

Less than two feet away sat a French couple whispering sweet nothings. He was about the sexiest man I had ever seen. He sat tall. A head full of dark wavy hair. Seated ever so close to him was a blond woman dressed in a backless white cotton dress that flowed to the ground. She looked as if ready to pose for a travel magazine cover. The sensual energy radiating off this couple moved around me. They introduced themselves and went back to enjoying each other as if I were the mirror on the wall.

Another couple, about my age, sat at a table in front of me. I overheard them speaking Spanish, so I assumed they were from Spain. I thought about getting up to introduce myself, but it seemed odd for a woman traveling alone to do so.

I tried to pretend to enjoy my dinner. I raised my glass as if toasting myself. When I finished the appetizer, the waiter served my entree. The intensity of my exposed aloneness made me wish I could shrivel into invisibility. Traveling in the company of strangers had seemed like a good idea when I packed for this trip. On my solo trip to India, I had met interesting, inspiring people. I assumed I would do the same in Egypt.

A river of emotions flowed and then gushed and overwhelmed me. Generally, I managed to stay on top of my feelings in public. I struggled tonight to hold emotion at bay, determined not to allow strangers to see me cry. I forced a smile but could not hold the tears that seeped out of the corners of my eyes. Lacking a tissue, I lifted my linen napkin to dab escaped moisture. It was a pitiful maneuver. When I turned to see if the sexy French couple had noticed, I concluded they had never even looked my way. Watching their affection toward each other made everything worse.

Glaring at the empty chair at my table, I imagined how much Charlie would have loved being here. Should I pretend to be talking to him? Should I run from the dining room sobbing like a soap opera star? No, I would stay and finish my meal. I would not interrupt anyone's dinner with my sadness or allow strangers to know the grief I tried to contain. I hurried to finish my chocolate mousse before dashing to a scheduled massage.

As I walked into the massage area, I tried again to numb my tears, but that wasn't happening. When I met Dalala, the massage therapist, her gentle presence unleashed what felt like the Nile River bursting through a leak in the Aswan Dam.

I began to weep. Nothing stopped my river of tears.

Dalala embraced me. I felt as though the Goddess Isis had wrapped her wings around me. Dalala's caring presence and her gentle massage opened me to depths of grief not yet acknowledged. I experienced the power of being validated by another woman, producing pleasure in the midst of pain.

I noticed she wore silver earrings with images of Isis and her wide-open wings. "Do you have a relationship with Isis?" I asked through my sobs.

"Yes," Dalala said. "Isis is her Greek name. We call her Eset," Dalala said, touching her heart.

I blew my nose in an awkward way with the tissue Dalala provided. I hoped this lovely woman would understand what caused my tears.

"It's not like me to fall apart," I said. "But I miss my husband. He died on my birthday, four years ago tomorrow. My birthday, the date of his death and our 46th wedding anniversary will happen while I'm in Egypt. I didn't know I held so much raw grief," I said, fumbling with my tissue.

"The heart has its own ways," Dalala replied.

My heart raced.

"At the Philae Temple you will see the bark that carried Eset along the Nile."

I pictured the painting on my jacket and imagined Eset/Isis traveling to visit the Temple of Osiris, built after his death.

"Eset wept at becoming a widow," Dalala reminded me. "When inside the Temple at Philae, you will feel embraced as if in her physical presence."

We hugged warmly. My tears stopped. Dalala had provided the presence I needed. I could not thank her enough.

The next morning, my body felt lighter. Under a cloudless day, I left the *Sanctuary Adventurer* to board a felucca, a small traditional Egyptian sailing vessel. It was this boat that would take me to the papyrus-trimmed landing dock leading to Philae and the Temple of Isis, where the Goddess first learned of Osiris' death.

I sailed over rippling waves, past lush green vegetation and the swaying palm trees flanking the Nile. The trees looked as if they had walked down from the desert, thirsty for a drink at the river's edge. Behind the palms, bare granite cliffs rose as if holding the desert in place.

Light winds allowed us to sail with only occasional thumps and bumps. Seated on an overstuffed pillow, I delighted as the crew sang to the accompaniment of a tambourine and a hand-held drum. The melodic, exotic, heart-stirring music heightened my anticipation. As the felucca came closer to the island, I watched the Nile flow as if following the rhythms of the stirring music.

Imagining Charlie holding my hand as I left the felucca, I thought about Isis after Osiris' death. I wondered if being present in the temple of another widow would bring me comfort.

When the boat docked, I glimpsed a reflection of the temple in a shadow floating on the river. I raised my head to take in the 3,000-year-old temple scene and the surrounding stone buildings. My awareness of not being alone in my loss carried me as I crossed over the Nile. Something from a place even deeper than the place I went to while watching Andrea Thomas and her "Goddess Isis moment" on a TV screen at the Oklahoma Health Science Center.

I pictured the Goddess holding her memories as she searched for parts of Osiris while working to resurrect his presence. I had traveled to Egypt to find parts of myself, ones I had been searching for my whole life. I sought yet another identity as a woman on my own. I needed to claim the confidence to complete my book by sharing what I was no longer willing to keep silent about. I'd used my writing as a way to express myself, but soon I would put my words out into the world and speak about them. Perhaps my stories would touch the universal or archetypal nerves the mythological stories of Isis touch. Managing these thoughts, I allowed myself to realize, like Isis, I was also gathering parts of my husband, the memories I would keep with me always.

After I stepped onto the island, I passed under the first of two massive pylons. I paused to breathe. For thousands of years, both rulers and ordinary people had come to this place seeking healing from a female deity, the embodiment of the Divine Feminine. Her power, essence, and energy came alive for me.

Long buried in the collective unconscious, emerging in my lifetime, I was encountering again what I'd sensed around the world and close at home. I thought about Dalala. Her devotion to the Goddess Eset that I knew as Isis. And about the values of the feminine. How they belong united with the values of the masculine.

In a courtyard inside the temple stood massive columns topped by capitals resembling papyrus blooms. They seemed to hold up the sky. The size, the complexity of the incised hieroglyphics on the walls, the sheer beauty and power dazzled me. I imagined how it might have looked when painted azure blue, green and gold. The same colors used to paint my jacket. Today slight remnants of the paint remained on the pillar capitals, but my mind's eye could picture stones glowing in the sun and shining under the moon and the stars. I felt an indisputable connection to the sacredness of life.

I imagined the fragrances of frankincense and jasmine incense flowing through the air as in ancient times. I pictured priestesses and priests moving about in long white robes, their senses awakened by the perfumes. I could almost hear ancient chants, prayers, and drumbeats. Dancers swirling through the space accompanied by sistrum sounds that echoed papyrus stems, blowing in the breeze.

While the scene played across my mind, I was struck by the contrast with what I often experienced inside my church as a young person. My congregation sang hymns without allowing their bodies to move. Hymns accompanied by an overpowering organ. I liked organ music, but not when too loud. One hymn, "Onward Christian Soldiers," reminded me of soldiers willingly or unwillingly risking their lives in unwinnable wars. I stood at the temple in sacred solitude and also remembered times when the sound of the choir singing hymns in church had touched me with loving and compassionate feelings for myself and others.

Holding a myriad of emotions, I proceeded through a series of chambers before entering the inner sanctuary, the holy of holies. The Goddess Isis's golden bark once stood mounted on the empty stone altar I touched. I thought about the bark painted on my jacket as I imagined the revered goddess floating along the Nile toward the temple built to honor her husband, Osiris. I sensed what must have been the longings she felt.

The secluded space, though lacking the goddess's statue or her bark, beckoned me for more reflection. Perhaps Isis could offer her wisdom to guide me toward a new vision for my future. Wasn't this what she had done for her worshippers across thousands of years? Maybe here I could find the depth of meaning and purpose Florence Nightingale found during her time in Egypt.

I removed my sunglasses and sun hat for a lingering gaze around the sanctuary. I softly spoke as if Isis could hear my words. "Being in your temple inspires me to seek the best way to live my life. I want not only an adventurous, but also a purposeful, significant life. A love story formed the core of your story as it has mine. Somehow I sense you understand my longings?"

I remained silent.

"Listen for inner guidance. What you seek will be revealed," a voice whispered.

Filled with awe and wonder, I watched more visitors arrive, some snapped photos while others lingered silently.

I had the distinct awareness that not only was a goddess present with me, but Charlie was present in support as well. I had what I needed to move forward. Inside this Sacred Feminine temple, I sensed and felt the capacity to become myself and to express the fullness of my power and radiance. If only I could hold inside my heart and soul each day this amplified vision of my true self.

All too soon it was time to return to the felucca for a trip back to the ship. As the sun began to fade, I put my hands on my heart to touch the depth of feeling it held.

Later that evening, seated at my table in the ship's dining room, I watched as the Spanish-speaking woman I remembered from the night before rose from the table shared with her husband. As I sat alone, awkwardly waiting for another gourmet meal, the smiling woman approached me.

"Hello, I'm Carmela," she said in perfect English. "My husband and I watched you come down the stairs last night. You looked lovely in your gold silk jacket. And the sparkle in your eyes filled the room." Tilting her head, she asked, "Would you like to join us for dinner?"

Without hesitation I moved to their table. I chose to believe it was not sympathy at my aloneness that caused the invitation. Both Carmela and her husband seemed genuinely interested in meeting me. I learned they lived in Peru and that Carmela was about to publish a book of table setting photography. Our mutual book publishing interest allowed two strangers to connect in a beautiful way. How marvelous to share a meal with such a charming couple! While delighted to interact with them, I found myself pretending not to feel odd being alone.

The dinner changed the trajectory of my trip. I never revealed the sparkles Carmela saw in my eyes had been tears. From that night on, I was treated by other passengers as if I were a celebrity, or perhaps like a rescue puppy, depending on how I chose to interpret my situation. I soaked up comments about how brave I was for traveling on my own. With this encouragement and renewed access to inner guidance, my story continued to expand.

A travel quote written on a card placed in my cabin fit my experience. "We travel not to escape life, but for life not to escape us." *Anonymous*

24

THE SANDSTONE FAÇADE

Dallas, Texas, 2023

I watched a full moon radiate through the window of my condo. After years living in Dallas, I looked forward to this one special night. Whether glowing on this perfect night or shining a silver sliver of promise on my doubting nights, or when hidden on my darkest nights, the mysterious orb beckoned me forward as I prepared to leave for this big night.

For a second time, I would wear the silk jacket my friend gave me for my return trip to Egypt. The painted Egyptian symbols across the front and the back pleased me as they'd done when I first wore it.

As I slipped on the jacket, I took a final look in the mirror. I liked what I saw. Freckles, the once detested spots scattered across my face, were now appreciated marks of distinction. My meandering wrinkles served as hieroglyphics telling tales of a life well-lived. Spaces between the wrinkles allowed me to believe I could look forward to more years for wrinkles to appear. Tousled auburn hair, woven with rays of gray, highlighted the exterior others would see. The richness of my interior landscape, my wonderful memories, my insights, I'd allowed these to flow onto the pages of my book.

One more thing to do. I opened the drawer and lifted out the little white box my sister brought me yesterday. "It's from Mother," Sarah told me. "For your big night. Promise you won't open it until then."

A gift Sarah saved after Mother died. What could it be? How did Mother trust this night would happen? With moist eyes and nervous anticipation, I accepted the box, placing it inside a drawer in my dressing area.

Tonight, I retrieved the box from the drawer before lifting a faded paper note from under a ribbon. As I read the words, I could hear Mother's voice, "For a fleeting moment that afternoon in Casablanca I watched the possibility of your life sparkle, but the shock of the filthy threads hanging from your ears almost made me faint. I rushed for my scissors. As I cut the threads, two tiny blue beads dropped to the floor. Do you remember your hissy fit? After you left the room, I picked up your beads and slipped them inside an envelope. Later, I tucked the envelope inside my jewelry box."

"Mother saved my beads!" I gasped.

"When I found the envelope buried at the bottom of my jewelry box," Mother's note continued, "I asked Sarah to take the beads to a jeweler. To make dangling earrings for you."

My hands shook. I untied the gold ribbon and opened the box. A pair of earrings stared back at me. Both with a single deep blue lapis lazuli bead. Each bead suspended by a chain dangling inside a gold hoop. I slipped on the earrings. A magical feeling came over me, and I felt Mother with me as I read the last lines of the note. "Promise to finish your book. And wear your earrings when you present it to the world.

"All my love, Mother."

Her love and nurturing came alive. "When a woman wears earrings," I said to myself, "she honors the Divine in herself, the Divine in others, the Divine throughout the universe."

I touched my earrings as a tsunami of grief enveloped me. Mother was gone, Daddy was gone. Charlie was gone. For years, I had imagined this night as I worked to create the pages of my book. Through my struggles, I never doubted I would have a book launch at the Crow Museum of Asian Art in the room I was about to enter.

Yet, I had not allowed myself to picture doing so holding such great loss. The kind felt beyond the moment of saying goodbye, or the difficult days soon after a loved one's death. The presence of a less raw grief arrives as the silent absence of loved ones weighs heavy on the heart. Yet in such a moment joy enters as a surprise presence to share space in the same beating heart. Those now gone I sensed cheering me on as I prepared to leave for the long-awaited event.

Once inside the museum, I prepared to stand in front of an 18th century Mughal Empire façade from a mansion—known as a *haveli*—constructed in the Jaipur area of Rajasthan, India. The massive Islamic inspired, hand-carved architectural piece stood about two stories high and covered the length of one wall. Intricate honeycomb-styled carvings incised into reddish gray sandstone covered the surface. The top portion contained open-worked sandstone screens. Some say the tiny geometric openings of these top screens allowed air to pass through providing better ventilation than from open windows. Tonight, I would share with my guests a different purpose for the carved screens.

The moonlight from adjacent museum windows shone onto the carved façade. The sandstone gleamed. The impact seized me as I waited for my moment to speak.

I imagined Charlie with me on our first visit to the Crow Museum almost twenty years earlier. While fascinated by the façade, on that day I did not grasp the true reason I was powerfully drawn to it.

This evening as I waited for the moment to walk into the

museum space, my mind returned to magical Jodhpur, a couple hundred miles from Jaipur. I had been there visiting the Mehrangarh Palaces, built six centuries before I arrived. The trip was a chance to prove to myself that I could draw on inner confidence to fly alone to India and join strangers for a three-week journey. A widow with wanderlust, I sought a new identity while fleeing grief that could not be left behind.

On the day I visited the Mehrangarh Palaces, sun rays caused both the sandstone walls and the stark Thar Desert to glow like Rajasthani jewels. Sky-blue, stucco homes stood below the massive walls around the palaces. The small, stacked-together box homes of ordinary citizens covered a swath of desert land.

I walked along a cobblestone street rising to the palaces. A female Rajasthani guide stopped to share tales of turbaned, bejeweled Maharajas and their silk-sari covered Maharanis.

"Unimaginably wealthy royals once occupied the palaces," she told me. "The cannon mounted on the sandstone walls kept the unwanted out. Had you been a Maharini during the centuries when they lived here," the guide added while snapping my photograph, "you would have ridden here on top of an elephant. Inside a howdah—an enclosed, curtained carriage attached to an elephant's back."

"Sounds exciting," I told her. "As long as the elephants were well treated."

"Maybe not so exciting," the young Rajasthani guide told me, explaining the howdahs kept women isolated and hidden. Muslim women—especially members of the wealthy, elite Mughal families—were not allowed to be seen outside, unless fully veiled and covered.

"Forced invisibility!" I said.

When I looked at what my guide called the "Palace of Peeps," I saw thousands of small geometric shaped openings carved into a sandstone façade creating latticework screens, rather than windows. Royal women peeped through the tiny openings. The courtyards below reserved for men only.

I stiffened imagining peeping at a world reserved for men. Touching my heart, I found the little girl in me. I remembered Casablanca where I peeped through a crack in the living room door, silent and invisible, wishing to enter my father's world.

My adult habit of feeling unseen and unheard resurfaced. It was time to leave that behind. Time to claim the deeper truth about myself. I was past peeping at the world. I was ready to be visible with voice and value.

I lost count of the steps climbed that day before entering a dim room located behind the carved screens of a magnificent palace. It was hot! Filtered light and shadows of golden sun appeared between the openings in the screens.

I considered the history of isolating women. Not only women during the Mughal Empire in India, but women in today's world. Today, however, an inner façade—a woman's inner glass ceiling—often blocks potential with the same certainty of the ancient sandstone façade screens. While with awareness, change happens.

I returned my mind to the Crow Museum and the 18th century Rajasthani Mughal façade showcasing the same architectural features I'd discovered in Jodhpur's Mehrangarh Palace. I was about to launch my book standing outside a façade that had once served to keep women hidden.

From my quest across external and internal barriers, after gathering women's stories, through pounding computer keys and thanks to a supportive husband, I'd found purpose and meaning. And I'd written an important book.

Alone inside the glass-walled hallway leading to the room containing the façade, I heard an often-forgotten voice in my mind.

"You'll probably embarrass yourself out there. You might flush. Or you'll forget what you wanted to say."

"You never give up, but I've got this," I said, standing tall without hesitancy to speak up. "Come with me. I'm entering with my voice, my value, and my vulnerability. I'm leaving the mind chatter, the constraints of excess thinking, to go deeper inside to where I have trust and confidence in what I am about to do."

For years, I'd imagined what it would feel like, sound like, look like for family and friends to gather with me for the launch of my body of work. I'd brought forward a dream to share what I had come to know. A global book tour might follow. I repeated to myself words from Sam Keen and Anne Valley-Fox's book, *Your Mythic Journey,* "And why deny that some force at least as intelligent as an Apple computer (and perhaps more tender) might be respon-sible for morning glories and the insatiable human appetite for significance?"

THE END THAT'S A BEGINNING

ACKNOWLEDGEMENTS

Remarkable, yet uncelebrated, women and men from around the world shared experiences woven into this novel. Without their stories there would be no book.

The writing and publication required a tribe of support. Enormous appreciation to James Bonnet, author of *Stealing Fire From The Gods,* for guiding me through his profound storymaking model. Eternal gratitude to Carolyn Flynn, owner of Soulfire Studios, for developmental editing that took my writing to a level beyond what I imagined. A warm shoutout to Jona Kottler for editing and revision suggestions and for unmatchable wit that provided relief during writing struggles. Amy Gottlieb, author of *The Beautiful Tomorrow,* deserves my gratitude for insights that pointed to a better place to open my story. High regards to Atmosphere Press and to Nick Courtright, Kyle McCord, Alex Kale, Ronaldo Alves, Senhor Tocas and the entire editing, layout and marketing team for making my road to publication exciting and rewarding.

Assistance, inspiration and encouragement came from special friends Marlene Kenneally, Diane Bonnet, Debbie Marks, Monica Reeves, Linda Johnson, Dotty Avondstont, Meribeth Sloan, Kay Murcer, Claudia Spears, Kirstin Joy Burch, Regine Oesch-Aiyer, Pam Glyckherr, Tuki Machado, Jeanine Hilkins, Lizzie Foster, Rose Allison, Jenny Diebold, Suzanne Jabour,

Gaye and Bruce Karish. Huge thanks to Jane Heers for trusting that a book launch would happen when she purchased a dress for the event years before I finished writing. Appreciation to Jeanette Korab for the author photo.

To my brother Dan Harkins and my niece Sarah Harkins for reading and commenting on an early draft. To Sarah Holbrook, the best sister a big sis could have, for constant belief in my project and for edits to numerous drafts.

A world of love to Amy, Kevin and Stanton Flick for the unceasing joy brought to my life. And for Gary Pribulsky, whose love and never-ending support changed my life over the course of our 46-year marriage. You had to leave us too soon, but your legacy as a devoted husband, father, father-in-law and grandfather blesses us and makes us smile.

AUTHOR'S STATEMENT

The *Possibility of Everywhere* is a work of autobiographical fiction written to share my truths. My lack of insight while living certain events caused me to saddle some characters with flaws that do not reflect the essence of their true selves.

Twenty-plus years passed as I wrote this debut novel. During this time, I traveled the world, traveled deep inside myself and traveled to the grocery store, the gas station, to my hairdresser, tax accountant and on and on.

After submitting my work to the publisher, I considered writing a non-fiction book entitled *How to Tell Your Story and Change Your Life in Twenty Years or Less*. After further consideration, I condensed my thoughts to share with you here:

May you always remember how much your story matters. May you discover the deepest truths of your story—though the process will take time. May you be ever aware that how you tell your story to yourself and to others shapes your life. And may you embrace both the brilliance and the imperfection that resides inside you and inside each of us.

Thank you for spending time with what I have written. I welcome your comments. Please contact me at: bethharkinswrites@gmail.com.

ABOUT THE AUTHOR

Beth Harkins is an inspiring author, storyteller, workshop leader and world traveler who has crossed six continents, 65 countries, including the USA, while gathering women's stories—the ones headlines miss.

A founding member of the Woman-Centered Coaching, Training and Leadership Institute, Beth also holds a master's degree in Humanistic Psychology. She applies her training, life experience and passion for the power of story to her writing.

A mother, grandmother, widow and wild wise woman, Beth lives in Dallas, TX surrounded by family, friends, books and treasures from around the world.

Contact her at: bethharkinswrites@gmail.com and visit her website at http://www.bethharkins.com.

ABOUT ATMOSPHERE PRESS

Atmosphere Press is an independent, full-service publisher for excellent books in all genres and for all audiences. Learn more about what we do at atmospherepress.com.

We encourage you to check out some of Atmosphere's latest releases, which are available at Amazon.com and via order from your local bookstore:

Dancing with David, a novel by Siegfried Johnson

The Friendship Quilts, a novel by June Calender

My Significant Nobody, a novel by Stevie D. Parker

Nine Days, a novel by Judy Lannon

Shining New Testament: The Cloning of Jay Christ, a novel by Cliff Williamson

Shadows of Robyst, a novel by K. E. Maroudas

Home Within a Landscape, a novel by Alexey L. Kovalev

Motherhood, a novel by Siamak Vakili

Death, The Pharmacist, a novel by D. Ike Horst

Mystery of the Lost Years, a novel by Bobby J. Bixler

Bone Deep Bonds, a novel by B. G. Arnold

Terriers in the Jungle, a novel by Georja Umano

Into the Emerald Dream, a novel by Autumn Allen

His Name Was Ellis, a novel by Joseph Libonati

The Cup, a novel by D. P. Hardwick

The Empathy Academy, a novel by Dustin Grinnell

Tholocco's Wake, a novel by W. W. VanOverbeke

Dying to Live, a novel by Barbara Macpherson Reyelts

Looking for Lawson, a novel by Mark Kirby

CPSIA information can be obtained
at www.ICGtesting.com
Printed in the USA
LVHW051112080523
746408LV00005B/519

9 781639 887026